THE SILENCE OF THE LIBRARY

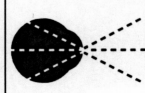

This Large Print Book carries the
Seal of Approval of N.A.V.H.

A CAT IN THE STACKS MYSTERY

THE SILENCE OF THE LIBRARY

MIRANDA JAMES

WHEELER PUBLISHING
A part of Gale, Cengage Learning

GALE
CENGAGE Learning·

Farmington Hills, Mich • San Francisco • New York • Waterville, Maine
Meriden, Conn • Mason, Ohio • Chicago

GALE
CENGAGE Learning®

LIBRARY OF CONGRESS CATALOGING-IN-PUBLICATION DATA

James, Miranda.
    The silence of the library : a cat in the stacks mystery / by Miranda James.
— Large print edition.
        pages ; cm. — (Wheeler Publishing large print cozy mystery)
    ISBN 978-1-4104-7040-9 (softcover) — ISBN 1-4104-7040-7 (softcover)
    1. Librarians—Fiction. 2. Authors—Fiction. 3.
Murder—Investigation—Fiction. 4. Large type books. I. Title.
PS3610.A43S55 2014
813'.6—dc23   2014023343

Published in 2014 by arrangement with The Berkley Publishing Group, a member of Penguin Group (USA) LLC, a Penguin Random House Company

Printed in the United States of America
1 2 3 4 5 6 7 18 17 16 15 14

With great respect and admiration, and with thanks for countless hours of pleasure and vicarious adventure, this book is dedicated to the memories of Mildred Wirt Benson, Margaret Sutton, and Julie Campbell Tatham. Without Nancy Drew, Judy Bolton, and Trixie Belden, I would never have had so much fun in childhood and adolescence.

ACKNOWLEDGMENTS

My thanks go as always to the members of my weekly critique group for their consistently valuable input: Julie, Kay F., Kay K., Laura, Millie, and Bob. Huge thanks as well to the Soparkar-Hairston clan for their hospitality in providing an inviting atmosphere for our meetings.

Without the support and patience of my wonderful editor, Michelle Vega, and my indefatigable agent, Nancy Yost, I would be lost. Berkley Prime Crime has provided a happy home for Charlie and Diesel, and I am thrilled with the consistently gorgeous covers. Diesel thinks the "cover cat" who serves as his body double is a handsome dude — though, of course, not nearly so handsome as he is!

Finally, my two dear friends and constant cheerleaders, Patricia Orr and Terry Farmer, patiently read each book, chapter by chapter, in spurts and deluges, and offer helpful comments and unfailing support. I am truly blessed to have such friends.

ONE

Lightning tore through the sky, and a brilliant flash of light struck the ground near the road. Sparks flew, and a massive tree split and started to fall. The pert red roadster trembled as Veronica Thane urged it forward.

The huge oak threatened to land on her car, and only the girl's swift reflexes saved her from sure annihilation. The car shot ahead as a section of the mighty tree struck the road behind it.

Veronica Thane's hands tightened on the wheel as she peered through the sudden deluge of rain on her windscreen that rendered her all but blind. When another bolt of lightning briefly illuminated the dark sky, the intrepid girl caught a glimpse of a driveway ten feet ahead.

Her heart thudded painfully as terror gripped her, but she called upon her deep reserves of fortitude and guided the roadster through the storm. Her breath coming in gasps, she jerked the wheel to the right, and her car shot into the driveway at a fast clip. More lightning, now mercifully farther away, offered her just enough light to see the dark, hulking outlines of a mansion some distance ahead.

Shelter lay before her!

Through the wind-whipped trees that lined the drive, Veronica spotted dim lights in several windows. Now she had only to reach the house, and surely the residents would offer her refuge from the wild turmoil of the storm.

The roadster shuddered to an abrupt halt as Veronica reached the impressive double front door. Lightning once again offered a fleeting look at the building that now loomed over her. Rain pelted down as the light faded, but the plucky girl had seen her goal.

She thrust her door open and stepped into the tempest. As she darted forward, instantly drenched, she recalled her handbag, still in the roadster. Now there was no turning back.

The girl pounded up the stairs of the portico that protected the massive front entrance. She raised the heavy, ornate knocker, shaped like a gargoyle's monstrous head, and banged it against the dark heavy oak. Surely, despite the fury of the storm, someone within would hear her and invite her inside.

I smiled as I closed the book and laid it next to me on the bed. I first read *The Mystery at Spellwood Mansion* over forty years ago when, on a rainy Sunday afternoon, I discovered my late aunt Dottie's collection of the adventures of Veronica Thane. I had finished my library books and was desperate for something to read, but the library was closed. Aunt Dottie sent me to one of the spare bedrooms on the third floor and told me to search the bookshelves there.

"That's where I keep some of my treasures." Aunt Dottie had smiled as she shooed me out of the kitchen. "Mind you, handle them gently." The words floated after me as I scurried away.

Odd how certain memories linger.

I recalled my headlong rush up the two flights of stairs and the moment when I turned on the light and beheld a wall of books. How had I missed this room before?

I don't know how long I stood and gazed at the hundreds of books, but I ended up seated on the floor in front of the shelves. My hands ran over the spines, all covered in

11

dust jackets, and the titles in one section tantalized me with words such as *mystery, secret, clue,* and *terror.*

Finally I stopped my fingers from roaming and pulled a book gently off the shelf. I examined the cover. A dark-haired girl stood under a tree in the foreground, her eyes focused on a spooky-looking manor. *The Mystery at Spellwood Mansion* stood out in bold letters, followed by *A Veronica Thane Mystery by Electra Barnes Cartwright.*

I stretched out on the floor, opened the book, and began to read.

From what I recall, I didn't move from the spot until I finished the book. By then, Aunt Dottie was calling me down for dinner. All I could talk about that evening was Veronica Thane, and Aunt Dottie joined in the conversation about her childhood favorite.

After that I always associated Aunt Dottie with Veronica and the other girl detectives whose adventures made up that amazing collection. Nancy Drew, the Dana Girls, Judy Bolton, Cherry Ames, Vicki Barr, Connie Blair, Penny Parker, and more besides. Then there were the boy sleuths: the Hardy Boys, Ken Holt, Rick Brant, and so on.

Over the next several years I worked my way through hundreds of those books before moving on to more adult fare, such as Sherlock Holmes, Hercule Poirot, and Henry Gamadge. Aunt Dottie sparked my love of mysteries and fed it with her huge collection. I still had every one of her books, each too precious ever to let go.

A large, furry creature leapt onto the bed near my feet and interrupted my reverie. My Maine Coon cat, Diesel, chirped at me, determined to capture my focus.

"Sorry to neglect you, boy, but I was reliving my youth for a few minutes there." I grinned as Diesel butted my head, still chirping. He loved attention, and he returned it with often energetic affection. He climbed onto my legs, all thirty-six pounds of him.

"Hang on a moment, boy, you're a bit heavy." Diesel muttered as I spread my legs. He slid between them and resettled himself, his head in my lap with his body stretched out. He purred loudly with a sound reminiscent of his namesake engine.

With the cat comfortably in place and myself reasonably so, I picked up my book, found my place, and delved into the story again.

Lightning rent the sky once more, and the bedraggled girl huddled in the meager shelter of the portico. She grasped the knocker, ready to knock a second time, when the door swung inward, quickly and silently. She stumbled forward into the dimly lit foyer, righted herself, and turned to greet the person who admitted her. The door creaked shut.

Veronica Thane stifled a gasp as her eyes beheld the cadaverous, elongated figure of the ancient man who stood before her. "He must be eighty years old," she thought. "And well over six feet tall."

"Good afternoon, miss." The butler — for so he must be, as he wore the usual garb of such a servant — spoke in a high, thin voice. "The mistress will be pleased that you managed to arrive early, despite the storm."

Veronica gasped. What could he mean?

A voice called my name, and I put the book aside with some reluctance. "Yes, Azalea, I'm in here." I sat up and tried to disentangle Diesel from my legs, but he wasn't interested in moving. I had to scoot myself backward a few inches before I was clear enough to swing one leg over him. Then I twisted until I sat on the side of the bed.

"What you doing all the way up here, Mr.

14

Charlie?" Azalea Berry, my housekeeper, frowned at me from the doorway. "And what you doing messing up that bed after I cleaned in here this morning?"

"Sorry, didn't mean to disturb things." I retrieved the book and tucked it under my arm before I stood. "Diesel and I were just reading. I came up here to look for something, and I got sidetracked by the books. I just had to lie down and read for a few minutes."

Azalea nodded as the ghost of a smile flitted by. "Miss Dottie used to do that, too. Sometimes I couldn't find her nowhere, and up here she'd be, stretched out on that bed, reading one of them books of hers."

I glanced at the four-poster, almost as if I expected to see my late aunt lying there. For a moment I could have sworn I saw the dim outline of a person, but when I blinked, the image faded. Diesel warbled and rubbed against my leg. I wondered whether he sensed another presence in the room as I had.

"Yes, she loved her books." I showed *The Mystery at Spellwood Mansion* to Azalea, and she glanced at the cover. "This series was one of her favorites. What I came looking for, actually. The public library is doing a special exhibit for National Library Week

15

next month, and it's going to feature the author. She would have been a hundred years old this year."

Azalea peered at the book again. "Miz Dottie loved those from when she was a little bitty thing. I reckon she told me about that Veronica girl a hundred times, how much she admired her when she was growing up."

I felt a sudden lump in my throat as another memory surfaced from a conversation with my aunt when I was about twelve. I asked her why she didn't have any children of her own, and she told me she once had a little girl, but the angels came for her when she was only six months old and took her back to Heaven with them. She had named her daughter Veronica.

Azalea must have sensed my sudden discomfort, and Diesel did, too. He warbled loudly and rubbed against my leg again as Azalea stepped back and motioned for me to follow her into the hall.

I clicked off the light and shut the door behind us. "You were looking for me, weren't you?" I asked.

Azalea nodded. "Yes, sir, you had a phone call from that lady at the library, Miz Farmer. When I couldn't find you right away, I told her I'd get you to call her back soon as I did."

"Sorry it took you so long to find me." I followed her toward the stairs, Diesel at my heels. "I'll go call her back right now."

Azalea continued down the stairs when we reached the second floor, but Diesel followed me into my bedroom, where I retrieved my cell phone from the nightstand.

I speed-dialed Teresa Farmer, director of the Athena Public Library. She answered right away. I identified myself, but before I could apologize for the delay, she spoke over me.

"Charlie, you're not going to believe this." I heard the excitement bubbling in Teresa's voice. "She's not dead!"

Two

Before I could respond, Teresa repeated her last statement. "She's not dead!"

Teresa had me flummoxed. "Who's not dead?"

"Sorry, Charlie." Teresa chuckled. "Electra Barnes Cartwright. I found out she's still alive and apparently sharp as the proverbial tack."

"That's amazing." I sat on the bed, and Diesel hopped up beside me. "She'll be a hundred on her birthday this year, whenever it is."

"That's right. I looked her up in *Contemporary Authors.* She'll be a hundred in May. How do you remember these things?"

"One of my habits, storing away useless trivia." I laughed. "There must be some connection between girls' mystery series and longevity. Both Mildred Wirt Benson and Margaret Sutton lived to be nearly a hundred."

"I know Benson wrote many of the early Nancy Drew books," Teresa said. "Who was Margaret Sutton?"

"She wrote the Judy Bolton books."

"I don't remember reading those," Teresa said. "They must not have been around when I first discovered and read books like that."

Teresa, in her midthirties, was a good fifteen years younger than I, and the Judy Bolton books were out of print by the time she came along. I mentioned this, and she laughed.

"Obviously I've missed a good series. You'll have to tell me more about them later, because you probably know all there is to know about Judy Bolton. Otherwise you wouldn't be advising us on our National Library Week exhibit."

I had picked up a fair amount of knowledge over the years about series books, such as Nancy Drew and the Hardy Boys, and I was delighted to put my seemingly arcane knowledge to good use for once.

"Now back to Ms. Cartwright." Teresa reclaimed my attention. "I started noodling around on the Internet. Came up with the number for an agent named Yancy Thigpen and thought I'd take a chance and call."

"What did you want from the agent?" I

asked. "Unless you suspected that Electra Barnes Cartwright was actually still alive."

"I thought that was unlikely," Teresa said. "I was hoping the agent might know of any artifacts or special materials we could use for the exhibit. I never dreamed she would tell me that the author was still living."

"That is a wonderful surprise."

"This whole thing is coming together like it's truly meant to be." I could picture her bouncing in her chair judging from the enthusiasm bubbling in her voice. "Now for the really big news — not only is she still alive, but Electra Barnes Cartwright lives nearby. How's *that* for amazing?"

I felt dazed. "I knew she grew up around Calhoun City" — a small town about a hundred miles south of Athena — "but from what little I remember reading about her, she left the South and settled in Connecticut when she was in her twenties. When did she come back to Mississippi?"

"About twenty years ago. Yancy said Mrs. Cartwright lives quietly out in the country with her widowed daughter and grandson, between here and Mineola. Do you know them? Marcella and Eugene Marter."

"No, can't say as I do." Diesel bumped his head against my arm to signal his need for attention. I rubbed my hand along his back as Teresa continued.

"Marcella has a library card but I don't think she uses it much. But that's neither here nor there. One more awesome thing." She chuckled.

When she didn't continue immediately, I said, "Okay, out with it before I pop a gasket here."

"If you aren't too busy tomorrow," Teresa responded, "how would you like to go with me to meet Electra Barnes Cartwright?"

I laughed heartily. "I think you can figure out my answer. What time and where shall I meet you?"

We arranged to meet at the library a little before nine for an appointment at nine thirty. The drive to the Marter home should take only twenty minutes at most.

"Bring Diesel along," Teresa said. "I asked whether Ms. Cartwright would have any objection to a cat, and Yancy told me she loves animals. Besides, he's such a good icebreaker if we need one."

"He definitely is that." Plus he always seemed to know when he was being talked about, because I noticed him staring intently at the phone. He chirped loudly several times, as if to tell me he would be happy to go along. "Did you hear that?"

Teresa laughed. "Yes, I did. He's given his

approval to the visit, too."

"That settles it. See you tomorrow." I rang off and stowed the phone in my pocket. "Come on, boy, let's go downstairs and get something to eat." I set the copy of *The Mystery at Spellwood Mansion* on the nightstand for bedtime reading before I followed Diesel out of the bedroom.

The sky on Tuesday morning promised heavy rain, and the clouds grew darker as Teresa and I departed the library in my car. I'd checked the weather report last night, and the forecast gave only a twenty percent chance of rain. More like eighty percent, it seemed to me as I examined conditions.

Diesel stretched out in the backseat, his purr a basso continuo to our thoughts. Teresa provided the directions, and I cast anxious eyes to the heavens as I drove. The weather reminded me eerily of the opening scene in *The Mystery at Spellwood Mansion*. No lightning yet, but I had a feeling the distant rumble of thunder presaged plenty of it to come.

"Yancy said Ms. Cartwright is a hoot to talk to. Definitely knows her own mind and isn't afraid to speak it." Teresa fiddled with the strap of the seat belt across her chest, and I could tell the weather made her as nervous as it did me. "She's also pretty active. Walks at least a couple miles a day, unless the weather's bad, or it's too hot."

"That's pretty amazing. Better than I usually do, and I'm almost half her age." The sky continued to darken, and I switched on the car's lights. I preferred being safely inside during a storm, not out in a car right in the middle of it.

"Not much farther." Teresa drew a deep breath, perhaps to calm herself, while Diesel had stopped purring and begun muttering instead. He had obviously picked up on our unease over the weather. "There should be a sign for the byroad." She consulted her printed directions. "It should say *Applewood Hill Farm.*"

I peered ahead as rain suddenly pummeled the car. I felt fur brush my sleeved arm as Diesel climbed over the center console and into Teresa's lap. "Sorry about that," I said as I kept my gaze focused on the road ahead. "He doesn't like storms any more than we do."

"No problem." Teresa got the cat to settle, but at thirty-six pounds, he easily overflowed her lap, and his tail rested across the console and extended into my lap. "It's okay, boy," she murmured in soothing tones, and Diesel's muttering slowed.

23

"There it is." The car's lights shone on a large sign about seventy yards ahead, and I slowed for the approaching turn. The rain, fierce at first, began to decrease in volume, and I sent up a thankful prayer that the storm seemed to be moving quickly over us.

"From here it should only be about two miles." Teresa peered at her directions while Diesel's tail twitched in my lap. "Then there's a driveway on the left, and the house is about four hundred yards up the driveway behind a stand of trees."

The sky lightened as we headed down the byroad, and the rain continued to slacken. There seemed to be no other houses close to the road, though I spotted three drive-ways before we reached one on the left. A small sign, about two feet by four, boasted *Marter Family Farm* in faded Gothic letter-ing.

"This is it." I pointed the car down the driveway, and moments later we drove through a stand of pine trees. On the other side the drive swept up a slight rise to circle in front of a rambling, two-story farmhouse. I figured it had been built sometime be-tween the two world wars, with maybe a few additions along the way. A wide porch extended across the front of the house, which faced south, and around on the western side as well. There were a couple of porch swings and three chairs. Light gleamed dimly in a window to the west of the front door.

Rain still sprinkled as I parked the car, and I debated whether to bother with an umbrella. "Hang on to Diesel for a moment, until I can get around to pick him up." He didn't like getting his pads wet, so I would carry him up to the porch.

Once I had Diesel in my arms, I let Teresa scurry up the walk ahead of us. Under cover of the porch, I put the cat down and stood aside as Teresa pulled open a screen door to knock on the wooden door behind it.

After a moment Teresa knocked again, and seconds later the door swung back to reveal a short, heavyset woman who appeared to be in her late sixties or early seventies. She scowled at the sight of Teresa and said, "What are *you* doing here?"

THREE

Thunder crashed, and I jumped as the rain poured down once again. What was wrong with this woman? We needed to get inside and out of the storm. I was thankful we had avoided getting soaked as we scurried from the car onto the porch, but if the wind picked up again, we would soon be dripping.

"I beg your pardon." Teresa stepped back from the door, obviously confused. "When I spoke to you yesterday, you said this morning would be fine."

Her posture rigid and her expression suspicious, the woman stared at Teresa a moment. She reached toward the wall inside the door, and the porch light flickered on. The woman's face relaxed, and she flashed a brief smile.

"I'm sorry, couldn't really see who you were." She stood aside and motioned for us to enter. "I thought you were that, um, salesman I talked to the other day. He just won't leave me alone, trying to sell me, uh, life insurance."

I followed Teresa inside, and Diesel almost got tangled in between my legs in his haste to enter the house. I managed not to stumble and moved out of the way. The woman closed the door behind us. I was grateful to be out of the storm but a bit skeptical of our would-be hostess's explanation of her earlier rude words to Teresa. She didn't sound particularly convincing — especially since Teresa in no way resembled a sales*man*. It wasn't *that* dark on the porch.

The woman's eyes widened as Diesel stretched and warbled a greeting. "I'm Marcella Marter, Mrs. Cartwright's daughter." She continued to stare at my boy. "What kind of cat is that? I surely don't think I ever saw one that big before, outside of a zoo." She brayed like a frightened donkey — her version of a laugh, I supposed — and startled the rest of us. Diesel drew back with a jerk, and I patted his head in reassurance.

"His name is Diesel, and he's a Maine Coon, the oldest natural breed of domestic cat in the U.S. They tend to be larger than other breeds, but Diesel here is well above average in the size department." When he heard his name, the cat warbled again as he looked up at me and then at Mrs. Marter.

"It's almost like he's talking." Again Mrs. Marter emitted that raucous laugh, and Diesel shifted back against me. "He's a beautiful thing. Mother will eat him up with a spoon."

"I'm Teresa Farmer, and this is Charlie Harris. We're really looking forward to meeting Mrs. Cartwright." Teresa spoke in a firm tone as Mrs. Marter had made no move to take us beyond the front hall.

Our hostess nodded. "Sure thing. Y'all come on through. Mother's having a good day, and I know she's anxious to talk to you." She turned and headed down the hallway that divided the house. As we followed her, I glanced around and noted that the hardwood floor, where it wasn't covered by rag rugs, shone with polish. The house had a pleasant smell, a light tang of citrus in the air. Whoever did the cleaning here appeared to be as meticulous as Azalea.

Thunder boomed directly over the house, or so it seemed, and the building shook. Diesel mewed anxiously, and I paused to calm him with a hand on his head.

Teresa and Mrs. Marter continued down the hall ahead of us and turned into a room on the left near the end of the corridor. I stepped into the doorway with Diesel by my legs, and I paused to get my first glimpse of my childhood idol. The room blazed with light — enough to make me blink — and several seconds passed before my eyes began to adjust. In addition to the overhead fixture, I counted seven lamps placed around the large sitting room, all glowing. The effect reminded me of family outings to the beach in Galveston with the summer sun that blazed without mercy. The glare was intimidating at first, and the resulting heat stifling. I could already feel the sweat on my forehead, and I knew my slightly damp clothing ought to dry quickly. I supposed, like many elderly people, Mrs. Cartwright liked the heat, but all these lights seemed an odd way to keep her warm.

Once I was able to focus, I spotted the reason for our visit ensconced on a sofa to my right, and my heart raced. This was a thrill I never expected to have. I absorbed as many details as I could without appearing rude.

Electra Barnes Cartwright, at nearly a century of life, appeared thin, but not unhealthily so. Clothed in trousers and a heavy cardigan over a collared blouse, neck swathed in a scarf, she looked ready for an outing. Dark glasses protected her eyes from the light, and her hennaed hair surprised me. I had expected — I realized — a fluffy, white-haired lady, but Electra Cartwright didn't project that image.

"Mother, here are those nice people from the library in Athena that we talked about." Mrs. Marter moved to within three feet of her parent and stood, hands clasped, in front of her. She waited until Mrs. Cartwright nodded before she made the formal introductions.

"Nice to meet you all." Mrs. Cartwright had a rasp in her voice, like that of a hardened smoker. "Especially this four-legged gentleman. Aren't you beautiful?" Diesel evidently agreed because he moved closer to her outstretched hand and warbled three times. Mrs. Cartwright laughed as she stroked the cat's head.

"Diesel likes attention." I noted the happy smile Mrs. Cartwright wore as she continued to lavish attention on the cat.

"He's not conceited," Mrs. Cartwright said. "He's simply convinced. Aren't you, sir?" She looked up at me, her hand finally still atop Diesel's willing head. "You're a fortunate man to have such a wonderful companion."

"Thank you, ma'am." I ducked my head in acknowledgment. "He has brought considerable joy to my family and me."

"Marcella, where are our manners?" Mrs. Cartwright's tart tone took me aback, especially when Mrs. Marter twitched into action and shoved a chair at Teresa. "Please pardon my daughter," Mrs. Cartwright continued. "We don't get many visitors these days, and our company manners sure aren't what they used to be."

That was an understatement, I thought. The relationship between mother and daughter appeared tense, and that made me feel uncomfortable.

"Thank you." After a swift glance at me, Teresa nodded at Mrs. Marter as she sat down. I found another chair and pulled it near. In the meantime Mrs. Cartwright patted the empty space beside her on the sofa and indicated that Diesel should join her. He glanced my way first, as if he sought permission. When I nodded, he climbed up beside Mrs. Cartwright and settled his head and front legs in her lap.

My eyes teared up every other minute or so from the intense light, and I wished mightily for a pair of sunglasses. This quirk of Mrs. Cartwright's made the room unpleasant for visitors, but I supposed that if I made it to the century mark, I ought to be allowed a few quirks.

"We really appreciate you taking the time to visit with us." Teresa leaned forward to address Mrs. Cartwright. "As your daughter might have told you, we are featuring you and your work in an exhibit for our upcoming National Library Week festivities next month. It was certainly a stroke of luck to find out that you were living so near Athena."

Mrs. Cartwright laughed. "That I'm still alive and kicking is what you really mean. I know that little fact will be a shock to some." She glanced at her daughter, who hovered behind Teresa. Mrs. Marter frowned at her mother before she turned and left the room.

Mrs. Cartwright called after her daughter. "Bring us something cold to drink." She focused on Teresa. "Exactly what are you going to do for these festivities?"

"Primarily an exhibit of your life and works, highlighting the fiction you wrote for children and young adults." Teresa nodded in my direction. "For example, thanks to his late aunt, Charlie has an amazing collection of the Veronica Thane series. He has offered to let the library borrow items from it for the exhibit."

Mrs. Cartwright stroked Diesel's back with her right hand. "Your aunt is a reader of mine?"

"Yes, ma'am, she was," I said. "She passed away several years ago, but she left her house and all its contents to me. She had a superb collection of juvenile mysteries, like the Veronica Thane series — her personal favorite — along with others like Nancy Drew and Judy Bolton."

Mrs. Cartwright snorted and startled Diesel into meowing. "That dratted Nancy Drew. She was the bane of my existence. I know my Veronica books could have sold even better if the syndicate hadn't interfered."

Teresa cast me a bewildered glance, no doubt thrown by the reference to a *syndicate* and the vitriol in our hostess's tone.

"I presume you're talking about the Stratemeyer Syndicate." I smiled, and Teresa's face cleared. I had given her the basic history of Edward Stratemeyer and his fiction factory when we first discussed our ideas for the Cartwright exhibit.

Mrs. Cartwright scowled. "Just hearing that name makes my blood pressure go up. I was lucky enough not to work for him, or receive the hack wages he paid. And the stories I heard from other writers who did, and had to work with those daughters of his." She glared at me, but I realized that I was not the target of her evident wrath.

"I believe I read in an article once that other nonsyndicate writers complained that the syndicate tried to get their series quashed so they wouldn't compete with Nancy Drew and the Hardy Boys, for example." Those claims, I reasoned at the time, might have been nothing more than the proverbial sour grapes, due to the phenomenal success of Nancy and the Hardys, but I didn't really know for sure. Mrs. Cartwright naturally had a right to her own opinion on the matter.

"I could tell you *plenty.*" The elderly author shook her head. "But there's no point in it now. Everyone else concerned is long gone." She flashed a sudden grin. "I've outlived them all."

Teresa addressed Mrs. Cartwright. "You and your work will be the focus of this exhibit. I want to assure you of that. We'll have examples of the other girl detectives, but you and your books are the centerpiece."

"That's good. If I've got pride of place, then I don't mind sharing." Mrs. Cartwright laughed again. "What other plans did you have beside the exhibit?"

"That was the sum of it originally," Teresa said. "But with your being so close by, we wondered whether you would be interested in some kind of public appearance."

"Meet my adoring fans, you mean." Mrs. Cartwright laughed. "Sure, I would love to do that. Haven't actually talked to one of them face-to-face in years. Had plenty of letters, though."

"That's terrific," I said. "One idea I had was a public interview. You wouldn't have to give a speech, unless of course you want to. More along the lines of my interviewing you in front of an audience, give them a chance to listen and perhaps ask a few questions of their own at the end."

"I think I'd like that. Less wear and tear on me. Count me in." Mrs. Cartwright smiled, obviously pleased. "It would be lovely to see a roomful of my readers."

"Absolutely not. That's a terrible idea." Marcella Marter plunked a tray of drinks down on a nearby table and glared at her mother. "I absolutely forbid it."

FOUR

Teresa and I exchanged startled glances. Neither of us had expected such unpleasant family dynamics.

"I beg your pardon." Mrs. Cartwright stuck out her chin as she gazed in Marcella Marter's direction. Her voice grew slightly deeper, perhaps from irritation, as she continued, "You *forbid* it? No, I don't think so."

I would have sworn I felt the temperature drop in the room when Mrs. Cartwright responded. Diesel, in obvious distress at the sudden tension, pulled away from Mrs. Cartwright. He sprang from the sofa and landed mere inches from my feet. He took refuge under my chair, and I leaned sideways to rub his back.

"Mother, I don't think you realize how exhausted you'll be if you try to do something like that. You're not used to going out in public anymore." Marcella, arms crossed

36

over her chest, regarded her parent intently. She didn't appear to be backing down, despite her mother's displeasure.

"I'm well aware of all that, you silly woman." Mrs. Cartwright's tone grew fiercer as she continued. "I will not tolerate your attempts to dictate the terms of my life. I have the Lord only knows how much longer on this earth, and I want some little bit of pleasure out of it before I go."

By now I figured Teresa was as uncomfortable and ready to get the heck out of this room as Diesel and I were, but there was little we could do.

"Are you going to keep standing there like a stone-faced baboon, or are you going to offer our guests a cool drink?" Mrs. Cartwright faced Teresa and me without waiting to see whether her daughter would comply with her command. "Marcella goes overboard trying to look after me. I'm old, but I'm not completely decrepit yet. I have more stamina than she thinks."

"We're delighted to know that you're in such good health." I decided I'd better speak in an effort to defuse the situation. "It's only natural that Mrs. Marter wants to take care of you."

"We'll make every effort to see that the events we're planning don't tax your strength too much," Teresa said. "And if at any time you don't feel up to participating, you just let us know. Everyone will understand."

"That's very kind of you." Mrs. Cartwright accepted a tall glass from her daughter. Mrs. Marter's expression remained mulish, but I supposed she had decided that protesting further in front of guests would not be seemly. "Marcella makes the best sweet tea. Y'all drink up. I'm sure you're parched by now."

That was the first kind thing I'd heard Mrs. Cartwright say about her daughter. I surely hoped they got along better in private than they did with company around.

Teresa and I accepted glasses, and I took a cautious sip. Mrs. Cartwright hadn't exaggerated. The tea was absolutely delicious, sweet, but not cloyingly so, and brewed to perfection. I drank half of my glass quickly, happy to feel the cold liquid sliding down.

"I brought water for your cat." Mrs. Marter plunked a bowl on the floor by my chair and poured water from a small pitcher into it. Diesel peeped out from under my chair and looked first at Mrs. Marter, then at me. "Go ahead, boy, if you want some," I told him. He sniffed at the bowl before he dipped his head and began to lap at the liquid.

"Thank you. It was kind of you to think of him." I held up my glass. "And your mother is right. This tea is wonderful."

"It sure is." Teresa smiled. "Hits the spot beautifully."

Mrs. Marter flushed, apparently embarrassed by the praise. "Thank you. There's more if you want."

Teresa and I both asked for refills, and Mrs. Cartwright regarded us benignly — or so I thought, since it was hard to read her expression thanks to her dark glasses. When you can't see a person's eyes, you can never truly tell what's going on in her head. At least she smiled at us.

Teresa set her glass on the floor beside her chair and then reached into her purse to extract a few pages. She examined them before she stood to hand one to Mrs. Cartwright. "This is a tentative schedule I drew up. Please look over it at your leisure, and let me know later if everything is okay. We can adjust it however you like."

Mrs. Cartwright accepted the paper and appeared to examine it. "At first glance this looks just fine to me, but I'll go over it with Marcella and Eugene and then let you know."

"Eugene is my son. He is such a comfort to me, and to Mother, of course." The quiet pride in Marcella Marter's voice revealed a more pleasant side to her personality than we had witnessed thus far.

Teresa must have decided it was time to bring the visit to a close. She thanked Mrs. Cartwright and Mrs. Marter for their hospitality. "We really appreciate y'all letting us barge in on you today. It has been such a pleasure meeting you both."

"It certainly has." As I stood, Mrs. Marter stepped closer to take my empty glass, and I flashed a grateful smile at her. "Mrs. Cartwright, I've loved your books ever since I first discovered them, and I know everyone is going to be thrilled to see you at the library."

Mrs. Cartwright cackled with laughter. "It's going to shake a few people up when they realize I'm still alive and kicking. I've been living such a quiet life here, out on the edge of nowhere, most people think I died years ago." She laughed again. "Ought to be pretty interesting when I show up at the library and see who's there."

The elderly writer's tone gave me pause. Was I reading more into it than was really there, or was there something slightly ominous in those words?

I decided I was imagining things. I had been involved in too many strange goings-on during the past year, and now I was making trouble out of thin air.

Diesel emerged from beneath my chair and approached the sofa. He chirped at Mrs. Cartwright, and she scratched his head. "I sure do hope you'll have this handsome boy at the library when I'm there. He's the sweetest thing. You'd better watch out, or I might steal him from you."

"He loves coming to the library with me." I observed the old lady's obvious pleasure as she bonded with Diesel. "He will remember you, and I know he'll pester you for more attention."

Mrs. Cartwright petted the cat, then smiled and held out her hands to me. I grasped them for a moment. She squeezed lightly, then I let go. Her hands were cool, despite the heated room, and I noted that, although wrinkled and spotted with age, her fingers were long and slender. I remembered how cruelly my maternal grandmother's hands had been twisted by rheumatoid arthritis, and I was pleased to see that Mrs. Cartwright hadn't suffered that indignity.

Mrs. Marter waited in the doorway to the hall, and Teresa and I moved in her direction. I called to Diesel, and he pulled away

41

from Mrs. Cartwright. He seemed rather taken with her, despite the earlier tension between her and her daughter. He followed us to the front door without any further urging on my part.

When Mrs. Marter opened the door to usher us onto the porch, I noted that clouds still scudded across the sky. The rain had stopped, though thunder rumbled far away. The air, refreshed by the storm, felt cool to the skin.

Teresa and I bade Mrs. Marter good-bye, and I carried Diesel to the car to keep his paws from being soaked. Neither Teresa nor I spoke until I headed the car down the drive away from the house.

"That was nothing like I expected." Teresa's laugh sounded strained.

"No kidding." I turned the wipers off now that the windshield was clear. From the backseat, Diesel added his opinion with a few warbles and a meow. "I always find situations like that unsettling. You don't know whether you should simply excuse yourself and leave, or sit there and pretend that you haven't heard anything rude or embarrassing."

"I suppose they have lived together for a long time." Teresa spoke with the tact that made her such an outstanding library director. "Not to mention that the weather could have affected them. I know violent storms always put me on edge."

"Perhaps that was it." I rather doubted the weather had anything to do with it, but we might as well leave it at that. I had to hope that, when Mrs. Cartwright appeared in public, she and her daughter would refrain from bickering. Otherwise the audience would be mighty uncomfortable.

"At least Mrs. Cartwright seemed pleased with our plans." Teresa sighed. "I'm going to cross every available appendage, just in case. I have the weirdest feeling about this after having met mother and daughter."

I wanted to reassure Teresa that all would be well, but I was every bit as uneasy as she was. "What's the next step?"

"As soon as Mrs. Cartwright confirms that the schedule I gave her is okay, then I want to move forward with the publicity. I thought I might go ahead and add a teaser to the library website today, though. I don't think that will be a problem. We might as well start to generate some interest around town." Teresa pulled a small notebook and pen from her purse and started to make notes.

That sounded reasonable to me. Fans of Mrs. Cartwright would be thrilled to know she would make a public appearance or two. A brief news item on the website surely wouldn't cause any problems.

FIVE

Three days later, on Friday afternoon, Diesel and I worked our usual volunteer shift at the Athena Public Library. He lounged by my feet as I manned the reference desk. Two of his library friends worked nearby, Lizzie Hayes at the circulation counter, and Bronwyn Forster at a computer terminal helping a patron. From time to time, Diesel evidently decided a change of person was in order, and he made a regular circuit every ten or fifteen minutes, going from Lizzie to Bronwyn and back to me. He was really soaking up the attention today.

The library was quiet this afternoon. School wouldn't be out for another hour, and then we would get a small flood of students dropping in to do homework or check out books. A few would wait here until a parent or elder sibling came by to pick them up for a ride home. I loved seeing young people in the library, though on occasion they could get a bit rambunctious.

The front door opened, and I watched as a plump woman who appeared to be in her sixties, perhaps a decade older than I, stepped inside. She removed her sunglasses and tucked them into her purse. After a cursory glance around, she made a beeline for me.

"Good afternoon," I said as she reached the desk. "How may I help you?"

She repeated my greeting. "I'm here to see the library director, if she's not too busy. It's about the event you're planning to have with Electra Barnes Cartwright." She smiled good-naturedly, and I had a feeling I had seen her before, but where I wasn't sure. She wore her thick gray hair braided in a coronet around her head. Her jewelry consisted of a gold wedding ring and a pearl necklace. She looked every inch the society matron come to take afternoon tea. All that was missing were a hat and gloves.

"I'll be happy to check with her. What name shall I give her?" I picked up the phone as I punched in Teresa's extension.

"Mrs. Carrie Taylor," the woman responded. "I'm president of the EBC Fan Club."

That stirred a faint memory as I waited for Teresa to answer the phone. When she picked up, I told her she had a visitor and explained who it was.

"She'll be right out," I said as I hung up the phone.

"Thank you." Mrs. Taylor smiled and wandered a few feet away from the desk to examine a nearby bulletin board that listed the library's upcoming events.

Diesel, ever curious, stood and stretched before he sauntered around the desk and over to where Mrs. Taylor stood. He sniffed at the hem of her midlength cotton dress. He chirped and evidently startled her because she stepped back as she gazed down at him. Then she smiled. "Who are you?" She bent slightly to scratch his head, and he warbled for her.

"His name is Diesel," I said. The memory finally surfaced. I'd seen her several months ago at the Atheneum, our local independent bookstore. She'd been talking about children's mysteries with the owner, Jordan Thompson. I thought at the time she sounded quite knowledgeable as she and Jordan discussed the various incarnations of Nancy Drew.

"He's a Maine Coon, isn't he? Melba Gilley has told me about him. You must be Charlie Harris."

I acknowledged that I was. I had gone to

school with Melba, and now she worked as administrative assistant to the head of the Athena College Library.

Mrs. Taylor beamed at me. "What a handsome fellow he is. But isn't he rather large even for his breed?"

"Yes, he weighs in around thirty-six pounds, definitely on the large side for a Maine Coon. He's a gentle giant, though." I smiled as I watched her continue to interact with my cat. Diesel obviously approved of her, to judge by the purring.

Teresa approached and introduced herself. Mrs. Taylor greeted her, and the two women went to the director's office. Diesel trailed after them.

I wondered what Mrs. Taylor wanted to discuss. Obviously something to do with Electra Barnes Cartwright, but that was as far as I could figure. Teresa would fill me in when she had a chance.

Ten minutes later a tall, lanky young man — thirty at most, I judged — entered the library. He stopped in the doorway to look around. When he spotted me, he walked over, thumbs hooked in the belt loops of his jeans. He sported cowboy boots that looked like ostrich hide, a silver belt buckle the size of a goose egg, and a deep crimson dress shirt emblazoned with the monogram *GB*.

His raven hair was close-cropped, as was his beard. He stopped in front of the desk and stared at me. His close-set eyes, shamrock green, blinked like they were still adjusting to the inside light.

"How may I help you?"

"Is it true what I read on your website?" He had a flat Midwestern accent. "You're going to have Electra Barnes Cartwright here soon?"

"Yes, she's going to take part in our celebrations for National Library Week. We're very excited about that."

"I have to meet her." He placed his hands on the edge of the desk, and I could see them tremble.

"You'll have a chance to do that on the day she is here for her public interview. The schedule approved by Mrs. Cartwright is on the website, and I can give you a flyer with everything listed, if you like."

He shook his head. "I can't wait that long. I need to see her like today. She's so old she might croak at any minute, and I've got a collection of books for her to sign." He gripped the desk harder.

I didn't like the arrogance of his tone, and my own turned frosty when I responded. "I'm afraid that's not possible. Mrs. Cartwright won't be available until the date

49

scheduled. We'll have to see, on the day, whether she's up to signing books."

"Have you met her?"

I wanted to answer in the negative, but I couldn't lie. "I have."

"Then I'll bet you know where she lives." He glared at me. "Come on, just tell me. I'll make it worth your while." He reached in his right front pocket and pulled out a small wad of cash. He stripped off five bills, all hundreds, and thrust them at me.

I stared at him, aghast. What kind of moron was he? Trying to bribe me, all for the sake of getting his books signed?

"Absolutely not." I folded my arms across my chest and glared at him, the way I used to do at Sean and Laura when they behaved badly.

He slapped down the five hundred dollars and then peeled off another five and added them to the stack. "Come on, that ought to be enough for anybody. What's it to you anyway? I'm being really generous here."

"Not to mention unbelievably offensive. Pick up that money, and stuff it back in your pocket." I couldn't remember the last time I'd been this angry.

By now both Lizzie and Bronwyn had caught on that there was an incident brewing at the desk, and they came up on either side of me. "Do I need to call the police?" Bronwyn spoke in an undertone.

The strange young man glowered at the three of us. "For crying out loud, don't call the cops. You hillbillies don't know a good thing when you see it." He snatched up the money and stowed it in his pocket. "Should have expected something like this in such a hick town." He turned and stomped over to the door and out of the library.

"What was *his* problem?" Lizzie frowned. "I didn't hear what he wanted. I can't imagine what would be worth trying to bribe you for, Charlie."

I shook my head. "In all my years working in libraries, that was a first. I have no idea who that young man is, but he is a complete and utter jerk." I started to explain what he wanted from me, but the voice of Carrie Taylor interrupted me.

"His name is Gordon Betts, and he's got more money than he knows what to do with." She grimaced. "If he's here, then the other nutcases can't be far behind."

Six

"Nutcases?" I asked, taken slightly aback. The young man was rude, but a nutcase?

Mrs. Taylor shrugged. "Sorry, but they sure seem like nuts to me."

"Who are *they*?" Teresa frowned as she stepped from behind our visitor.

"Collectors." Mrs. Taylor rolled her eyes. "They can be absolutely nutty when it comes to children's series books. Well, at least some of them are. I don't want to make you think they're all lunatics, like Gordon, but there are a handful who go to extremes to complete their collections."

"I didn't realize books like that are so collectible." Bronwyn leaned on the reference desk as she regarded Mrs. Taylor.

"What kind of extremes?" Lizzie wanted to know.

Diesel had wandered over to sit in front of Mrs. Taylor. He meowed plaintively, and she glanced down with a smile. "Cats don't care about these things, do they, sir?" She turned to regard Lizzie and Bronwyn. "Oh, my, yes, these series, especially Nancy Drew and the Hardy Boys, are very collectible. Those are probably the two most famous, but there are plenty of others that collectors go after."

Like the Veronica Thane books, I thought. A couple of weeks ago, in preparation for lending items from my collection for the library's exhibit, I checked values for a few books on the Advanced Book Exchange website. Early copies of the first two Veronica Thane books in fine condition were going for mid–three figures.

"But what about the extremes?" Lizzie asked.

"I know of at least two cases when collectors hounded the families of authors for memorabilia and copies of books the authors might have had in their own collections." Mrs. Taylor shook her head. "I imagine some families might be glad of the money collectors are willing to pay, but it still seems indecent to me to badger people because they don't want to deal with you."

"Are these children's books really expensive?" Teresa asked. "Along the lines of first editions of literary fiction, for example?"

Mrs. Taylor shook her head. "I have no idea what kind of prices literary first editions might command. I'm not really interested enough in them, frankly. But yes, a really fine first edition of one of the first Nancy Drew books, especially one signed by Mildred Wirt Benson, might go for six or seven thousand or more."

"Dollars?" Bronwyn almost squeaked the word out.

I decided to rejoin the conversation. "Avid collectors with enough money will pay what they have to in order to get what they want." I had bought a few first editions of treasured adult mystery novels over the years, though I never spent anything even close to a thousand dollars for one book, much less six or seven thousand.

"I think I'm going to look through my mother's trunks in the attic this weekend." Lizzie grinned. "She had some Nancy Drew books when she was a girl, and I could be sitting on a small fortune."

"That's entirely possible." Mrs. Taylor smiled. "But if they've been up in your attic for very long, they may not be in the kind of condition that collectors will shell out much money for. Plus they need to have intact dust jackets."

Lizzie's grin turned into a frown. "Well, there goes my fortune. With the humidity here and the hot summers, there's no telling what books packed away in a stuffy attic for twenty years will look like now."

I almost groaned at the thought of books stored in those conditions. A woman who worked in a library ought to know better, but from experience I realized that librarians weren't always as careful about their own books as they might be. One of my staff members in Houston, I had discovered to my horror, had a first edition of *Gone with the Wind* she kept on a shelf above her kitchen sink where the sun could hit it. The dust jacket had been discarded long ago, and the binding was riddled with spots and damage from the sun. A sad state for what could have been a valuable book, alas.

"Back to these collectors you were talking about." Teresa frowned, and I could see she was concerned. "Will there be more people like this Gordon Betts showing up?"

"Without a doubt," Mrs. Taylor said. "The news that Electra Barnes Cartwright is alive and going to appear at the library is probably all over the Internet — at least as far as the children's book collecting community is concerned." She smiled. "I helped spread the word, actually. Once I saw the information on the library's website, I sent out a special electronic edition of the EBC newsletter I publish. There are several hundred subscribers to that."

Teresa closed her eyes, and I knew she was centering herself with slow, deep breaths. She always did this when she was upset or worried. As a former public library director myself, I could easily imagine her thoughts. I was envisioning some of the same possibilities myself — hordes of rabid Veronica Thane fans descending upon Athena, desperate to see the author and demand that she sign their books.

To my chagrin, I realized we should have considered this possibility before we even went to talk to Mrs. Cartwright. I'd been so carried away by my own excitement over meeting her and having her involved with the library's events that I hadn't stopped to consider the implications. On the other hand, having Electra Barnes Cartwright appear at the library wasn't on the order of hosting a superstar singer or actor, who could draw thousands of raving, out-of-control fans. In our situation, though, even a few determined — or even obsessed — readers surely wouldn't wreak much havoc.

I'd been wrong before about situations like this, however, and I had the uneasy feeling I was wrong now.

While Lizzie and Bronwyn asked Mrs. Taylor further questions, I motioned for

Teresa to step aside with me. In an undertone I said, "We should talk to Mrs. Cartwright about this and rethink our plan. She may not realize the furor that her public appearance could cause."

"If Mrs. Taylor isn't exaggerating." Teresa grimaced. "That one person aside, do we really think everyone will behave that way? Surely he's an extreme case."

"Mrs. Taylor *could* be exaggerating, I suppose, but she doesn't impress me as that kind of person." I paused to examine the lady again. Nothing in her demeanor set off any alarm bells with me, and I had many years of experience dealing with the public.

Teresa folded her arms across her chest. "Wishful thinking on my part. You're right either way. We need to talk to Mrs. Cartwright. I'll go call her daughter and discuss the situation with her."

"Good plan. If necessary, we can just say that Mrs. Cartwright will do the interview but is unable to sign books because of her health."

Teresa nodded before she headed for her office. I turned back to the conversation with Mrs. Taylor.

"I never heard of Connie Blair," Bronwyn said. "But I read Betty Cavanna's books and never knew she wrote under another name."

The Connie Blair series, written under the name *Betsy Allen,* featured a young woman who worked in advertising. Connie, like Cherry Ames the nurse and Vicki Barr the airline stewardess, was one of the "professional" girl detectives.

"I read some of those," Lizzie exclaimed. "Didn't the titles all have a color in them?"

"Yes, they sure did." Mrs. Taylor beamed at Lizzie. "Connie was more sophisticated than most of the other girl detectives."

By now several other library patrons had drawn near to listen to the discussion. Two of them were women about Mrs. Taylor's age, and another was a girl who looked about fourteen.

"Mrs. Taylor, we definitely need to include you in our programs for National Library Week. Perhaps a talk on the different girl detectives? I think our patrons would enjoy that." I glanced at the bystanders and was pleased to see the teenager nod enthusiastically.

"I know my book club would love to come to something like that." This came from one of the older women. She turned to her companion. "Don't you think so, Martha?"

Martha nodded. "I surely do, Kathryn. There are about twenty of us, and I know most of us read Nancy Drew and Veronica

Thane growing up."

Mrs. Taylor appeared delighted at their enthusiasm. "I'd love to give a talk. That was one of the things I discussed with your director, and she was interested."

"Then we will definitely set it up," I said. Once again beside me, Diesel rubbed against my leg and warbled loudly. Everyone laughed, and he warbled again. He enjoyed being in the spotlight when it suited him.

"Excuse me, who's in charge here?"

The loud voice startled me, and I noticed a similar reaction from Mrs. Taylor and a few of the others around us.

While we were talking, a woman I'd never seen before had come into the library. She stood at the reference desk and appeared slightly aggrieved over the lack of attention she was receiving.

I stepped forward past Mrs. Taylor, Lizzie, and Bronwyn, who had blocked my view of the desk. "How may I assist you, ma'am?"

Diesel followed alongside me, and as he became visible, the woman spotted him. She paled, and her mouth opened, but only strangled sounds, not words, came forth.

Then she turned and fled out the door.

SEVEN

"What on earth is the matter with *her*?" Lizzie, like the rest of us, stared at the door as it closed behind the stranger.

"Severe ailurophobia," Mrs. Taylor said before she took off after the woman. She pushed open the door and strode out. We could her hear shout, "Della, come back here."

"Severe what?" Bronwyn asked.

"Ailurophobia," I replied. "It means an abnormal fear of cats." I looked down at Diesel, and he regarded me almost quizzically, like a child might do. "Sorry, boy, but there are people who are terrified of kitties."

"Sounded like Mrs. Taylor knows her," Lizzie said. "Poor woman. Imagine being afraid of a sweet boy like Diesel."

At the sound of his name, Diesel chirped, and Lizzie and Bronwyn nearly bumped heads as they bent to pet him. "You first,"

Bronwyn said with a grin.

While Lizzie and Bronwyn took turns rubbing the cat's head, I went to the door and walked outside. I could see Mrs. Taylor with her arm around Della's shoulders, and the stranger appeared calmer now. I noticed that she wore a well-tailored skirt and jacket, both a bright yellow, with an emerald green blouse. The colors complemented her dark hair, cut in an old-fashioned bob that framed an attractive face.

I debated whether to approach them, but when Mrs. Taylor spotted me, she motioned me over.

"Della, dear, this is Mr. Harris," Mrs. Taylor said. "Mr. Harris, Della Duffy." She gave the other woman's shoulders a brief squeeze and then released her.

Della Duffy held out a hand that felt cold and clammy in mine as I gave it a gentle shake. "How do you do, Mr. Harris? I'm sorry but I couldn't stay in there with that cat." Her mouth twisted in a grimace. "I'd like to know what the heck a cat was doing here. They shouldn't let animals in the library."

I dropped her hand and resisted the urge to pull out my handkerchief to wipe it. My tone was stiff as I replied, "No need to apologize, Ms. Duffy. Diesel is pretty large for a domestic cat, and he's been known to startle people before. He's a gentle giant, though, I can assure you, and has always been welcome at the library."

Ms. Duffy's grimace lingered. "Is he yours?"

I nodded.

"Sorry, but I can't stand cats. He might be gentle, but if I go back in there, I'll just have another panic attack." Mrs. Taylor patted her shoulder.

Despite my irritation at her brusqueness, I felt sorry for her. Irrational fear can wreak havoc in a person's life, and I could only imagine the terror she felt because of her phobia. "Perhaps I could help you now, out here, so that you don't have to go back in the building. Or I can take Diesel home, and you can get help from one of the other library staff."

Ms. Duffy shook her head. "No, don't bother. If there's somewhere to sit outside, you might as well help me here. At least the weather is pleasant. Not too hot, with a little breeze." She glanced about and spotted the bench in front of the shrubbery near the front door. She headed for it, and Mrs. Taylor and I followed. I would have to overlook the woman's less-than-gracious behavior.

The two women sat, and I stood in front

of them because the bench was made for two. Mrs. Taylor spoke for the first time since her introduction. "Della is a collector, Mr. Harris. I've known her for a dozen years or so."

"Charlie, please." I forced a smile, though Mrs. Taylor had been anything but rude. I addressed the other woman. "I suppose you read about the library's planned event with Electra Barnes Cartwright."

Ms. Duffy nodded. "Carrie here also e-mailed me, and I can't tell you how excited I was to hear such wonderful news. I've been a fan of Mrs. Cartwright's since I was ten years old, and the thought of actually getting to meet her . . ." Her voice trailed off.

"We know, dear." Carrie Taylor patted the other woman's arm. "Both Charlie and I are fans of EBC's, too."

"Do you always refer to her as *EBC*?" I asked Mrs. Taylor.

She grinned. "I'm so used to it now I hardly realize I'm doing it. It's convenient shorthand, and the readers of my newsletter are used to it, too."

"Her full name is rather a mouthful." I turned to Ms. Duffy. "What can I help you with, ma'am?"

Her response was tart. "I want to know

when I can meet Mrs. Cartwright."

"There will be a public interview with her. The schedule will be up on the library's website soon." I regarded her warily. Was she going to be like Gordon Betts and demand that she be given Mrs. Cartwright's address for a private visit?

"That's not good enough." Ms. Duffy frowned. "I have one of the most extensive collections of Veronica Thane and EBC books of any collector I know, and I want her to sign as many of them as possible."

I did my best to suppress my irritation as I answered. "We don't know yet whether Mrs. Cartwright will be able to sign books. I doubt she could sign a whole collection anyway. You do realize that she is about to turn a hundred soon?"

"Is she so decrepit that can't write her name?" Ms. Duffy glared at me. "If she's strong enough to come and do an interview, then she ought to be able to sign her name."

Mrs. Taylor and I exchanged glances. I wondered if she was as appalled at Della Duffy's callous disregard for Mrs. Cartwright as I was. I had a good mind to tell her what I thought of her demands, but generations of good Southern manners made that difficult. Instead I settled for milder words. "Mrs. Cartwright will be the one to decide that, and we will all have to abide by her wishes. Now, is there anything else I can do for you?"

"Obviously not. I guess I'll just have to find EBC on my own. I'll make it worth her while to sign her name as many times as I need." Ms. Duffy flashed what I took to be a smile of self-satisfaction and conviction.

Beside her Mrs. Taylor sighed and shook her head gently. "Della, you and Gordon are going to have to realize that you can't just bully your way into getting what you want. Throwing money around isn't going to accomplish anything, either. Charlie is right. EBC is an old woman, and I can't believe you're truly that blindly selfish."

Before Ms. Duffy had a chance to respond, a voice hailed us from behind me. "What ho, ladies? What are you two lovely specimens of the gentler, fairer sex up to this beautiful day?"

Wondering who on earth talked like a character out of a third-rate English novel, I turned to find out.

An elderly man who had the appearance of an overripe cherub stood about six feet away. He beamed at the women like a chubby sun emerging from a cloud. No more than five feet tall, he sported a gray suit that wouldn't have been out of place on

Madison Avenue in the 1950s.

"Oh, goody, just what this little shindig needed." The venom in Della Duffy's tone startled me. "Winnie, shouldn't you be back in your hobbit hole finding another dead writer to rip off?"

"Good morning, sir." The cherub advanced toward me, smile intact, hand extended. "I don't believe I've had the pleasure of meeting you before. Winston Eagleton, publisher."

I shook his hand as I responded to his cheerful introduction. "Charlie Harris, librarian. Pleased to meet you, sir."

He nodded and moved toward the bench. "Carrie Taylor, what a sight for an old man's eyes you are, to be sure. Lovely and girlish as ever."

Mrs. Taylor regarded Eagleton blandly. "You're as full of the blarney as ever, Winston. Either that, or you're decades overdue for an eye exam."

"You and Della-the-ever-delightful will have your little jokes." Eagleton offered Ms. Duffy a smile no less genial than those he gave Mrs. Taylor and me. "Della, you know very well indeed that I reprint only out-of-copyright material, or copyright material with the appropriate permissions." He wagged a finger at her in a playful gesture.

"You really must stop saying such things, or Winnie might have to sue."

"Tell *Winnie* that he knows *very well indeed* that I have enough money to hire a lawyer who will bury him in that hobbit hole for the rest of his smarmy little so-called life." When she finished delivering that mocking, menacing statement, Della Duffy got up from the bench and pushed her way past Eagleton and me. She headed down the sidewalk to the parking lot, got in her car, and peeled out of the lot while the rest of us watched in silence.

"I don't know who did a wee in her porridge this morning," Eagleton observed in a cheery tone, "but our Della is in a right old slather."

"Isn't she always when she doesn't immediately get what she wants?" Mrs. Taylor sounded tired. "Put her and Gordon in a gunnysack, shake them up, and who knows which one would fall out first."

I hadn't heard that expression in a while, and I couldn't argue with Mrs. Taylor's observation. Della Duffy appeared to be every bit as arrogant and self-centered as Gordon Betts, and with the two of them around, our event with Electra Barnes Cartwright could end up a disaster.

"How quaint." Eagleton sat down beside

Mrs. Taylor. "Carrie, I have the most wonderful news, and I wanted you to be the first to hear it as the publisher of the EBC newsletter."

"What wonderful news?" Mrs. Taylor didn't appear all that interested.

Eagleton chuckled merrily. "Why, the news that I'm going to publish the long-lost volumes of Veronica Thane's adventures."

EIGHT

Mrs. Taylor snorted in an unladylike manner. "Winnie, where did you get such an idea? A few years ago EBC wrote to me and told me that when the publisher canceled the series, she was happy to move on and write different things."

Eagleton continued to beam, and I began to wonder if the man was on medication that kept him in a permanently sunny mood. Nothing seemed to deflate him. "Carrie, dear Electra might have told *you* such a taradiddle in the past, but I happen to know better." He laid a finger to the side of his nose and winked. "I have another source who tells me that there is a trunk in the attic — I'm speaking metaphorically, you understand — that has five unpublished Veronica Thane novels. *Five.* Isn't that astounding?"

"That's one word for it," Mrs. Taylor muttered.

Despite Mrs. Taylor's obvious disbelief, I had to hope that Eagleton's source was right. After all these years, how fun it would be to have new Veronica Thane adventures to read! Perhaps childish enthusiasm on my part, but I had loved the books fiercely as a boy. Many adults, I supposed, had a small corner inside them that occasionally longed to relive the pure joys of a childhood experience.

I decided to give the man encouragement. "That's exciting news. I would love to have copies when they're published."

"Who is this so-called source of yours?" Mrs. Taylor's voice had a snarky edge to it. Her reaction might perhaps stem from jealousy because Eagleton had scooped her on this. With her position as the editor of a newsletter dedicated to all things EBC, she would be annoyed she hadn't heard about the unpublished books first.

"Dear EBC's daughter, of course." Eagleton sounded gleeful as he continued. "Even you, Carrie dear, must admit that the great lady's own daughter should, above all others, know what she's talking about."

Mrs. Taylor's tone was grudging when she responded. "I suppose you're right, Winnie. If anyone knows the truth about it, Marcella certainly would. I have to hand it to you.

When are you going to publish these manuscripts?"

For the first time Eagleton lost his overly perky demeanor. He frowned. "We haven't settled the details yet, but I hope to take possession of the books sometime in the next few days. Marcella promised she would call as soon as the great lady is ready to receive her humble servant."

"In other words, EBC hasn't agreed to let you have the rights to publish them." Mrs. Taylor grinned. "You scurried down here all the way from Ohio because you're hoping to snap up the rights before a bigger publisher comes calling with a fat bankroll."

"The big houses in New York won't be stumbling over one another to publish these books." Eagleton appeared cheered by this thought. "As much as *we* admire and revere EBC and Veronica Thane, the books *have* been out of print for thirty years. No other publisher has expressed interest in them before now, and I really can't see that I'm going to have competition."

"There are precedents for both small and large press reprints of books like the Veronica Thane series." I decided that a few pertinent facts couldn't hurt. "In recent years Applewood Books reprinted the whole Judy Bolton series, and they even published a title cowritten by two fans and illustrated by one of Sutton's daughters." Warming to my theme, I added, "Springer reprinted the Cherry Ames series, and Random House reissued Trixie Belden, though I'm not sure whether they're still available."

"I know about all those." Mrs. Taylor's expression made it clear she wasn't all that impressed with my knowledge. "With the exception of that one new Judy Bolton title, however, they weren't continuing the Cherry Ames or Trixie Belden series. And they certainly weren't claiming to have a trunk full of unpublished manuscripts in the attic. That sounds more like the plot of one of these series books than actual fact."

"I suppose I shall have to start calling you *Doubting Thomasina* instead of Carrie." Eagleton proffered another sunny smile. "You shall see, my dear Thomasina, you shall see and be amazed."

Mrs. Taylor appeared unmoved by Eagleton's claim. "I think I would have heard about these manuscripts before now. After all, I've known Marcella for over a decade. She's never even mentioned your name when we chat."

Eagleton shrugged. "My dear Carrie, far be it from me to fathom the deep mysteries of the feminine mind. I have not been

72

acquainted with Marcella as long as you, but in our recent conversations she has been *most* charming and *quite* forthcoming with details about her mother's work. Not to mention eager to see her mother's name in print once again so that a new generation of readers can discover the joy of such an engaging and endearing heroine as Veronica Thane."

Mrs. Taylor stood in an abrupt movement. "I think I'll just call Marcella and check this story with her. I think there's something odd going on. And if you're involved, Winnie Eagleton, it's really, really odd." With that, she moved quickly away, and I called "Good-bye" after her. She didn't appear to hear me.

Eagleton shook his head. "Poor Carrie. For years she has prided herself on this deep, personal connection to the great lady and her family although they have never met face-to-face. I can imagine how distressing it must be for her to discover that she is not clasped as firmly to the Cartwright bosom as she believed."

I had no desire to insert myself into this odd contest between Eagleton and Mrs. Taylor. The man had come to the public library, and I presumed he had a reason for his visit. "Was there anything in particular you were seeking at the library? If you'd like to come inside, I'll be happy to help you."

Eagleton beamed at me as he stood. "Yes, young man, there is." I had to suppress a smile at being called *young man.* "I need access to older issues of your local paper as well as those of national papers like the *New York Times.*"

"I can certainly help you with that." I nodded in the direction of the front door. "Come on inside, and we'll get you started. Our local paper went online in 1998, and we have microfilm of older issues. We also have access to the *Times* and other papers online through various databases. I can show you how to find them."

"Smashing, absolutely smashing." Eagleton beamed as he followed me to the door.

Diesel awaited right inside the library. He often became anxious when I left him for more than a few minutes. Usually he was happy with Lizzie and Bronwyn, but I figured he had picked up on the tension when Della Duffy made her abrupt exit.

"Everything is okay, boy." I scratched his head, and he rewarded me with chirps and meows.

"Who is this fine fellow?" Eagleton stared at my cat, evidently fascinated. "I don't recall that I have ever seen such a large domestic feline. I suppose he is a Maine Coon, is he not?"

"Yes, he is." A point to Eagleton for recognizing the breed. "His name is Diesel, and he accompanies me everywhere. He's big even for his breed."

Diesel sidled closer to the stranger to allow his head to be rubbed, and Eagleton complied. I waited a few moments to let the two become acquainted while Bronwyn and Lizzie watched. Then I gently directed Eagleton toward the small room where we kept the microfilm of the pre-1998 issues of the *Athena Daily Register.* "If you'd like to start with these," I said, "I can show you how to load the microfilm into the reader, if you need me to."

"Thank you, young man, but that won't be necessary." Eagleton nodded at the equipment. "I am quite familiar with this technology. I rather think I will start in here, and perhaps later you can show me to a computer and help me get started with the papers online."

"Certainly," I said. Diesel and I left him humming as he examined the drawers in which the film was stored.

Eagleton emerged from the microfilm room about ten minutes before Diesel and I completed our volunteer shift for the day. I got him settled at a computer station, logged him in, and guided him to the links for the newspaper databases.

Diesel climbed happily into the backseat for the short drive home. Nothing was very far from anything else in Athena, one of the distinct advantages of living in a smaller town. Sean's car was in the garage when I pulled in beside it, and I was surprised he would be home at a little past three-thirty in the afternoon.

In the kitchen I went straight to the refrigerator for a cold drink while Diesel visited his litter box in the utility room. I spotted a folded note with *Dad* scrawled across it stuck to the fridge door with a daisy magnet. As I sipped at my diet drink, I opened the note and scanned the contents.

Sean had written in his precise, bold hand, "News to share. Come to the back porch, and I'll tell you."

I tucked the note in my pocket and headed for the back of house. Diesel caught up with me before I reached the door and jogged past me. He turned his head toward me and warbled.

"Go ahead." I grinned because I knew what he wanted. My boarder Justin Ward-law had taught him how to open doors with his front paws, and Diesel liked showing off his skill. He reared up on his hind legs and twisted the knob. The door popped open, and the cat and I stepped onto the screened-in porch that ran the length of the rear of the house.

I had already picked up the fragrant smell of my son's cigar. This was the only part of the house in which he was allowed to indulge his habit, and when I couldn't find him elsewhere inside, I knew he'd be out here. I'd rather he gave it up entirely for his health, but I knew better than to argue with him about it. At least he smoked only where there was plenty of air circulating.

"Hey, Dad." Sean turned and smiled, cigar in one hand and champagne bottle in the other. "Time to celebrate."

NINE

"Celebrate?" What was he talking about? Did this mean he had finally asked Alexandra Pendergrast to marry him? We had all been expecting this for months now.

"I know what you're thinking." Sean shook his head. "No, Dad, I haven't asked her yet. I'm talking about the state bar exam." He popped the cork on the bottle.

Of course. How could I have forgotten? Sean had taken the Mississippi bar in February, and the results were expected this month.

"You passed," I said. I had never doubted he would. My son, I could say without boasting, was an extremely bright young man.

"I did." Sean stuck the cigar in his mouth and picked up two champagne flutes. He filled one and handed it to me before filling his own.

"To Mississippi's newest legal eagle." I

raised the glass and smiled. "I'm proud of you, as always."

Sean beamed back at me as he raised his own. He drew on the cigar and expelled the smoke. We watched it waft away in the breeze coming through the screens as we sipped the champagne.

"Thanks, Dad." Sean downed the rest of the amber liquid. "How about a refill?"

"No, thanks, one glass is enough for me," I said.

Diesel sat in front of him and chirped. Sean glanced down and smiled. "Sorry, big guy, but I don't think champagne is good for cats. Dad might have a fit if I give you any."

The cat's head turned in my direction, as if to ask my permission. "No, boy, Sean is right. No bubbly for you."

Diesel made a rumbling noise — his method of signaling irritation when he didn't get his way. Sean and I shared a chuckle over the cat's behavior.

"I'm sure Alexandra is pretty excited about the news." My son had been working with her and her father, the legendary Q. C. Pendergrast, as an assistant. Q.C. had promised to make Sean a partner when he passed the bar. I figured the old man was getting ready to ease off on his legal practice and let the youngsters take over.

"I haven't told her yet." Sean's expression turned serious. "I wanted to tell you first, Dad."

Suddenly a lump in my throat made it difficult to speak. A year ago my relationship with my son had floundered, with me clueless as to the reason. We resolved the problems between us, however, and these days I felt closer to Sean than I had since his childhood.

Diesel warbled, and I had to smile. He always sensed when my mood shifted suddenly. I rubbed his head to reassure the cat. "Thank you, Son. I'm glad you did. Hadn't you better tell Alexandra now?"

"I will, tonight at dinner." Sean looked away from me and focused instead on the backyard. He drew on his cigar and expelled the smoke.

Judging by his tone, he didn't sound all that eager to talk to Alexandra. Had there been some rift between them that I didn't know about?

I kept my tone nonchalant when I queried him. "What's wrong? Have you two had a fight?"

Sean glanced back at me. He shook his head. "Not a fight, merely a strong disagreement." He had another sip of champagne.

"It's this plan of her father's to turn over the firm to Alex and me. *After* we're married."

I sat on one of the wicker sofas, and Diesel jumped up beside me. He stretched out, with his head and front legs on my lap. "Do you feel like he's trying to push the two of you into marriage? Is that what's bothering you?"

Sean shrugged and smoked in silence for a few moments. I kept quiet and stroked Diesel's back.

"I *want* to marry Alex." Sean's tone was clipped as he deposited ash into the ashtray on a nearby table. "She knows that, even though I haven't asked her yet. Q.C. knows I'll get around to asking her eventually. I just don't want him to hand over his practice because I'm married to his daughter." He stuck his cigar back in his mouth and drew hard. He looked angry as he blew smoke toward the screen. "I have money saved. I can buy into the practice on my own."

I should have realized before now that this would be an issue for Sean. He had always been proud, insistent on being independent. He wanted to earn whatever he had, and I in turn had always been proud to have reared such a self-reliant son.

"Have you expressed any of this to Q.C.

81

and Alex?"

"When the subject first came up."

Sean's wry delivery of that line didn't fool me. There had probably been a heated discussion. Sean had a bit of a temper — slow to ignite, but fiery when it burst forth. He took after me in that respect.

"What did Q.C. say when you told him how you felt?" I kept my tone mild as I continued to rub Diesel along his spine. Happy warbles repaid me for my attentions to His Majesty.

"Nonsense, my boy. After all, we can't have you working for your wife. What would the folks around here have to say about that?" Sean did a fair imitation of Q.C.'s deep voice and broad drawl.

"And how did you respond?" Temperately, I hoped.

Sean cut a sideways glance at me. "Politely enough, despite the fact that I was blazingly angry. Insisted I didn't want to be a partner on those terms, but he didn't pay any attention to my objections. I figured there was no point in arguing, so I dropped it. For the time being."

"Do you think he'll start pushing again when he finds out you've passed the bar?" Perhaps I should have a word with Q.C., explain how proud Sean was, and ask him

82

to back down. No, I decided after a moment's reflection, if Sean ever found out I did that behind his back, he would find it hard to forgive.

"Probably." Sean laughed, but there was no mirth or joy in the sound. "As long as I don't propose to Alex, though, he won't go through with it." He paused. "At least, I don't think he would."

That was another trait Sean inherited from me — stubbornness, occasionally to the point of folly. I worried that he would break up what had so far been a happy and loving relationship. I understood his position, though, and I couldn't blame him for resenting Q.C.'s high-handed behavior.

"Don't worry. I know what you're thinking. I am *not* going to screw this up. Alex is the best thing that ever happened to me, and I'd be a world-class idiot to let her get away."

"You'll work it out somehow, I'm sure." I gently moved Diesel from my lap so I could stand. "If there's anything I can do, you know all you have to do is ask."

"I know." Sean dropped his cigar in the ashtray and came over to give me a quick, fierce hug. "Thanks, Dad."

That lump was back. I swallowed hard as Sean stepped away to pick up his cigar.

"I have things that need doing," I said, my voice a little hoarse. "So Diesel and I will leave you to it. Come on, boy, back in the house."

Diesel followed me, but I opened the door this time. As Diesel ambled through, I glanced back at my son. He stared out at the backyard and smoked. I sighed as I closed the door.

Time to box up the books I was lending for the exhibit of juvenile series books at the library. The cartons I needed were in the utility room, and while I was there, I added some dry food to Diesel's bowl and rinsed out his water bowl and refilled it. I pulled two medium-sized cartons from the shelf and left Diesel noisily crunching as I headed for the stairs.

Happy to note that I wasn't breathing all that hard by the time I reached the third floor, I decided I wasn't in such bad shape after all.

Moments later, when I squatted in front of the shelves to retrieve a few books from the bottom, I revised my opinion. My knees creaked, and I had to grab on to an upper shelf to pull myself up. I moved stiffly as I put the books in a carton atop the bed.

I turned to examine the shelves and let my eyes roam over the spines. *Where are the*

Cherry Ames books? I wondered. I finally spotted them in the upper left corner, against the back wall of the bedroom. I couldn't reach the books without an uncomfortable stretch, so I retrieved the upholstered ottoman from its place in front of an old easy chair.

I stepped onto the ottoman and tested my balance. Confident that I could reach up without straining, I retrieved a couple of the volumes from the shelf — one of the older ones with a dust jacket and the green-spined final book in the series, *Cherry Ames, Ski Nurse.*

When I pulled the latter book down, I spotted what looked like a scrapbook at the end of the shelf. *What is that doing here?* I wondered. It seemed out of place. I reached for it and tugged, but the cover had stuck to the varnish of the shelf. I set the two Cherry Ames books on the shelf and reached with both hands to prize the darn thing loose. No telling how many years the scrapbook had been there, adhering to the wood.

Finally, with a forceful effort, I loosened it. Bits of the vinyl cover stuck to the shelf. I would have to try later to remove them. I scooped up the Cherry Ames books with my free hand and stepped down from the ottoman. Once again I set Cherry aside and turned my attention to the scrapbook.

I fanned the browned pages, and as I did, I could see that a few of the newspaper articles Aunt Dottie had pasted in were loose and about to flutter out. With more care I examined some of the pages and found to my delight that the items were apparently all related to children's books. I spotted clippings from magazine articles along with the newsprint. Mildred Wirt Benson, who late in life finally gained long overdue recognition for her role in creating Nancy Drew, was featured heavily. I wondered whether Aunt Dottie had managed to find anything on Electra Barnes Cartwright. I didn't have time now to delve thoroughly through the scrapbook, and with some reluctance I stuck it in one of the cartons and turned back to my task of choosing books for the exhibit.

Ten minutes later, satisfied that I had a representative selection of both well-known and nowadays obscure series books, I stacked one carton atop the other and carried them downstairs. I had to move with care because I couldn't see my feet. I made it safely enough to the second floor and took the cartons into my bedroom. Since I hadn't planned to take them to the library until tomorrow morning, they could stay here for now.

My cell phone rang while I headed down to the kitchen, and I pulled it from my pocket as I reached the first floor. According to the number that appeared on the display, Teresa was calling from her office at the library.

I barely had a chance to say "Hello" before Teresa burst into speech. "Charlie, can you come back to the library right away? Mrs. Cartwright's daughter called. She and her son are on the way here to discuss Mrs. Cartwright's fee for next week."

I knew Teresa had no money in her budget to pay an author for appearing at an event. Neither Mrs. Cartwright nor her daughter had broached the subject when we visited them. What could we do about this? Especially after we'd already advertised on the library's website that Mrs. Cartwright would appear.

I assured Teresa I would be there in a few minutes. "We'll figure something out." I tried to sound confident, but unless Mrs. Marter was reasonable about the amount, we would have to cancel.

TEN

Diesel chirped away in the backseat during our second trip of the day to the public library. My daughter, Laura, laughingly claimed he was conversing with us when he did that, because sometimes he was quite voluble. He would occasionally pause, cock his head to the side, and gaze up at the recipient of his confidences as if he expected a response. There were even times when I figured I knew what he was attempting to tell me, but now wasn't one of those times. I let him chatter on until I parked the car at the library.

"Come on, boy. Let's go in and see your buddies again."

Diesel hopped over the seat and climbed out as I held the door open for him. Finally quiet, he padded beside me as we entered the library.

Bronwyn looked up from the reference desk as we neared. After greeting us in turn

— Diesel first, as usual — she said, "Teresa is in her office. She's really upset. Do you think she'll cancel the whole exhibit?" Diesel disappeared behind the desk, and I knew he went to rub against Bronwyn. That would make her feel better.

Bronwyn had put in many hours preparing for the exhibit. She had a flair for art and had created the posters, besides the work she had done getting our exhibit cases cleaned and ready. "We'll do our best to resolve things with Mrs. Cartwright and her family." I spoke with more confidence than I felt, but I wanted to erase the worried look from Bronwyn's face. She nodded and attempted a smile.

I heard Diesel warble at her, and with her attention diverted to the cat, I headed to Teresa's office.

When I walked in, I found her seated at her desk, glaring at her computer screen. "There's no way. Absolutely no way."

"Looking at the budget, I presume." I sat in one of the chairs across from her.

Teresa nodded wearily as she turned to face me. "The money just isn't there. Even if they were asking only a few hundred dollars."

"How much do they want?" I wasn't sure I wanted to hear the figure.

"Seventy-five hundred." Teresa still sounded shaken as she spoke the words.

"Good heavens." Far worse than I'd imagined. "How do they think a small public library could come up with money like that?"

"You tell me." She closed her eyes and massaged her temples with her fingertips. "I knew that big-name writers often get paid for doing talks at libraries, but I've heard they will sometimes waive their fees in special cases. This is as about as special a case as I can imagine."

"Perhaps we can bargain with them, get them to drop the price." I tried to sound encouraging. "Maybe even persuade them to drop their demand for a fee at all."

"I wouldn't count on it. When Mrs. Marter called to inform me about the fee, she sounded firm. I don't think they'll budge."

"In that case we will simply tell them the exhibit will go on but without any appearance by Mrs. Cartwright. That would be a shame, but we have no other choice."

Teresa nodded. "I thought about calling Miss An'gel and Miss Dickce, but they're so generous as it is. I hate to go to them with my hands out yet again."

The Ducote sisters — known to everyone in Athena as Miss An'gel and Miss Dickce

— were the town's richest citizens and the mainstays of all charitable efforts. They might be happy to oblige such a request, but I understood Teresa's reluctance to approach them in this instance.

"I called Carrie Taylor," Teresa continued, "and asked her to join us. I may be grasping at straws, but since she has devoted so much of her time to Mrs. Cartwright and her work, I didn't think it would hurt to have another person to make an appeal on our behalf."

"Good idea. Let's hope you're right." I was about to say more, but Teresa looked past me at the doorway. I turned to see Mrs. Taylor paused there. I stood and offered her my chair and pulled another one near the desk for myself.

Teresa quickly filled Mrs. Taylor in, and the older woman frowned when she heard the details. "That's outrageous. I dearly love Mrs. Cartwright and her books, but they ought to be ashamed for trying to stick the library with such a crazy demand." She sniffed. "I'll be willing to bet you EBC doesn't know a thing about this. It's that greedy grandson of hers. Never could hold down a job from what I've heard tell."

Mrs. Taylor evidently knew more about the family than I realized. I wondered who the source of her information was. I was about to ask when she forestalled me. "I'm in frequent contact with EBC's agent, Yancy Thigpen. She's been a lot more informative about things than the man who used to represent EBC."

Gossiping about a client didn't sound at all ethical to me, but it didn't appear to faze Mrs. Taylor.

"Of course, there are things I can't print." Mrs. Taylor gave us a smug smile. "Yancy tells me my little newsletter is the best of its kind she's ever seen, and she doesn't mind sharing these little tidbits with me. I'm sure she has EBC's permission anyway. She knows I won't spread them around."

Teresa and I glanced at each other and then quickly away. The irony of her claim appeared to be lost on Mrs. Taylor.

"What about this agent?" I asked. "Should we call her and explain the situation? She must have dealt with this kind of thing before."

"I have her number written down somewhere." Teresa hunted through three small stacks of paper on her desk until she found what she needed. She punched in the digits on her office phone while Mrs. Taylor and I waited in silence.

"Good afternoon. I'd like to speak to

Yancy Thigpen please." Teresa paused for a moment. "Teresa Farmer, director of the public library in Athena, Mississippi. I've spoken with Ms. Thigpen before." Another pause, much longer this time. Finally Teresa said, "I see. Thank you very much." She put down the receiver.

"Oh, dear," Mrs. Taylor said, "she wouldn't talk to you, would she?" She sounded upset.

"No, it wasn't that." Teresa smiled. "Actually, it's probably good news. The assistant, or whoever he was, told me Ms. Thigpen is flying down to Athena today." She checked her watch. "In fact, she should have arrived at the airport in Memphis by now. She ought to be in town in an hour or so, unless she gets lost on the way."

"Do you think we should try to postpone this discussion with Mrs. Marter until the agent is here and can take part?" That would be the best thing to do, I thought.

"Too late," Teresa said in an undertone. She stood and nodded toward the doorway. "Good afternoon, Mrs. Marter." She came from behind her desk to approach the visitor.

Mrs. Taylor craned her neck around to see. I stood to offer my chair to Mrs. Cartwright.

"Marcella, move out of the way." Mrs. Cartwright's voice sounded from outside the office. "I need to sit down."

"There isn't much room in my office," Teresa said as Mrs. Marter moved aside at her mother's command. "Why don't we go to our small meeting room instead? It's only a few feet farther."

"Very well." Mrs. Cartwright allowed Teresa to take her left arm as she leaned heavily on the cane in her right hand. Though slightly stooped, she was an inch or so taller than Teresa, who was about five-five. Marcella Marter trailed behind them, and Mrs. Taylor and I brought up the rear.

Teresa flipped the light switch as she guided our guest into the room and helped her to a chair. She sat next to the elderly woman around a smallish rectangular table that could accommodate ten people. Mrs. Marter took the chair on her mother's free side, while Mrs. Taylor and I went to sit across from them.

Mrs. Cartwright, swathed in black, with a black scarf around her neck and black gloves on her hands, sported large-framed dark sunglasses. The red hair provided a sharp contrast to her clothes, and her face had been expertly — though heavily from what I could tell — made up. I supposed she was vain enough about her appearance that she didn't want to look like a centenarian in public.

"This is an unexpected pleasure, Mrs. Cartwright." Teresa smiled. "I thought your grandson was coming with you."

"Eugene had something else to do." Mrs. Cartwright bumped her cane against the edge of the table. "Besides, this is my business, not any of his. Nor any of my daughter's. Isn't that right, Marcella?"

"Yes, Mother." Marcella stared at her lap and spoke in a whisper.

"Good afternoon, Mrs. Cartwright. It's so wonderful to finally meet you in person." Mrs. Taylor's voice, quavery at first, grew more assured as she continued. "I thought I wouldn't get to meet you until next week, but here you are."

"Who are you?" Mrs. Cartwright sounded brusque. "I know Mr. Harris there" — she nodded at me — "but I don't know you."

Mrs. Taylor giggled. "Oh, dear, I have completely forgotten my manners, haven't I? I'm Carrie Taylor, the editor and publisher of the EBC newsletter, *The Thane Chronicles.*"

"Then I suppose I should thank you for all the work you've done to keep Veronica Thane's name alive." Mrs. Cartwright smiled. "I've been happy to know that there are readers out there who still remember me and my little books."

"Oh, there are, there are. Millions, probably. If you only knew how much people love you and your writing." Mrs. Taylor bobbed up and down a bit in her chair.

"That's wonderful to hear." The author turned to Teresa, and beside me Mrs. Taylor stopped moving. "Now, about the speaker's fee for my appearance next week. Marcella said there is a problem."

"I'm afraid so." Teresa paused for a breath. "Before we discuss that, though, I wonder if you could tell me why you didn't mention a fee when we visited you the other day. We proceeded with our plans in all good faith that you were happy to appear without one."

"I thought you had already discussed that with my daughter." Mrs. Cartwright frowned. "At least, that is what she led me to believe."

"We did not talk about a fee at any time." Teresa shook her head. "We simply don't have that kind of money in our budget. We can't afford to pay you."

"That's outrageous." Marcella Marter's head jerked up. "You have to pay what we're asking. You've already told everyone my mother will appear here next week."

"Yes, we have," I said to offer Teresa my support. "It's unfortunate, but small public libraries like ours can't afford to pay speakers such a large amount."

"Dear EBC, please consider your fans. You don't know how much it means to us to hear you talk about your life and career. Could you possibly see your way to appearing for free?" Mrs. Taylor's impassioned plea startled us all. Before anyone could respond, Mrs. Taylor continued. "And think of the publicity this will generate. There could be several hundred people here next week to hear you. When publishers get wind of this, one of them might want to reprint the Veronica Thane series."

There was a long, tense moment of silence while we waited for the author or her daughter to respond.

"That's a very good point, Marcella, don't you think?" Mrs. Cartwright prodded her daughter's arm with a gloved finger. "Think of the publicity for the unpublished manuscripts. I could get a lot more money than that fool Eagleton is offering."

ELEVEN

"Unpublished manuscripts?" Teresa sounded bewildered, as well she might.

Mrs. Taylor squealed — with delight, I presumed. "Oh, my goodness me. You mean Winnie Eagleton wasn't making it all up?"

"When did you talk to Eagleton?" Mrs. Cartwright's tone was sharp. "He was not supposed to discuss this with anyone."

"Winnie and I have known each other for years." Mrs. Taylor surged blithely on, apparently oblivious to her idol's irritation. "He knew he could trust me with the news. Of course I didn't believe him, but I am absolutely *thrilled* to death to know he was right. Your readers will be ecstatic to know there are five more Veronica Thane books."

"I told you we shouldn't talk to that stupid little man." Marcella Marter might have thought no one could overhear, but her tone was a little too heated for private remarks.

"Oh, do hush, please," Mrs. Cartwright

snapped back at her daughter. "He was the only one willing to offer any money, no matter how pitiful." She turned back to Teresa. "I think we will reconsider the speaker's fee. My agent is coming down from New York today, and I'll discuss it with her. She's young and seems to understand the way publishing works these days better than I do. The world has changed so drastically since I started out writing my little books in an old garden shed of my house in Connecticut."

"Thank you for reconsidering, Mrs. Cartwright," Teresa said, and I echoed her. I felt the knot in my stomach loosen, and I was sure Teresa experienced a similar relief. The decision about the fee wasn't final yet, but I decided to be hopeful Mrs. Cartwright would forgo the money in favor of the publicity and the potential impetus to finding a higher-profile publisher.

Another worry occurred to me suddenly. What would happen if we didn't have a large crowd turn up for the event? *Tomorrow,* I told myself in best Scarlett O'Hara fashion. *I'll think about that tomorrow.*

While I wool-gathered, Mrs. Taylor talked. I tuned back in to hear her say, ". . . that darling little garden shed. I know I have a picture in my EBC archives somewhere at home. I'll try to find it so we can show people at the talk next week. Wouldn't that be wonderful? I know I have other pictures that your fans would love to see."

In Mrs. Cartwright's presence she sounded more like an adolescent rock 'n' roll fan than a Southern matron. I had felt a bit giddy with excitement myself at my first meeting with Mrs. Cartwright, but I think I disguised it better.

Mrs. Cartwright looked puzzled. "Goodness gracious, I'm afraid I don't remember any pictures." She glanced at her daughter, then focused again on Mrs. Taylor. "When you're as old as I am, you tend to forget a lot of things. I just can't imagine —"

We never heard what she couldn't imagine because there was a sudden loud argument taking place in the doorway. When I looked over there, I saw Bronwyn attempting to block a man from entering the room.

"I told you already, sir, this is a private meeting, and you cannot go in there." Bronwyn had a fierce temper when roused, and by the tone in her voice, I figured she was about ready to take the man's head off.

"Let me in there, you stupid woman. Get out of my way." The voice sounded familiar. Then I caught a glimpse of a furious, bearded face, and I recognized Gordon Betts.

Teresa rose hastily and joined Bronwyn, adding her voice in protest. I hurried around the table to help them. I was not going to allow the jerk to get away with his bullying tactics, even if I had to pick him up and carry him out of the library myself.

I raised my voice. "Let me handle this, ladies." Teresa and Bronwyn glanced at my face and promptly moved aside, leaving me almost toe to toe with the slightly shorter man. He looked up at me, and evidently what he saw there alarmed him because he started backing away.

I reached for his arm and grabbed it.

"Ow, that hurts." Betts glared at me and tried to shake loose.

"What in heaven's name is going on? And who is that loud young man?" Mrs. Cartwright's voice stopped me before I could drag Betts toward the front door. We froze in place.

In the ensuing quiet, all I heard was my own heavy breathing and the same from my captive, until Mrs. Cartwright wheezed heavily near me.

Betts shook loose as Mrs. Cartwright stepped around me to confront her overeager fan. She leaned on her cane as she glared at the young man. "Who are you?" she demanded.

"Gordon Betts, Mrs. Cartwright." He shot me a glance of triumph. He had succeeded after all in meeting his quarry. "I have the largest collection of your books in the world. Every foreign edition, as well as examples of the different printings and formats. Five hundred and seventy-three items, to be exact."

Marcella Marter appeared at her mother's side. "Well, goody for you." Her tone was nasty. "Do you want a blue ribbon?"

Betts paid her no attention. He seemed focused completely on the author. "When I found out you lived nearby and were going to appear at the library next week, I boxed everything up and brought it with me from Chicago. I'd like you to sign my books."

"*All* of them?" Mrs. Cartwright was clearly taken aback by the demand.

"What's it worth to you?" Marcella moved closer to Betts, as if to shield her mother from him. "My mother is a hundred years old. If you want her to spend that much energy, then you'd better be willing to pay her to do it."

I heard a couple of gasps from behind me. Mrs. Taylor, Teresa, and Bronwyn had crowded near to witness the bizarre scene.

"Marcella, really." Mrs. Cartwright frowned.

"Hush, Mother." Marcella focused a laser stare on Gordon Betts. "How much?"

"Five thousand." Betts glared defiantly back.

"Make it ten." Marcella's blatant avarice shocked me.

"Seventy-five hundred," Betts shot back.

"Done." Marcella stuck her hand out, and Betts grasped it. They shook. "Cash."

"Just show me the way to the nearest bank." Betts smirked at me.

"Come with us, and we'll take you there." Marcella grasped her mother's arm and started to tug her along.

Mrs. Cartwright's lips were compressed in a tight line. I had expected further protests from her, but she remained silent. She jerked her arm free from her daughter's grasp, however, and walked on her own power beside Marcella. Betts stayed right on their heels.

The rest of us stood rooted to the floor. Bronwyn looked stunned, Teresa furious. I was taken aback as well. There was nothing we could do after Betts managed to claim Mrs. Cartwright's attention. Marcella Marter showed she was made of sterner stuff than I would have guessed. I felt rather sorry for Mrs. Cartwright, though I suspected she could have put a stop to it if she had really wanted to. Were they that desperate for money?

They certainly could be, I realized, because none of Mrs. Cartwright's books had been in print during the past thirty years. No income there — and I had no idea if she had managed to save anything substantial during her career. It really was none of my business, I also realized, and further speculation would get me nowhere.

"I'm going back to the desk," Bronwyn muttered as she stepped past me.

"I have to be going, too," Mrs. Taylor said. "That Gordon is an embarrassment to the rest of us. He thinks money will get him whatever he wants."

"In this case it seems to have worked," Teresa commented wryly. "I wish I could throw money around as easily as he seems to."

"If you had an incredibly wealthy father like Gordon's, you could." Mrs. Taylor sounded disgusted. "Gordon has probably never worked a day in his life. He inherited untold millions so he thinks he can do anything he likes."

"What's the source of the father's wealth?"

I had to ask. I was way too curious to let it go.

Mrs. Taylor shrugged. "Manufacturing, some huge conglomerate that makes all kinds of things that everybody has to have, apparently." She glanced at her watch. "Oh, dear, as late as that? I really must be going. I have some research to do. I want to dig in my files and find that picture I mentioned." She smiled suddenly. "Not to mention I have a few really interesting items in my collection. Gordon may think he has everything, but I know better."

Teresa and I had no chance to bid her good-bye because she hurried to the door. We turned to each other with tired smiles.

"Thank the Lord that's over, at least for now. I don't think I can take one more crisis over this exhibit." Teresa brushed her hair away from her face as she often did when she was tired or frustrated or, in this case, both.

"I know what you mean." As I patted her shoulder, I heard warbling. I glanced down, and there was Diesel, rubbing against her legs.

Teresa laughed and scratched the cat's head. "Thank you, sweet kitty. You know how to make me feel better."

"I'm going to be the optimist here," I said.

"Mrs. Cartwright's agent will advise her to forget about the speaker's fee, and everything will go smoothly from then on. We'll have a wonderful turnout for Mrs. Cartwright, and everyone will be thrilled, just as Mrs. Taylor said. No glitches, all smooth sailing."

I should have kept my mouth shut.

Twelve

I found my place in *The Mystery at Spell-wood Mansion* and resumed reading. As I recalled, Veronica had just been told by the creepy butler that she was expected.

Veronica gasped. What could he mean?

The raven-haired girl was about to voice that very question but the butler suddenly glared at her, and Veronica read menace in his steely gaze.

"If you know what's good for you," he hissed like a snake about to strike, "you'll leave as soon as the storm lets up and forget you ever came to this house."

The old man might think he could frighten her with his eldritch words, but Veronica Thane did not scare easily. Though she had known adversity in her life, with the loss of her adventurous parents in darkest Africa when she was a young child, she had all the mettle of those two departed relatives. It would take more than a weird servant and a spooky mansion to discompose Veronica.

She had intended to apprise the man of his misconception, for she was a thoroughly honest and straight-forward young woman, but she scented a mystery. Veronica liked nothing better than a mystery and had had some small successes in solving a few.

The young woman who was expected was obviously a stranger, else the butler would surely have realized his mistake by now. That girl had no doubt been delayed by the same storm that brought Veronica here, and there was no way of knowing when she might arrive.

In the meantime, Veronica decided impulsively, she would pretend to be that girl in order to determine whether there was actual danger in this house.

In a tone that brooked no argument, Veronica spoke. "That will do. You will please show me to a room where I might dry myself and make myself ready to meet your mistress."

Recognizing an authoritative voice when he heard one, the butler recoiled slightly. "Very well, miss. If you will come with me."

Satisfied that she had won her point,

Veronica followed the servant up the stairs and to a suite on the second floor. "You will find everything you need here, miss. I will advise Mrs. Eden that you have arrived."

Veronica nodded in dismissal, thinking how unlike Fontaine, her guardian's butler, this man was. Mrs. Buff-Orpington would never allow Fontaine to treat a guest in her house in such a manner, and the butler himself would not deign to act that way.

As she dried herself with the purple towels she found in the bathroom, Veronica reflected fondly on her estimable guardian. Mrs. Araminta Buff-Orpington, a widowed Englishwoman who had long resided in the American South, had been at school with Veronica's late paternal grandmother. When the elder Mrs. Thane died suddenly after hearing the grim news of the deaths of her only son and his young wife, it was discovered that Mrs. Buff-Orpington had been named Veronica's guardian until she came of age.

"Aunt Araminta," as Veronica called her, was an elegant, though reclusive, widow of considerable means, and she looked upon her ward as one would upon one's own child. The relations between woman and girl were warm and affectionate, and

Mrs. Buff-Orpington trusted in Veronica's courage and good sense to carry her through any situation.

As she rang the bell to summon back the butler, Veronica knew she would have to keep her wits about her.

The servant appeared quickly, and Veronica followed him with grim determination to a sitting room on the ground floor. He motioned for Veronica to wait, and he opened the door and stepped inside. Veronica moved closer, intent on hearing anything the man said.

"Madam," he intoned, "Miss Derivale is here. Are you ready to receive her?"

A trembling voice responded. "Oh, yes, Bradberry, show her in immediately."

Veronica stepped back, and not a moment too soon. The door swung open wide, and the butler motioned her in.

"Madam, Miss Derivale."

Veronica entered the room and paused a moment to survey her surroundings. The furniture and the appointments of the room called to mind the trappings of the Victorian age. Heavy, ornate, and, Veronica suspected, somewhat dusty. She suppressed a sneeze as she approached a middle-aged woman who reclined on a damask-covered chaise longue.

"That will be all, Bradberry," Mrs. Eden spoke in a firmer tone.

"As you wish, Madam." The butler withdrew, closing the door behind him.

Veronica gazed at her hostess, struck by the woman's unhealthy pallor and feverish gaze. Why, Mrs. Eden appeared positively ill. Was the expected Miss Derivale a nurse, by any chance? she wondered.

Mrs. Eden forced herself upright and stared hard at Veronica. "Oh, dear, you are younger than I expected, but I am in such desperate straits, you will have to do." Her voice broke into a sob, and Veronica hastened to comfort the distraught woman.

"How can I help you, Mrs. Eden?" she asked. "I will gladly do whatever I can to aid you, but you must confide in me."

The older woman's body trembled under Veronica's comforting grasp. "I am in terrible danger, but I dare not leave this house."

I grinned as I closed the book and put it aside. As an adolescent, I had found those chapter endings completely thrilling, and I always had to turn the page to see what happened next. Over four decades later I recognized melodrama when I read it, and tonight I was too tired to read further.

I glanced at the bedside clock. Quarter after ten. I figured Helen Louise might be home by now, so I picked up the phone and punched in her number.

The phone rang five times, and I was getting ready to leave a message when Helen Louise, slightly out of breath, answered and said, "Hello, love. Are you and Diesel already in bed?"

I glanced at the large feline at rest beside me. As usual, Diesel had his head on the pillow, turned toward me. He opened his eyes sleepily and meowed twice. "Yes, we are, and Diesel said to tell you hello. Did you just get in, sweetheart?"

Helen Louise chuckled, a warm, throaty sound that made my stomach do an odd lurch. How I had come to love that chuckle of hers. "Yes, I was walking in the door when I heard the phone. I knew it was you."

"Oh, and not one of your other boyfriends?" I laughed, feeling like a giddy teenager.

"They never call this late." Helen Louise giggled. "Oh, love, I missed seeing you today."

"Me, too." I pictured her dear face, lined with fatigue. She worked so hard at the bakery, but her business was better than ever. "You need another assistant, honey. You're wearing yourself out."

"I know." She expelled a heavy breath, and I heard the exhaustion behind it. "You wouldn't believe how hard it is to find reliable help. I've tried employing students part-time, but the last one never could turn up on time. The one before that was always calling in sick. At least Debbie is reliable and a hard worker." Debbie Coulter was a young divorced woman who had been working at the bakery for about six months now.

"Too bad you can't clone Debbie," I said. Surely there had to be another hard worker somewhere in Athena.

"That would be nice. I'll simply have to keep looking and pray that someone suitable turns up," Helen Louise said. "But enough of that. What did you two get up to today?"

I gave her a shortened account of the events of the day, and she listened without comment until I finished. "*Mon Dieu,* what a mess. I know how you hate all these tense scenes, my love, but something tells me you ain't seen nothing yet."

"I wish you hadn't said that," I responded wryly. "Teresa and I both are nervous enough as it is."

"Sorry, love." Helen Louise sounded contrite. "Remember, though, you can't control others, especially when they're intent on causing mischief."

"I know." I suppressed a sigh. The problem was, I always had a hard time letting go of my intense desire to make things run smoothly.

Helen Louise chuckled again. "My dearly beloved control freak, try to relax. Do what you can, and let the Good Lord look after the rest." She paused. "I didn't realize you knew Carrie Taylor."

"Not really," I replied. "She got in touch with Teresa once we posted the information about Mrs. Cartwright on the library website. Do you know her?"

"Only slightly. Her bosom buddy is Melba Gilley, though."

"Mrs. Taylor did mention her." I could imagine the knowing smile on Helen Louise's face. Melba was perhaps the biggest gossip in Athena, and if she and Carrie Taylor were that close, well, enough said, I reckoned. "I'm sure Melba will be on the phone first thing tomorrow, pressing me for details." I was very fond of Melba, but she could be exasperating.

"Sorry, my dear, but I figured I had better let you know."

After that we chitchatted for a few minutes, then, hearing the tiredness in Helen Louise's voice, I admonished her to get some rest. We bade each other good night.

As I put down the phone, I felt a paw on my left arm. Diesel yawned and snuggled up to me. He liked to make sure I stayed close. He might disappear during the night to visit with another member of the family, but he didn't want me going anywhere without his knowing about it. I drifted off to sleep, determined not to let my brain get caught up in worries over the events of the day.

When my bedside phone rang the next morning, I came out of a sound sleep and fumbled for the receiver. I mumbled a greeting, and an all-too-familiar voice barked in my ear.

"Mr. Harris, Kanesha Berry. Sorry if I woke you up."

Kanesha, my housekeeper's daughter, also happened to be the chief deputy in the sheriff's department. Calls from her never boded well. Suddenly I was more alert.

"Doesn't matter." I glanced at the clock — ten minutes after seven. "What's going on? Is there an emergency?"

"You could say that." Kanesha sounded peeved — as she often did when she talked to me. "How well do you know a Mrs. Carrie Taylor?"

"Not that well. She's been helping us at the library with an upcoming exhibit and an event." I had a sick feeling in my stomach now. "Why do you ask?"

"She's dead, and it looks like murder." Kanesha pulled no punches. "She had your home phone number scribbled on a notepad by her desk, where her body was found."

THIRTEEN

"Dead?" I woke up fast. Beside me, Diesel warbled anxiously. I rubbed his head as I continued. "I can't believe it. I saw her just yesterday. Twice as a matter of fact."

"I want to talk to you, but it'll have to wait until I'm done here. Maybe about an hour. You'll be at home." That last statement didn't sound much like a question, more like a command.

"I'll be here." The dial tone buzzed in my ear. I wondered if Kanesha even heard me. I hung up the phone and stared at Diesel. He had stuck his face right up in mine and chirped as he rubbed his head against my chin. I put an arm around him and hugged him, and he bore it for a few seconds before pulling away. "I'm okay, boy, don't worry."

Evidently reassured, Diesel sat back and commenced cleaning one front paw. I watched him while my thoughts raced.

Carrie Taylor, *murdered.* That was terrible.

Why on earth would someone murder her? She had seemed like a nice lady who wouldn't make enemies easily.

I recalled what Helen Louise told me last night, that Mrs. Taylor and Melba Gilley were bosom buddies. She couldn't be that close to Melba without loving to gossip the way Melba did. Perhaps the roots of her death could be traced there. What could she know, however, that made someone angry enough — or desperate enough — to kill?

Poor Melba. She would be devastated by this. I started to pick up the phone to call her but stopped myself when I realized how bad an idea it was. For one thing I couldn't tell her news like that over the phone. Not to mention the fact that Kanesha would have me strung up by my thumbs if she found out I had done such an idiotic thing.

No, Melba would have to find out the news some other way. I'd have to tell Kanesha, naturally, about their friendship. I knew she would want to question Melba to discover whether she knew anything pertinent.

Then a horrible thought struck me. Melba could be in danger, too, if the killer knew about her closeness to the dead woman. What if Carrie Taylor had shared with Melba the information that led to her death?

Perhaps I should call Melba after all.

Diesel meowed anxiously again, and I realized he had picked up on my rapidly escalating unease.

Get a grip, Charlie, I told myself sternly. *Don't get hysterical. Melba is probably fine and in no danger whatsoever.* I scratched the cat's head to calm him, and he settled down to groom his other paw.

I decided I'd better get up and in the shower. Kanesha might be here sooner than the predicted hour, and I ought to be ready. Besides, I discovered I was hungry despite the horror of the situation.

Diesel disappeared while I was in the shower — not an unusual occurrence. He was either down in the utility room, doing his business and munching on dry food, or snuggled up in another bed, probably Laura's.

The aroma of fresh coffee hit my nose as I entered an empty kitchen. Stewart Delacorte, the second of my two current boarders, had probably prepared the coffeemaker last night and set it for the morning, bless him. I poured myself a cup, added some half-and-half and sweetener, and had a few sips before I went out to fetch the paper.

I decided on cereal and fruit for breakfast — a healthy change from the delicious, but cholesterol-laden, meals Azalea prepared during the week. I kept telling myself I should make more of an effort to eat healthy during the week instead of only on the weekends, but Azalea's old-fashioned Southern cooking was irresistible. Now that she had recovered from the health problems she suffered around Christmastime she seemed more indefatigable than ever. She didn't even ask her sister Lily to help out, as she had done for a couple of months after her brief hospital stay.

While I munched my cereal and read the paper, I did my best to avoid thinking about poor Carrie Taylor for the moment. With the grilling I'd soon get from Kanesha Berry, I wouldn't be thinking of much else.

No other member of the household — not even my cat — had put in an appearance by the time I rinsed my bowl in the sink and stuck it in the dishwasher. For Saturday mornings, this quiet was typical. I was the only early riser on the weekend. Just as well today, I thought, because Kanesha wouldn't want anyone else in the room when she questioned me.

The doorbell rang about ten minutes after eight as I was enjoying my second cup of coffee. My stomach lurched. *Back to reality,* I told myself as I went to answer.

Kanesha Berry, grim-faced as ever, stood on the front doorstep. Her ever-present shadow, Deputy Bates, was not in evidence this morning, and I wondered where he was as I invited her in.

Kanesha followed me into the kitchen. "Sorry to have to bother you so early on a Saturday morning, Mr. Harris, but murder can't wait."

"I understand," I said as I reached for the coffeepot and a fresh mug. "Would you like some coffee?"

"Yes, please." Kanesha pulled out a chair and sat, and I noticed how weary she looked, her face drawn and almost haggard. "No cream or sugar."

I ventured a question. "Have you been up all night?"

She nodded as she accepted her mug. "Domestic dispute on the north side near the county line, and then we got the call about Mrs. Taylor around five this morning."

I decided to risk another question. As tired as she was, she might let me get by with it. "Who found her? Since she's a widow, I thought she lived alone."

Kanesha stared at me over the rim of her mug while she drank. She set the mug down before she responded. "She did, except for a dog. Little yappy thing, like that poodle of Mr. Delacorte's. He was barking his head off, and her neighbor went over to complain. Looked in through the back door when Mrs. Taylor didn't answer the knocking and saw her slumped over her desk in a corner of the kitchen. Turned out she'd been strangled to death."

I nodded as I offered her a refill, and she accepted. I sat down across from her and waited for the questions to start.

"You saw her twice yesterday, you said. What was she doing?" She sipped at her coffee and regarded me intently.

"She came to the library — the public library, that is — for meetings with Teresa Farmer and me about an event for National Library Week." I went on to explain the nature of the event and the participation of Electra Barnes Cartwright. "Mrs. Taylor published a newsletter devoted to the author — she always referred to her by her initials, *EBC*."

Kanesha frowned. "That explains part of the note that was puzzling me. Above your phone number and your name she — or someone — had written *EBC*."

"Maybe she was planning to call me about something to do with Mrs. Cartwright," I said. "When she left the library the second time, she said she was going home to look through her EBC archive."

"What was she looking for? Did she say?" Kanesha drained the last of her coffee, but waved away the offer of another refill.

I thought for a moment. "She had a picture she wanted to find, of the garden shed where Mrs. Cartwright used to write when she was younger." There was something else, but what? I dug into my memory. "Oh, and there was a remark about Gordon Betts."

"Who is Gordon Betts?" Kanesha frowned. "I don't remember a family in Athena called Betts."

"No, he's not from around here. Chicago, I think I heard him say. He's one of the book collectors who showed up because of the information on the library website. He's a rabid fan of Mrs. Cartwright's, and he has a large collection of her Veronica Thane books." I related briefly the two incidents with Betts. "The last thing Mrs. Taylor said was that she had items in her own collection that Betts didn't know about. The way she said it, I took her to mean that he would want them badly if he knew about them."

I had a sudden horrible feeling. Would Gordon Betts want these mysterious items badly enough to kill?

"Do you have any idea what these items were, or how valuable they might be?" Kanesha had pulled out a small notebook and a pen and was jotting down notes.

"No, I don't. She didn't explain, and we didn't really have a chance to ask."

Kanesha looked up from her notebook. "What about this Betts? If he's a collector, does he have a lot of money?"

"According to Mrs. Taylor he does. Inherited from his father, something to do with manufacturing. She said he has never had to work." I shrugged. "This is all hearsay, because I have no idea whether her information is accurate, or where it came from. These collectors all seem to know one another."

"There are others?"

I nodded. I told her about Della Duffy and said that we expected more — perhaps many more — to turn up in time for Mrs. Cartwright's appearance at the library.

Kanesha looked disgruntled at the news. "If Mrs. Taylor's death is connected to Mrs. Cartwright in some way, that means potentially way too many suspects. I've had nightmares like this."

I couldn't believe she said anything so personal, because usually she was careful

124

not to let her feelings show. Particularly to me.

"Maybe her death is completely unrelated to Mrs. Cartwright and her books. You should talk to Melba Gilley. According to Helen Louise, they were really close. Melba will be able to tell you if Mrs. Taylor had any enemies in town."

That news seemed to cheer Kanesha up slightly. Her expression became a tad less morose. "Thanks for the tip. I'll check with Ms. Gilley." She stood. "Thanks for the coffee, too. I'll probably have more questions for you later, but you've given me a lot to work on."

"Glad I could help." I escorted her to the door. We exchanged nods as she departed.

Back in the kitchen, I poured another cup of coffee — the last in the pot — and started to make a fresh one. While I did so, I thought again about the collecting bug and the lengths to which some people would apparently go to acquire highly desirable items.

What Mrs. Taylor had said about her own collection niggled at me. What if Betts had found out about the unique item or items she claimed to own? He might have tried to buy them, she refused, and then he killed her in a fit of rage and took what he wanted.

125

Nasty, but plausible, I decided, based on my interactions with Betts. He seemed to be short a card or two in his deck, as my mother would have said. Mrs. Taylor didn't deserve what happened. Memories of her enthusiasm for Mrs. Cartwright's books and her excitement over the planned public appearance made me determined to do what I could to identify her killer.

Time to track down Mr. Betts and ask him a few questions.

FOURTEEN

The Farrington House was the finest hotel in Athena, and I figured that must be where Gordon Betts was staying. I looked up the number and jotted it on a notepad. Before I could place the call, however, Laura breezed into the kitchen with Diesel trotting beside her.

"Morning, Dad." She kissed my cheek and gave my arm a quick squeeze. "Seems like ages since I saw you." She poured herself a cup of coffee. "What have you been up to?"

Both my children were avid mystery readers like me, and I knew Laura would be interested in hearing about the murder of Carrie Taylor. I wasn't ready to talk about it with her, however — at least not right this minute. I was more interested in catching up with my daughter. *Push the awfulness away for at least a little while,* I thought.

"I'll tell you all about it later," I said.

"Right now, why don't you bring me up to date on the wedding plans? You haven't asked for my checkbook for at least two weeks now." I grinned to show her I was only teasing.

She had a sip of coffee before she spoke. "I've picked out my wedding dress. It's an absolutely stunning Badgley Mischka." She batted her eyes at me. "I'm sure you'll love it."

"What's a Badgley Mischka? Sounds expensive." I thought she might be teasing me, but with brides and their dresses, you never knew.

"Badgley and Mischka are designers who work together. And yes, their dresses can be expensive." Laura giggled. "But don't worry, I have a friend who got it for me wholesale through somebody she knows in Memphis. It really is gorgeous. I've got some fittings coming up, and then everything will be set."

"You'll look beautiful no matter what you wear. Your mother . . ." I felt my eyes sting suddenly as I envisioned escorting Laura down the aisle. How excited her mother would have been to see it, too.

Diesel, back from a visit to the utility room, meowed at me and rubbed against my legs. Laura came to me and gave me a hug. "I know, Dad. I've been thinking a lot about her lately. But I know she'll be there with us."

I slid my arm around her and held her close for a long moment. I cleared my throat. "Yes, I'm sure she will."

Laura smiled at me as I released her. She picked up her coffee and moved over to the table. We sat across from each other. "All the arrangements are pretty much set now. The chapel at the college is reserved, and the chaplain is all set, too. My best friend, Dodie, will be my maid of honor, and Helen Louise offered to cater the reception. Now we just have to wait for June ninth to get here." Laura leaned back in her chair, obviously pleased with her plans.

"I won't have any trouble remembering your anniversary," I said. June ninth was my maternal grandmother's birthday. "Have you decided where you're going on your honeymoon? Last I heard you were leaning toward New York."

"We were at first. We thought about California, too," Laura replied. "But I've had enough of Hollywood for now, and I've never been to London. Frank has been several times, and he wants to show me around."

"London would be perfect — the West End and all the wonderful shows." I drained the last of my coffee. "I'm sure you'll want to experience the London theater scene." Jackie and I could never afford to take our children abroad, but we did take them to New York and Hollywood, among other places.

"Absolutely. I can't wait to see *The Mousetrap.*" Laura laughed. "I know it's probably hokey, but as a mystery lover, I can't pass up the chance."

"I'd love to see it myself," I said. Agatha Christie's play, the longest running in theater history, had entertained audiences for over six decades now.

Laura grinned slyly. "Maybe you can go to London on *your* honeymoon. And then of course over to Paris. I'm sure Helen Louise would love to show you her favorite city in the world."

I gazed sternly at my daughter. "None of that, now. I have to get *you* married and off my hands first. Sean, too. You've both been hanging around this house *unmarried* far too long. I need grandchildren to spoil. Then maybe I can think about Helen Louise and a wedding of my own."

At the mentions of Helen Louise's name, Diesel — who had been dozing quietly under the table — perked up and meowed. He adored Helen Louise, and she pampered him whenever we visited her bakery. She always had tidbits of chicken for him.

Laura held up her hands in mock surrender. "I'm not getting married for two months yet, Dad. You're going to have to wait a year or two for a grandchild."

We laughed together, and Diesel chirped along. "I don't mind waiting awhile longer. But at the rate things are progressing with Sean and Alexandra, I'm sure you'll produce the first sprig of the next generation."

"Oh, they'll work everything out." Laura shrugged. "Sean's just being stubborn, but he'll come around. Alexandra will sort out her father, and peace and happiness will reign once again for my big brother."

"I sure hope so," I said. "I'm keeping out of it."

"So am I," Laura replied. "Enough about weddings. Tell me what you've been up to. How's the exhibit shaping up?"

For the next ten minutes I shared with my daughter the events of the past couple of days. Her eyes widened in excitement when I told her about meeting Electra Barnes Cartwright. Laura had read the Veronica Thane books and loved them. She held back her comments, though, until I finished with the last, most horrible, event, the murder of Carrie Taylor.

"How awful." Laura shook her head. "That poor woman. Why would anyone do that to her? From what you've said, she sounds like she was a nice old lady. Was it a robbery gone wrong, do you think?"

"It might have been." I told her my suspicions of Gordon Betts.

"That's downright crazy," Laura said as I got up from the table to retrieve the piece of paper with the hotel phone number on it. "It's not like we're talking about a fabulous piece of art here, like a Renoir or a Rembrandt. Do you really think anyone would kill over a collection of children's books?"

"It does sound pretty senseless, doesn't it?" I shrugged. "People have killed for less, though. What might sound nutty to you or me might not sound that way to a rabid collector perhaps. The lust to possess has driven many to murder."

"I guess," Laura said, "but you have to wonder if there isn't something else going on, something no one knows about yet."

"That's entirely possible," I said. I brandished the piece of paper. "I was about to call the Farrington House when you walked in. I thought I would see whether Gordon Betts is staying there."

"And if you can track him down, you'll

try to talk to him, won't you?" Laura shook her head. "I don't blame you for being curious, but do you think you should? Won't Kanesha have a fit if she finds out?"

"Kanesha is probably going to have several fits with me before this is over," I said with as much nonchalance as I could muster. "I'm not going to be able to stay out of this."

"No, I don't imagine you will be. Just be careful that Kanesha doesn't lock you up." Laura's wry tone caused us both to smile.

I wouldn't have admitted it to my daughter right then, but I hadn't actually considered how the chief deputy would react. Laura's questions gave me pause, however, because I didn't want to get caught in the crosshairs over this. Kanesha might seek my help, as she had done on occasion when she thought I had access to information she needed. On reflection, I decided I probably ought to wait to talk to Gordon Betts until after I was sure Kanesha had questioned him first.

My cell phone rang, and I pulled it from my pocket. Melba Gilley's name popped up on the caller ID. "Morning, Melba. How are you?"

"Oh, Charlie, just awful," Melba wailed into the phone. "I'm so upset about Carrie, I can't tell you." She paused for a sobbing breath. "I've got to talk to someone. Carrie told me all about helping you with the exhibit at the library. I know that's what got her killed."

FIFTEEN

"Melba, honey, where are you?" If I didn't get her to calm down, she'd be in hysterics in three seconds flat. "I promise I'll help you, but you've got to try to settle down."

I heard her draw a deep, albeit shaky, breath. "Thanks, Charlie. I'm at home. Can you come over right away? I've really got to talk to you."

"I'll be there as quickly as I can. Diesel and I will look after you."

Melba thanked me again, and I ended the call. After a quick explanation to Laura, I grabbed my keys and headed for the garage. Diesel didn't need an invitation. Whenever he saw me pick up keys, he was ready to go.

The drive took almost ten minutes, since Melba lived across town in a section of Athena about fifty years newer than the neighborhood where my house stood. Diesel warbled from the backseat, and I told him we were going to see his buddy Melba.

He probably thought we were headed to the college library, since that's where he normally saw her — she was the administrative assistant to the director — but we usually walked the few blocks to campus. When I stopped the car in Melba's driveway, he looked out the window, then turned his head toward me and meowed. Did he remember coming here with me a couple of times? I had no idea.

Melba, dressed in a shabby orange bathrobe and matching fuzzy slippers, swung the front door open before I could raise my hand to ring the bell. Her tearstained face and unkempt appearance startled me. I had never seen her like this. She always dressed so neatly, her hair and makeup immaculate. My heart went out to her.

She motioned us in and shut the door. Then she sat on the floor and gathered Diesel in her arms. The cat started warbling and chirping for her, doing his best to cheer her as she rocked back and forth with him. After a moment I knelt by them and touched Melba lightly on the shoulder. She looked up at me, tears streaming from her eyes. She pulled a sodden handkerchief from her pocket and wiped her face.

I stood and held out a hand to her. "Come on, Melba," I said gently. "Let's get you into the kitchen and make you some coffee or maybe some hot tea. You've had a terrible shock."

She nodded and let me lift her up as Diesel moved out of her lap. I put my arm around her, and she leaned heavily against me as we walked down the hall to her kitchen at the back of the house. Diesel meowed anxiously as he followed us.

The windows over the sink faced east, and the morning sun streamed in. I settled Melba in a chair at the elderly oaken table, and Diesel sat beside her, his head in her lap. She stroked his head and sighed. "I'm feeling a little better."

"Good. Now, which would you rather have, tea or coffee?" I glanced at the counter by the sink and spotted a coffeemaker, its pot empty.

"I'd rather have a few shots of bourbon." Melba spoke with a vestige of her usual spirit. "But it's too early for that. Coffee will be fine. It's in the canister there behind the coffeemaker."

I got the coffee going, and in the meantime let Diesel work his therapeutic magic with her. By the time the coffee was ready a few minutes later, she was looking much less distressed, almost calm.

"Thanks." She raised her mug, with its

heavy dollop of cream and three sugars, and sipped several times. "Ah, that is better. I'm beginning to feel warm again." She set the mug down.

"I'm really sorry about Carrie Taylor," I said. "I didn't know her all that well, but she seemed like a sweet, decent person."

Melba nodded. "She was about ten years ahead of us in high school, so there was no reason you would have known her, I guess. I only got to know her myself about fifteen years ago, but she was probably my best friend." For a moment she appeared as if the tears would start up again, but she drew a deep breath to steady herself. "She'd never in a million years hurt anyone, and I can't imagine why someone would kill her. It just doesn't make any sense."

"I know, it never does," I said. "I guess Kanesha Berry has already talked to you?"

Melba shook her head. "No, I haven't heard a word from her. It was Carrie's neighbor, Thelma Crocker, who called. She's a busybody like you wouldn't believe, but at least she's taking care of Carrie's poor little dog." She paused. "I guess I'll take him. Thelma isn't that good with animals."

I was surprised that Kanesha hadn't talked to Melba yet, but since I wasn't privy to the

138

details of the investigation, I had no idea what Kanesha was doing. She wouldn't be happy that I talked to Melba before she did, but that couldn't be helped. I certainly wasn't going to turn my back on one of my oldest friends just to make the chief deputy happy. "I'm sure Carrie would be glad to know her dog will have a good home."

"That's the least I can do." Melba shrugged and drank more of her coffee. "What I'd really like to do is get ahold of the bastard that killed her and beat the crap out of him with a baseball bat. But I know Kanesha won't let me."

That sounded like the feisty Melba I knew. "No, I don't imagine she would." I decided she was calm enough now for me to ask a few questions. "When you called, you told me you knew it was her involvement in the exhibit at the library that got her killed. What did you mean by that?" I thought she could be right, but I wondered what she might know.

"It had to have something to do with the exhibit." Melba sounded convinced. "There was nothing else unusual going on in her life these days. As soon as the library put that notice on their website about Electra what's-her-name, Carrie was beside herself, like a kid about to get the best birthday present ever."

"She didn't have any enemies that you're aware of?" That sounded like a question Kanesha would ask. "From another aspect of her life?"

"No, she sure didn't. She was one of those Golden Rule kind of people. She treated everyone like she wanted to be treated. She was always nice to everybody."

Carrie Taylor hadn't been particularly nice to Winston Eagleton, as I recalled. She also had a penchant for gossip, at least from what I had seen. Since Melba was herself an inveterate gossip, I wondered how to approach the subject tactfully.

Melba saved me the trouble. "Now, Carrie was curious about people. She did like to know what was going on in their lives." She cut a shrewd glance at me. "Guess that's one reason we got along so well. But there wasn't anything malicious about it. You know me, Charlie, I talk about people, but I don't go around spreading dirt just for the heck of it."

That much was true. Melba liked to talk, but in general she didn't bad-mouth people — unless they deserved it, in her estimation. Then she could be merciless.

"I understand," I said. "But a person who didn't know Carrie well might not look at it quite the same way. Might not be happy if he or she thought Carrie knew something they didn't want anyone else to know. Do you see what I mean?"

Melba didn't answer straightaway. Instead she got up and poured herself more coffee. Diesel padded after her, evidently determined to keep an eye on her in case she needed more comfort. Melba leaned against the counter and regarded me over the rim of her mug as she sipped. Diesel sat at her feet and looked up at her.

"Yeah, I do see what you mean. But it's hard to imagine that she knew something worth killing her over." Melba shrugged. "I certainly don't know anything."

"When was the last time you talked to her?"

"Night before last," Melba said. "Usually we talked for at least a few minutes every night, but last night my allergies were driving me crazy. I took one of my heavy-duty pills, and it zonked me out by eight o'clock. I usually sleep for nine or ten hours when I take one." She shook her head. "And then I feel groggy for half the day afterward."

"So if she called you last night, you wouldn't have heard the phone ring?"

Melba's eyes widened. "Oh, my Lord, I hadn't thought about that. No, I wouldn't

141

have heard." She stuck her hands in the pockets of her robe. "Where the heck is my cell phone?"

The search of her pockets yielded nothing except the sodden handkerchief. Melba gazed around the kitchen, but the cell phone didn't appear to be anywhere in sight.

"Did you use it to call me this morning?" I asked. I hadn't paid attention to the number. She could have used her landline.

"No, I didn't. Carrie's neighbor doesn't have my cell number. I called you right after I hung up with her." Melba ran her hands through her hair, smoothing it back. "I must have left it in my purse when I got home yesterday. I'll go check."

She disappeared down the hall, and Diesel followed her, a faithful shadow. I realized I was thirsty, so while I waited, I found a glass and filled it with water from the tap. I had just set the glass in the sink when Melba returned, cell phone in hand, manipulating it as she walked. Diesel was right beside her.

"Still in my purse, and my purse was in the living room. No wonder I didn't hear anything." She looked up at me. "Carrie did call me, around nine forty-five, and there's a voice mail message." She sat at the table and motioned for me to do the same. She punched a few buttons, then turned on the speaker before setting the phone on the table between us.

Carrie Taylor spoke clearly in the silence. "Hey, Melba, just me. Thought I'd check in and see how you're doing. I know your allergies are playing up something awful. I'll bet you took one of your pills and you're sound asleep by now." She paused for about three seconds. "It's a shame because I really do need to talk to you. So much has been going on the past few days. I would've tried to call earlier tonight, but I actually had people over. First time in ages anybody besides you and Thelma have been in here. Oh, now hush, Zippy." There was the sound of a barking dog in the background. "There must be somebody at the front door, otherwise he wouldn't carry on so. I'll just go see who it is."

There was another pause, of perhaps six or seven seconds, then she spoke again. "There is somebody at the door, but I can't imagine who it could be at this time of night. Hang on a second while I check who it is." Another pause, only a couple of seconds this time. "Now what on earth does he want? Hush, Zippy, it's okay. Listen, honey, I'll talk to you tomorrow. Better get this over with so I can get to bed. 'Bye."

The call ended, and Melba and I stared at each other. I was sure we shared the same thought, and it was an utterly chilling one.

Had we just heard Carrie Taylor say " 'Bye" before she opened the door to admit her killer?

SIXTEEN

While Melba and I stared at the phone, the voice mail program directed Melba to punch various numbers, depending on what she wanted to do with the messages. Though her hands shook, Melba picked up the phone and made a selection — to save the message, I presumed. She set the phone back on the table. We both stared at it.

"That had to be the person who killed her." Melba's voice came out barely above a whisper. Her eyes filled with tears, and she pulled her hanky out of her pocket and scrubbed her face.

I felt pretty shaken myself. Diesel quickly picked up on our mutual distress and meowed anxiously. He came to me and rubbed his head against my thigh, seeking reassurance. I scratched his head as I tried to collect my thoughts. Diesel quieted under my ministrations.

Melba continued to sniffle, and I felt helpless in the face of her grief and horror. I would not soon forget the sound of Carrie Taylor's voice as she left that final message for her best friend. I took a deep breath to steady my own nerves before going around the table to bend over my friend and give her a hug.

Melba clung to me, and I muttered, "It's okay, honey, I'm here," over and over. Slowly she calmed, and I felt her relax in my arms. I released her gently, and she gave me a tremulous smile. I patted her shoulder before I went back to my chair opposite her.

"Thank you, Charlie. I don't know what I'd have done if I had been alone when I heard that." Melba sighed. "I'll have nightmares about that phone call. If only I'd been awake and able to talk to her, she might have told me who was at the door."

I felt a deep chill all of a sudden as a terrifying thought struck me. Had the man at the door seen Carrie Taylor on the phone? If he had, would he try to track down the person she had been talking to? Melba could be in grave danger if the killer thought Carrie had identified him to someone.

Did I dare share that thought with Melba right now? She was upset enough, and I had no idea how she'd react if I told her she could be a target for the killer as well. I needed to talk to Kanesha. This was a job for the professionals.

Melba apparently had not noticed my brief lapse of attention. She pushed back her chair. "Excuse me a minute. I'm going to wash my face. Lord only knows what I must look like by now. I'm ashamed to let you see me like this." She scurried out of the room before I could voice a disclaimer.

Diesel warbled at me, seeking more reassurance, and I rubbed his head and told him what a sweet boy he was for being so good to his friend Melba.

The doorbell interrupted our little chat, and Melba called out, asking me to see who it was, if I didn't mind.

My pulse raced as I headed for the front door. My fears for Melba's safety dominated my thoughts. What if the killer had come to call?

I quickly dismissed that notion, because what killer would be stupid enough to call on someone in broad daylight, when there was a car in the driveway?

Nevertheless, I paused in front of the door. I couldn't believe Melba had no peephole. That wasn't a good idea for a woman living alone. I took a deep breath and opened the door.

"Thank the Lord," I said when I saw

Kanesha Berry standing there.

She did not look happy to see me, however, as I stood aside and waved her in. Diesel greeted her with a loud meow, and she muttered "Hello, cat" before she focused her attention on me again.

"What are you doing here, Mr. Harris?" Kanesha glared at me.

"Who is it, Charlie?" Melba called from her bedroom. "Tell them I'll be out in a minute."

"It's Kanesha Berry." I had to raise my voice to make sure Melba heard me clearly. "We'll be in the kitchen when you're ready."

I motioned for Kanesha to precede Diesel and me down the hall. Her laser stare became even more intense, but after a moment's hesitation, she headed for the kitchen.

"To answer your question," I said as we stepped into the sunny room, "Melba called me about forty minutes ago. She had just heard about Carrie Taylor's death, and she was terribly upset. She asked me if I would come over, and I couldn't say no to her. She's one of my oldest friends."

Kanesha's eyes closed as she dropped into a chair. If anything, she looked even more exhausted than she had when I saw her earlier that morning. I could understand her frustration with me, but I hadn't deliberately sought Melba out in order to interfere in the investigation.

The chief deputy's eyes popped open. "There's nothing I can do about it now. I'll have to deal with the situation like I always do." She frowned at me. "I hope I don't have to warn you again about sticking your nose into things you shouldn't."

Diesel sat on the floor in front of her and stared at her. She pretended not to notice, but I could tell she was slightly unnerved by the attention. Her eyes flicked down to him every so often though she mostly focused intently on me.

"I have no intention of getting involved in your investigation." I kept my tone even, although I was worried and irritated. "It's not something I deliberately do because I can't think of any other way to occupy my time. These things just happen, and somehow I end up in the middle of them."

Before she could respond to that, I hurried on. "Listen, I'm worried that Melba could be in danger. She had a voice mail from Carrie Taylor that ended with Mrs. Taylor answering her door. She didn't say who it was, but it was a man. It might have been the killer. I haven't said anything to Melba because I didn't want her to get any more upset than she already is, but something needs to be done about it."

Kanesha rubbed a hand wearily across her eyes. "Let me talk to Mrs. Gilley and hear this message for myself. Then I'll decide what to do." She expelled a sharp breath. "I'm not about to let anything happen to her if I can help it, but first I have to determine whether there's a legitimate threat. Understood?"

I nodded. "Certainly. Do you want me to leave now so that you can talk to her alone?"

Kanesha hesitated, obviously torn. I figured she would love to tell me to go home and mind my own business, but she might also have been thinking that Melba would find it easier to talk with me there.

"No, you can stay if Mrs. Gilley wants you to." Kanesha shook her head. "Even if you didn't, I'm sure she'd be on the phone to you the minute I walked out the door."

"Good morning, Deputy." Melba sounded more like her usual self when she entered the kitchen. She also looked more like her usual self. She had dressed in jeans and a sweater, combed her hair, and applied a little makeup. "Would you like some coffee? I think there's still some in the pot, or I could make some fresh."

"Thank you, Mrs. Gilley, but I'm fine. Mr.

Harris told me earlier this morning that you were a close friend of Mrs. Taylor's, and I wanted to talk to you about her. First, though, let me tell you how sorry I am about the death of your friend." Kanesha's sympathy sounded sincere, not the rote words of a stranger observing the social niceties.

"Thank you." Melba resumed her place at the table, and I chose the chair to her left. Diesel gave up his close observation of the deputy and stretched out on the floor between Melba and me. "I'm glad you came by. There's something I want you to hear."

Melba picked up the cell phone and played the eerie voice mail message for Kanesha. I found it even more affecting than I did the first time I heard it. If anything, my fears for Melba's well-being increased.

Kanesha sat stony-faced until the message ended. "Can you forward that message to me, Mrs. Gilley?" She pulled a business card from her pocket. "Here's my number at the sheriff's department."

"Certainly," Melba said as she picked up the phone. "I'll do it right now."

Kanesha and I waited until the task was complete and Melba set the phone aside once more. In the meantime the deputy had pulled out her notebook and pen and jotted something down in it.

"Was that the only contact you had with Mrs. Taylor yesterday?" Kanesha asked.

"Yes," Melba said. She went on to explain the reason why she hadn't taken the call. "I did talk to her the day before, but offhand I can't think of anything she said to me that could have any bearing on this."

"Please think carefully about the conversations you had with her recently, and if there's any odd detail you remember that could be connected, let me know." Kanesha flipped back a couple of pages in her notebook. "Mrs. Taylor mentioned having people over last night. Her neighbor Mrs. Crocker told us she saw a couple of people going in the front door around eight last night. She couldn't see them clearly but thought they might have been two women. Any idea who they could have been?"

Melba frowned as she considered the question. "It could have been some of the ladies from church, I guess. Carrie was real involved in church work the past couple years. You might check with Althea Sprayberry. She and Carrie worked together lately on raising money for foreign missions."

Kanesha wrote in her notebook. I hesitated to interrupt, but I had a suggestion as to the identity of the two female visitors. "Deputy, I have an idea you might also want to follow up."

Kanesha glanced at me and nodded, so I continued. "It's possible that the visitors were Marcella Marter and her mother, Mrs. Electra Barnes Cartwright." I described the meeting at the library yesterday. "Perhaps Mrs. Cartwright wanted to talk to Mrs. Taylor about the newsletter she put out, or maybe her collection of material related to Mrs. Cartwright."

"Mrs. Cartwright and her books were some of Carrie's main interests," Melba said. "I can imagine how thrilled she was to meet her favorite author." She paused. "I wonder why she didn't mention her in the message, though. I'd have thought she'd be chattering all about it."

"We'll follow up on both those leads." Kanesha tapped the notebook with her pen.

My cell phone rang, startling me. "Sorry," I muttered as I pulled it from my pocket. Teresa Farmer was calling. "Excuse me. I need to take this." I wondered whether she had heard the news yet about Carrie Taylor.

Kanesha and Melba nodded as I stepped out of the kitchen and walked a few feet down the hallway. I answered the call.

"Charlie, sorry to bother you," Teresa said. "But I thought I should let you know that Winston Eagleton would like to get in touch with you. He asked me for your cell phone number, but of course I couldn't give it to him without your permission."

"Thanks," I said. "Did he say why he wanted to talk to me?"

"Eventually. Goodness, how that man can ramble," Teresa said. "He wants to invite us both to a dinner party this evening."

SEVENTEEN

"Dinner party?" Had I understood Teresa correctly? "Why on earth is he having a dinner party? Hasn't he heard what happened?"

The moment I said the words, I realized I shouldn't have. Teresa probably didn't know about the murder, and here I went, blabbing it without Kanesha's permission. Too late to retract what I'd said, though.

"What are you talking about, Charlie?" Teresa sounded puzzled.

I sighed heavily. I heard warbling and looked down to see Diesel staring up at me. If a cat could look concerned, he sure did right then. I rubbed his head as I replied to Teresa. "The news hasn't spread yet, but Carrie Taylor was found dead in her home this morning. She was murdered."

Teresa gasped. "How horrible. The poor woman. Who would do such a thing?"

"Yes, it's hard to imagine why anybody

would want to kill such a nice person."

"Does she have any family?" Teresa asked. "I know she was a widow, and I never heard her mention any children."

"I don't know," I said. "Right now I'm at Melba Gilley's house, and Melba was apparently Mrs. Taylor's best friend. She'll know if there's anyone. Actually, Kanesha is here talking to Melba. I can't say anything more at the moment."

"Of course. Let me know if there's anything I can do. Poor Melba." Teresa still sounded shocked. "I'm beginning to think this exhibit is cursed. Should we cancel it?"

I understood Teresa's concerns. I had wondered the same thing myself, but I finally concluded we should go ahead with our plans. I had a hunch that the murder was connected to Mrs. Cartwright somehow, and if we canceled everything, the investigation might stall. I didn't know how Kanesha might feel about that, but I certainly wasn't going to ask her.

I realized Teresa was waiting for a response. "No, I don't think so. I considered that, too, but I believe we should go ahead. For one thing, we can dedicate the events to Mrs. Taylor's memory. It's not much, but it's something we can do for her sake."

"I suppose you're right." Teresa didn't

sound completely convinced. "In the meantime, what about Mr. Eagleton? Surely he
won't want to hold a dinner party when he
finds out about Mrs. Taylor."

"That'll be up to him, I guess." I was curious to speak to the man, but before I did, I
wanted to check with Kanesha. Eagleton
could be a suspect, unlike Teresa, and I
didn't want to step on official toes. "If he
calls you back, don't say anything to him
about Mrs. Taylor. You can give him my cell
number, but in the meantime, if you have
his, will you forward it to me? I'll probably
call him."

"Sure, I can do that. I won't tell anyone
else about Mrs. Taylor's death, either."

We said good-bye, and I stuck my phone
back in my pocket. Diesel had stopped talking to me, but he still looked a little anxious.
I rubbed his head a few times and told him
I was fine and not to worry. He padded after
me as I rejoined Kanesha and Melba in the
kitchen.

"I think we're done for now," Kanesha was
saying as I sat down. "I appreciate your
time, Ms. Gilley. If I have any other questions, I'll let you know."

"I'll help any way I can." Melba's eyes
flashed. "I want you to catch the bastard
who did this to my friend."

"We will," Kanesha said. "In the mean-time, y'all be careful, and stay out of trouble." She looked straight at me as she offered that bit of advice — or was it a warning?

Kanesha headed down the hall. I told Melba I'd be right back. I had to talk to Kanesha before she left. I followed her out the front door.

"Deputy," I said, "I need to talk to you a minute."

Kanesha turned back and scowled at me. "I'm in a hurry, Mr. Harris. Can it wait?"

"No, it can't." I folded my arms over my chest. "I'm still worried as all get-out about Melba's safety. Have you made a decision yet about protecting her?"

Kanesha rubbed the back of her neck. "I'll talk to the police chief, see if he can have a patrol car keep an eye on her around the clock. Our department might be able to pitch in."

"Thank you," I said, feeling greatly relieved. "Do you think I should say anything to her? I don't want to terrify her, but at the same time, she certainly ought to be on her guard."

"You know her a lot better than I do," Kanesha said. "How do you think she'll react if you tell her?"

"Ordinarily I'd say she could handle it because she's a tough nut, but she's pretty shaken up over this."

"Use your best judgment." Kanesha shrugged. "We'll do our part, but it might not be a bad idea if she stayed with someone instead of staying in the house alone."

"I'll talk to her."

Kanesha nodded and turned to walk away, but I stopped her. "One more thing."

She glowered at me when she turned back. "Yes?"

"It's about Winston Eagleton. The publisher? I think I told you about him this morning."

She fairly barked out her response. "What about him?"

"Have you talked to him yet?"

"Not yet. He's on my list. Why do you ask?" She looked suspicious.

"He's apparently been trying to get in touch with me to ask me to a dinner party he's planning for tonight." I shrugged. "At some point I'll have to talk to him, but once he knows about Mrs. Taylor, he may reconsider his plans. I didn't want to give anything away by talking to him before you did."

"Thank you." She glanced at her watch. "I'll track him down soon. He's staying at the Farrington House. Give me at least an hour before you get in touch with him, all right?"

"Sure thing."

Kanesha raised a hand in farewell before she trudged down the walk toward her car. After she drove away, I went back in the house. She had better get some rest soon. She looked about done in.

Melba was feeding Diesel what looked like chicken. The cat scarfed it down happily. Melba grinned at me. "Don't you ever feed this poor boy?"

"Con artist," I said to the cat. He ignored me. Then I addressed Melba. "Does he look like he's starving?" I had to grin back.

"Not exactly." Melba dropped the last piece of meat and went to wash her hands at the sink. I was wondering how to broach the subject of her potential danger when she addressed the issue herself.

"If you're worried about me staying here on my own, Charlie, don't be," she said, her expression calm but determined. "I'll blow the jerk's head off if he tries to get in here. I'm going over to see Thelma Crockett right now and take Zippy off her hands. He's a loudmouthed little cuss, and he'll raise a ruckus if anybody tries to break in here. So don't you worry about me."

I went over and gave her a hug. "The main thing is, I want you to be safe. And if at any time you don't feel safe here, you pack a bag, put Zippy in the car, and come on over. We have plenty of room in the madhouse for you and the dog. You know that."

She hugged me back briefly, then pushed me away. "You're a good man, and a good friend. If I need to, I'll come. But that jerk isn't going to run me out of my own house. You can bet on that."

Diesel meowed as if he agreed, and Melba and I laughed. "Come on, boy, let's get going." I pecked Melba on the cheek, Diesel warbled at her, and the cat and I headed for the front door.

Once we were in the car, I decided we might as well go visit Helen Louise at the bakery. I informed the cat of our destination, and he meowed in approval from the backseat.

"No more chicken for you, though," I said, glancing into the mirror. He started muttering. "You've had enough this morning, thanks to Melba." He moved over to the passenger-side window and gazed out, ignoring me.

I had a quiet chuckle as we headed for the town square. After I found a parking spot, I called Diesel into the front seat with me so

I could put on the spare harness and leash I kept in the car. I wasn't worried about his darting out into traffic, because he was far too smart for that. If people saw him walking around loose in town, there were bound to be complaints, however. So into the harness he went.

The bell on the door chimed as we walked in. Both the cat and I sniffed happily at the wonderful aromas that suffused the air in the bakery. I thought longingly of the marvelous *gâteau au chocolat* that was one of my sweetheart's specialties. She never failed to have it on offer, and I knew there was always an extra one hidden away in case I dropped by unexpectedly. I needed to watch my calories, though, and I would do my best to resist the temptation to indulge.

Midmorning Saturday was generally a busy time at the bakery. Customers dropped by to pick up special treats for the weekend, and Helen Louise and her assistant, Debbie, filled a seemingly constant stream of orders from behind the counter. Helen Louise stood at the cash register when we entered. She glanced briefly at the door, and when she recognized us, she smiled.

I waved and smiled back, and Diesel started chirping, although I doubted Helen Louise could hear him over the chatter in the bakery. A few heads turned, and several people nodded in greeting as Diesel and I made our way to our usual table in the corner near the register. On occasion, a customer made the mistake of objecting to the cat's presence in the bakery, but Helen Louise quickly apprised that person of his or her error in judgment. By now the regulars were so accustomed to seeing me and my big kitty that they probably thought nothing of it.

There was a line of five people at the register, so it would be a few minutes before Helen Louise could get away to talk. If many more people joined the queue at the register, I would get in line myself. But for now Diesel and I got comfortable, I in my chair and he at my feet, and waited.

The line was down to one person when my cell phone rang. I pulled it out and glanced at the number. Not one I recognized, and there was no name on the caller ID. I debated whether to answer it, but then remembered it could be Winston Eagleton. "Hello, this is Charlie Harris."

A high tenor voice with a heavy drawl I didn't recognize replied. "Hi, there, Mr. Harris. This here is Eugene Marter. We ain't met yet, but I was kinda hoping to remedy that situation this morning. I'm running errands in town here and wondered if you got a few minutes to talk about Grandma and her big do at the liberry."

Eighteen

For a moment I was too taken aback by the identity of the caller to say anything. Then I realized he was waiting for an answer. "Good morning, Mr. Marter. I'd be happy to talk with you. Right now I'm at the French bakery on the square. Do you know the place?"

He assured me he did and would be along in a few minutes. I told him to look for me at the corner table by the register, then ended the call.

I was certainly curious to meet Mrs. Cartwright's grandson. He had been mentioned several times but thus far hadn't appeared. I wondered why he wanted to talk to me instead of, say, Teresa.

Then another question hit me. How did he get my cell number? I couldn't remember giving it to his mother or his grandmother. I would have to find a tactful way to ask.

In the meantime I decided to get something to drink, so I ambled over to the refrigerated counter near the register and chose a bottle of still water. Diesel remained by the table while I got in line to pay.

The last person ahead of me in the queue dithered for a moment, scrambling through an oversized purse in search of her wallet. When she found it, she couldn't decide whether to use her credit card or write a check. People like this — male or female — drove me nuts. The rest of her life must have been a sad trial if she couldn't cope any better than this with what seemed like such an innocuous decision.

At last she left — she used her credit card, by the way — and I stepped up to the register.

"Bonjour, mon amour," Helen Louise said with a wide smile. "I'd give you a big kiss if there weren't people in line behind you."

"Hello, sweetheart." I mimed a kiss, and her smile grew even wider. "Maybe things will slow down in a few minutes, and we'll have a chance to talk." I handed her money for the water, and she tried to wave it away. I insisted, and she finally took it.

"As soon as I can," she promised. She pulled a bowl from beneath the counter and handed it across to me. She kept one nearby for Diesel in case he was thirsty.

I resumed my seat at the table with what Laura would call my "goofy" smile in place. Helen Louise had that effect on me. It had taken me a while to realize the truth — and the depth — of my feelings for my dear friend, but now that I had, well, I occasionally felt like a gangly adolescent with his first crush. I poured water in the bowl and set it on the floor. Diesel sniffed at it, then started lapping it up. When he finished he curled up by my chair and closed his eyes.

Eugene Marter ought to be here any minute now, I reckoned while I sipped my own water. The buzz of numerous conversations swarmed around me, but I paid little attention. Perhaps three minutes later, the bell on the door chimed, and I looked up to see a youngish man, perhaps in his late thirties, walk in, stop, and look around.

When he spotted me in the corner, he smiled broadly and headed my way. This had to be Eugene Marter, and I observed him with curiosity as discreetly as I could. I judged him to be about five foot six, and he had dark, close-clipped hair, and a pale face that reminded me vaguely of his grandmother. He wore faded jeans, worn sneakers, and a flannel shirt that had been through the wash a few times too often. He had the appearance of a man who had little money to spend on himself. Or was he an eccentric who preferred to dress this way? Neither his mother nor his grandmother looked shabby.

I stood as he neared the table. "Good morning. You must be Eugene Marter." I stuck out my hand.

He grasped it firmly and gave it two quick, hard shakes. "Morning, Mr. Harris. Mighty nice to meet you. Grandma sure does think you're a gentleman." His bland countenance split in a brief but charming smile.

"Please, have a seat." I indicated a place at the table. "Would you like something to drink?"

"Well, I could probably use some water right about now. All this running around's made me kinda thirsty." He glanced over at the counter. "I'll just get me a bottle of that fancy imported stuff and be right back."

I nodded, and he walked away. I resumed my seat, and Diesel, alerted by the presence of a stranger, sat up and stretched. When Eugene Marter came back with his bottle, Diesel went around to him. The cat waited until Marter was seated, then laid a paw on the denim-clad knee. Diesel chirped at the man, and Marter stared at him.

"Hey, there, big guy. Mama and Grandma told me about you. Ain't never seen a kitty cat this big before." Marter glanced up at me. "He got some kind of gland problem? Or is he s'posed to be that big?" His touch was tentative as he stroked Diesel's head.

"He's large for his breed," I said. "He's a Maine Coon, and they are generally larger than most domestic cats."

"Well, I'll swan." Marter shook his head, and I struggled to hide my amusement over an expression I hadn't heard since my own grandmother passed away thirty-five years ago.

"You mentioned on the phone that you wanted to talk to me about something." I thought a gentle prompt wouldn't hurt, since Marter seemed in no hurry to talk. Instead, he sat staring at the cat, and Diesel seemed equally fascinated by him.

Marter focused on me. "Huh? Oh, yeah, matter of fact there was something I wanted to talk to you about." He leaned forward. "According to Grandma, you're a pretty sharp guy. She also said she'd read in the paper where you was some kinda detective or something. That right?"

I felt like squirming in embarrassment. I had managed — mostly — to keep my name out of the local newspaper, thanks to the cooperation of Ray Appleby, reporter for the *Athena Daily Register.* But my name had been mentioned a couple of times in connection with some recent investigations, plus I knew my good friend Melba had been busy on the grapevine, singing my praises. I had begged her not to, but I knew she hadn't really listened to me.

"I'm not a detective," I said, trying to keep the irritation out of my tone. "It's true that I've been involved in helping the authorities solve several murder cases. But I'm a librarian, not a gumshoe."

Marter frowned. "I reckon that's all right. Long's you ain't a real detective, it figgers you don't charge nobody for helping, right?"

"I certainly would not charge anyone for helping them." Had he planned to hire me to be a detective? I could hear my grandmother saying, *Don't that beat all!*

"That's good, 'cause I sure ain't got the money to pay you." Marter grinned. "Been outta work awhile, and just between you and me and the fencepost, Grandma ain't too liberal with the spending money."

Where was he going with this? I wondered. I was beginning to feel uncomfortable, especially when I recalled Carrie Taylor's dismissal of the man as being lazy and shiftless, more or less.

"That's too bad," I said with as much sympathy as I could muster — and it wasn't very much. Perhaps Mrs. Taylor had been right about him. He looked more than healthy enough to be holding down a job.

"It's like this, see." Marter leaned forward, his elbows on the table. He glanced around, perhaps to see whether anyone was within earshot. "Mama and Grandma told me about these here collector-type people, and how crazy they are about getting to Grandma. That don't sound right to me. All she did was write those old books, and I don't think they should be bothering her."

I started to say something but Marter didn't appear to notice as he continued. "She's as old as Methuselah, and she ain't got the energy to deal with all that crap. They're like to kill her with all this crazy-ass stuff. Just between you and me and the cat here, I'm kinda worried they might cause her to have a heart attack and die on us."

"I respect your concern for your grand-mother," I said. What was it he actually wanted from me? "And if she doesn't feel up to doing the event, then of course we will understand." My stomach knotted at the thought of having to cancel, but we couldn't insist Mrs. Cartwright go through with it, not at her age.

Marter rolled his eyes. "You don't know

my grandma. She's loving every bit of attention she's getting, like an old coonhound soaking up the sunshine. People done been ignoring her so long, and now all they want to do is hang around her like she's some little tin god or something. She probably ain't got many years left, and I don't want one of them crazy fans of hers to kill her off before she's due to go."

"Is her heart really as frail as that? The two times I've seen her, I have to say she looked like she was in pretty good shape for someone who's about to be a hundred years old."

"Her heart's okay, far as I know. She ain't been to the doctor in years, though. Don't believe in 'em." Marter stared hard at me. "But what I'm talking about here is an actual honest-to-goodness lowdown threat."

NINETEEN

"Has someone actually *threatened* harm to your grandmother?" I could hardly believe what I was hearing. Diesel, upset by my obvious agitation, pushed against my legs and meowed. I stroked his head while I waited for Marter to explain his provocative statement.

"Yes siree Bob, they sure have." Marter nodded several times as if to emphasize his point. "That funny little guy that claims he's a publisher, what's-his-name? Eagleton, that's it." His head bobbed again. "He got downright ugly on the phone with me last night. He was carrying on all about how Grandma done promised him he could publish those books of hers — you know, the ones ain't never been published before?" When I nodded, he continued. "He said he ain't gonna stand for Grandma going back on her word now that she thinks one of them big New York City outfits might be interested."

Marter sat back in his chair, arms crossed over his chest, and focused his gaze on me. He nodded two times more, as if to say, *See, what did I tell you?*

"I'm sure he was angry with your grandmother" — and privately I thought Eagleton had a right to be, if she was planning to renege on an agreement with him — "but I'm not sure that constitutes an actual threat. Was that all he said, he wasn't going to *stand for it?*"

"No, he said more than that." Marter scowled. "He said, 'Miz Cartwright don't want me mad at her.' In fact, he musta said that two or three times."

I had to admit, those words did sound like a threat. A vague one, but still a threat. I said as much to Marter.

"It don't sound that vague to me." Marter's tone was heated. "That little bastard means to do my grandma harm if she don't do what he wants."

Surely the man realized he was talking to the wrong guy. "If you're really worried that Eagleton might do something violent, you should go to the police. I don't see what I can do about it."

Diesel didn't like the tension he could sense. He scrunched up against my legs again and meowed plaintively. I kept petting him, hoping he would relax and not be so worried.

Marter's glance shifted sideways, then back again. "Well, it's kinda like this." He paused. "Me and the police don't get along too good. I kinda had a little trouble with 'em now and again, and I don't figger they'd take too kindly to me coming and bothering 'em. I got what you might call a 'credibility gap' when it comes to the law." He glanced away again.

Now I could see what he was getting at, coming to me instead of going to the authorities. He must have thought I had a good working relationship with the police since I was some kind of detective. I suppressed a deep sigh as I put those thoughts into words. "So you figured if I talked to the police, they would pay more attention?"

Marter nodded, suddenly willing to face me again. "Yeah, that's it. Can you do it and keep me out of it?"

"I could mention it to Chief Deputy Berry — she's with the sheriff's department — but there's one problem."

"What's that?"

"I wasn't the one who heard Eagleton threaten your grandmother." I paused. "Even if I went to the deputy with your story, she'd still have to talk to you to confirm it. She wouldn't accept it on my word alone."

"Couldn't you just say you heard him say that somewhere?" Marter gave me a weak grin.

I shook my head. "No, I can't. I'm not going to lie to the police."

"That ain't much help." Marter looked disgruntled. "Done wasted my time talking to you." He stood.

"Sorry, but I still think you should talk to the police yourself. Call the sheriff's department and ask for Chief Deputy Berry. Tell her your story, and you can tell her I said to call her." That was the best I could do under the circumstances.

Marter sighed. "Well, I reckon I'll think about it." He bobbed his head in my direction before he turned and strode off.

He was barely out the door before Helen Louise walked up behind me and startled me by putting her hands on my shoulders. She chuckled. "Sorry, love, didn't mean to make you jump like that." She kissed my cheek before taking the seat vacated by Marter.

Diesel immediately sidled up to her and started chirping. No doubt he was explaining how he was at the point of utter starvation and that only tidbits of chicken, straight from her hands to his mouth, would save him.

Helen Louise started to rise — headed for the kitchen and the chicken, I was sure — but I forestalled her. "He's already had his chicken treat this morning, thanks to Melba Gilley."

Helen Louise pursed her lips and glared, first at me, then at the cat. "*Sacrebleu!* Fickle, the both of you. Here I am, slaving away, making treats just for you, and then you go and take up with that woman." She tossed her head. "I never in my life knew two such faithless males."

Then she spoiled the effect by giggling. Diesel warbled at her. He probably thought she was serious, but he looked relieved when she laughed. I grinned at her. She had a silly side that I found appealing.

"How is Melba, by the way? I haven't seen her in weeks." Helen Louise rubbed Diesel's head, and he rewarded her with his rumbling purr.

"Not so good." I informed her of Carrie Taylor's murder, and she was duly shocked. "She and Melba were really close, and Melba's taking it hard."

"What on earth could Carrie Taylor have done that would make somebody want to kill her?" Helen Louise shook her head. "If she was that close to Melba, she obviously liked to gossip like I like French wines. Otherwise, she was about as inoffensive a woman as I've ever met."

I had a lot to tell Helen Louise to bring her up to date, and I made it as concise and quick as I could. Activity inside the bakery had slowed; otherwise it wouldn't have been possible to claim her attention for more than a few minutes. Helen Louise didn't interrupt, and by the time I'd finished, I had the beginnings of a headache. I realized it was lunchtime, and I was hungry.

"So that was Mrs. Cartwright's grandson." Helen Louise looked thoughtful. "Do you think he's right to be worried about potential violence against her? It sounds far-fetched to me."

"Before Carrie Taylor was murdered, I would have agreed with you." My head began to ache in earnest now. I rubbed my right temple. "After having met these groupies of Mrs. Cartwright's, though, I'm not so sure Eugene isn't right. They all seem slightly deranged to me."

"Poor baby, you look like your head's really bothering you. Need some aspirin?" Helen Louise patted my knee, her concern obvious.

I managed a weak grin. "Food and caffeine would do the trick, I think."

She laughed. "And you say Diesel's the con artist in the family. Hang on, love, I'll be back in a flash with treats for both my guys." She got up and headed for the kitchen.

Diesel chirped because he heard the word *treats*. He had figured that one out early on.

"Yes, I guess you can have a bit more," I told him. "But only a bit."

The cat stared at me for a moment, then held up a paw and licked it. *We'll see about that.* I could almost hear him saying the words.

Helen Louise appeared with a small tray of food and drink. More water and some chicken for Diesel, an iced Diet Coke and a small quiche for me.

"Thank you, sweetheart," I said. "The quiche looks wonderful. What kind is it?"

"Spinach, onion, and Gruyère cheese. No bacon or sausage, I'm afraid." She grinned.

"Sounds heavenly." I cut into it with my knife and fork while Helen Louise doled out chicken. The flavor of the first mouthful made me happy, and I chewed with enthusiasm. Helen Louise watched and then relaxed when I smiled broadly. *"Très délicieux."*

My accent was execrable, no doubt, but I knew she appreciated my effort. She wanted to take me to Paris one day, and I had no argument with the plan, but I was determined to learn a bit of French before we went.

She fed Diesel the last of the chicken and wiped her fingers on a napkin. Her assistant, Debbie, called her then, and she shrugged an apology. "Later," she promised as she went back to work.

Diesel grumbled because there were no more treats forthcoming. He stared hopefully at me, but I couldn't let him have anything with onions and cheese in it. Onions in particular were not good for felines. "Sorry, boy, this is not Diesel-appropriate. You've had more than enough goodies for today."

When he realized I wasn't going to give in and let him have a bite, he stretched out under the table, his head facing away from me. He could sulk all he wanted but he wasn't getting anything more to eat.

I finished my quiche, savoring every bite, and polished off the Diet Coke as well. My headache disappeared, and I felt much better. Activity in the bakery had picked up again, and I figured Helen Louise would be too busy for a while to chat any further. I managed to catch her eye and wave good-bye. She smiled and waved back. I didn't try to pay for my lunch. I had won a minor skirmish over the bottled water, and I decided not to press my luck.

"Come on, boy, time to go home." I called Diesel from under the table and picked up his leash to lead him out to the car. He refused to move for a moment, but after I tugged on the leash three times, he relented and came with me. He was single-minded when it came to chicken, the stubborn little cuss.

The cat hopped in the backseat and stared out the window. I carefully backed out and headed the car toward home. About halfway there my cell phone rang. I didn't like to talk while driving, so I pulled over to the curb on a residential street and retrieved my phone.

I didn't recognize the number, but it wasn't the same as Eugene Marter's. This one had an unknown area code. I answered it and identified myself.

Winston Eagleton's cheery voice came through clearly. "Good afternoon, Mr. Harris. I do hope I find you in good health and spirits this fine day."

"I'm doing well, Mr. Eagleton. How are you?"

"Not tip-top, I must confess. In fact I am rather distraught over the sad news of the death of dear Carrie Taylor." His cheery tone gave the lie to his words, I thought. But perhaps he was putting a brave face on things. Given his mode of speech, I figured that's how he would have put it.

"Yes, it's terrible. I didn't know her well at all, but she seemed like such a nice person."

"Oh, she was, she was, let me assure you. Salt of the earth, dear, dear Carrie." Eagleton sighed heavily. "One simply cannot imagine why a psychopath would attack such a defenseless creature. It boggles the mind, does it not?"

I agreed that it did even as I wondered whether he would ever get to the point of this call — unless discussing the sad event *was* the point.

"There are those, one must presume, who would think me callous in the extreme for what I am about to tell you, Mr. Harris." Eagleton paused, and I waited, unsure whether he expected a response. "Er, that is, I had decided late yester eve to hold a small soiree at my hotel, the Farrington House, and invite those who, like myself, are drawn to the works of dear Electra Cartwright. A select group, of course, because one cannot have the *hoi polloi* to dine with one."

"Certainly not," I murmured, wondering at the man's lung capacity. He hardly seemed to pause for a breath when delivering these long sentences.

"One hopes that you will not think it too gauche of me to go forward with these plans, but perhaps we can raise a toast to the memory of dear Carrie and celebrate all that was good and fine about her life and contributions. That would be fitting, would it not?"

"Yes, it would be." Before I could say anything else, he was off again.

"Dear Electra has promised to attend, and I have secured promises from Gordon Betts, Della Duffy, and your delightful cohort from the library, Teresa Farmer. Dare I assume that you will join us? One would also suggest that you bring that charming feline of yours, but I gather the hotel frowns upon that sort of thing. And Della does have that unfortunate fear of all things feline."

"Yes, that is regrettable," I said. I would not have considered taking Diesel with me anyway. There are times when it is not appropriate to bring him along, and this would be one. "I will be there. What time does your soiree commence?" Good grief, I was starting to sound like him.

"Shall we say seven, for seven-thirty? There will of course be cocktails and hors d'oeuvres beforehand. No black tie necessary." He chuckled. "One mustn't be too formal."

"That sounds fine. I'll see you there."

"Good-oh," Eagleton said. "I shall look forward to it. *Au revoir.*"

I put the phone down but didn't immediately pull out into the street again. Instead, I sat there wondering what the true purpose was for this get-together of Eagleton's. Perhaps I was being overly suspicious, but the man was up to something, I was sure.

But what?

TWENTY

The rest of the way home I pondered the motive behind Eagleton's dinner party but realized that I didn't know the man well enough to discern what lay behind any of his actions. Based on what Carrie Taylor had said, I suspected he might be doing his best to woo Mrs. Cartwright so that he could wring a contract from her for the unpublished Veronica Thane novels. That seemed the most likely.

The garage was empty when I pulled in, and no cars lined the street in front of the house. That meant Diesel and I had the house to ourselves. While the cat visited the utility room, I headed upstairs. I felt like putting my feet up for a bit and doing my best to think about something other than Carrie Taylor's untimely death.

Diesel returned from his pit stop, hopped on the bed beside me, and stretched out while I made myself comfortable, propped up against a couple of pillows. I picked up *The Mystery at Spellwood Mansion* and found my place, the beginning of the second chapter.

Veronica felt a chill creep along her spine as Mrs. Eden uttered those ominous words. What kind of danger did the poor woman fear?

The plucky girl's sturdy common sense took hold. Mrs. Eden's appearance proclaimed her an invalid of some years' standing. Perhaps she suffered from a nervous disorder, and her mind was disturbed by fears that came only from a fevered imagination.

The girl decided she must ascertain as adroitly as possible the truth of Mrs. Eden's claims. If the poor lady was truly in terrible danger, then Veronica resolved to do her best to assist Mrs. Eden. Should the danger prove imaginary, however, Veronica would need to use every ounce of her considerable tact. Adversity had tempered the girl with a maturity beyond her years.

Veronica spoke gently to the woman. "What is the source of your danger, Mrs. Eden? And why do you dare not leave the house? Does the danger come from without?"

A small moan escaped Mrs. Eden's quivering lips. "Oh, Miss Derivale! Dare I trust you? I feel so alone, betrayed by those who should instead tend to my well-being." She gazed hopefully into Veronica's eyes.

Veronica knew she must gain Mrs. Eden's trust if she were to be able to help her. Therefore she decided to make a bold move and declare her true identity. "You are under a misapprehension, Mrs. Eden, one I did not bother to correct until now. I am not Miss Derivale, whoever she may be. I am Veronica Thane, and I happened upon this house when I needed refuge from the storm."

"Veronica Thane," Mrs. Eden gasped. She gazed more intently into her guest's eyes. "I believe I have heard of you. Were you not the girl who aided Mrs. Finison Webster in tracking down her lost jewels?"

"Yes, I was able to assist Mrs. Webster," Veronica replied modestly.

"Then I will trust you," Mrs. Eden said impulsively, her hands clutching at Veronica's. "I need a friend so desperately, and there is none in this accursed house."

Unbeknownst to the two conferring on

the chaise longue, there was a secret listening post, constructed in the days of the War Between the States, when Spellwood Mansion was the home of a notorious Confederate spy. As Veronica and Mrs. Eden talked, an unseen presence listened to every word spoken between them.

"Veronica Thane." The listener barely whispered the name. Recognizing the threat implicit in the girl's true identity, the listener stole softly away to make certain nefarious preparations. The girl must be dealt with, and at once!

"Tell me, Mrs. Eden, the source of the danger," Veronica urged once again.

I turned the page, thinking I remembered the sad tale of Mrs. Eden's situation, but my cell phone interrupted my reading. Mrs. Eden and Veronica would have to wait, because I recognized the public library's main number.

Bronwyn barely waited for me to say "Hello" before she spoke. "Sorry to bother you, Charlie, but I wondered when you were going to bring the books you promised me for the exhibit. I don't have to have them today, unless you just happen to be out and about this afternoon. Monday morning

188

would be fine."

I couldn't believe I hadn't remembered to take the cartons this morning as I'd originally planned. The thought of running over to the library this afternoon didn't appeal much. "If you're sure Monday morning is soon enough," I said, "I can bring them by first thing, before I go to work at the college."

"Sure, that's fine," Bronwyn said. "But I really do need to have the books that morning. All I have left is to make labels for them before I put them in the exhibit cases."

I felt guilty because I should have taken them today. She would have to rush on Monday morning to get things done if I waited until then. But I so didn't want to get in the car again right now.

Inspiration struck — a solution good for each of us. "I tell you what, I'll e-mail you with the titles and authors and a brief note about each book. How does that sound?"

"That would be great." Bronwyn sounded relieved and happy. "That way I can cut and paste to make the labels. So much faster, and besides, you know more about the books than I do, Charlie. Thanks."

"You're welcome," I said. "I'll get on it right now." I glanced regretfully at *The Mystery at Spellwood Mansion* when I ended the call. Instead of finding out about Mrs. Eden's terrible danger, I would have to work.

No reason I couldn't be comfortable while I did work, however. The two cartons were here in my bedroom. All I had to do was retrieve the laptop from the den, and I'd be set.

"No need for you to come with me." I grinned at Diesel, dozing on his side of the bed. He opened one eye, yawned, closed the eye, and appeared to doze off again.

I chuckled as I headed down the stairs.

A few minutes later, I had one of the cartons at hand and the laptop booted up and ready to go. I pulled a book from the carton and set to work.

For each book, I typed in the title, the author, the series, and the basic publication information. If I knew the name of the illustrator, I added that. One of the best known was Russell H. Tandy, a professional artist who did the covers and the internal illustrations for the first twenty-six Nancy Drew books. As I typed that information for an early printing of *The Secret of the Old Clock,* the first Nancy Drew book, I felt the faint stir of memory. Something about Russell Tandy and a particular Nancy Drew book. What was it?

I did a quick Internet search and found the Nancy Drew Sleuth website. It didn't take long to find the information. Tandy had not illustrated the eleventh book in the series, *The Clue of the Broken Locket*. That was what that little niggle of memory was about. I revised my information in the e-mail and moved on to the next book.

By the time I finished the books in the first carton, I had begun to realize I'd pulled too many for Bronwyn to use effectively. There were sixteen in the first carton and probably as many in the second one. I pictured the exhibit cases in my mind and figured that twenty books would be about right for the space, by the time Bronwyn added the labels.

I set the laptop aside and went over to the second carton. After a quick examination of the items in it, I pulled three to go with the sixteen I had already written up.

Fifteen minutes later I was finished with those three. I read back through the e-mail, checking the titles and authors represented. I discovered that among the titles were two Veronica Thanes, but not the first, *Spellwood Mansion*. That one had to be included because it launched the series. Maybe I could finish rereading it over the weekend. Otherwise I would have to wait until the exhibit came down.

I picked up the book and examined it carefully. I pulled off the dust jacket to look at the binding. I frowned. There was no silhouette of Veronica and her two sidekicks, Lucy Carlton and Arthur "Artie" Marsh, on the front cover. That was strange. From what I recalled, all the books had sported the silhouette as part of the design.

I did another search, this time on Veronica Thane, and found a website with several pages devoted to the series. With the enthusiasm for these series books, I figured someone must have researched the publication history, and I was right. There was a page with pictures of the covers of every book in the series, and there were examples of the variations in binding.

And there it was, a picture of a Veronica Thane book sans silhouette. I scanned the long paragraph of information and learned that this particular binding was used only on so-called breeder sets for the first two titles in the series. There was an explanation of breeder sets, which sounded vaguely familiar. The publishers brought out the first two or three volumes in a limited print run to test the waters with readers, to see if the series might catch on. According to the website, the technique worked for Nancy Drew in 1930. The series was an immediate hit. Veronica had a more modest debut two years later.

What I read next made me sit up and whistle.

Diesel muttered in protest. I supposed my whistling disturbed his beauty nap. He rolled over on his back and stretched, and his tail switched back and forth. He stayed in that position with his head twisted to one side and went back to sleep.

I reread the paragraph that had piqued my interest.

A few years ago a collector and expert on the history of the Veronica Thane series, Jennifer Fisher, brought to light a little-known variant in the first printings of the first volume in the breeder set. This was recently confirmed by Mrs. Carrie Taylor, the publisher of *The Thane Chronicles,* the newsletter devoted to the author and her works, who reported that she has a copy in her extensive collection. In the final paragraph of this variant edition, the next volume of the series is named as *The Clarevoyant's Clew.* The correct title is, of course, *The Clairvoyant's Clue.* The error must have been caught quickly and corrected, though a number of the volumes with the wrong title did make it into the hands of readers. Copies of the book with the incorrect title have rarely surfaced, but recently a collector was reported to have paid over twenty thousand dollars for a near-pristine copy of the highly sought after item. Though the price seems extravagant, the purchaser certainly has the satisfaction of knowing he (or she) possesses a true rarity.

I wondered uneasily whether I had just discovered the motive behind Carrie Taylor's murder.

Twenty-One

Would anyone really kill in order to obtain a rare copy of *The Mystery at Spellwood Mansion*? Even if a collector had paid twenty thousand dollars for one?

I didn't want to believe it, but I knew people murdered for far less and for even more bizarre reasons. Kanesha needed to know about this. I copied the link for the page and e-mailed it to her with a brief explanation. All she had to do was check Carrie Taylor's collection, and if the copy with the incorrect title turned up, then the book wasn't the motive. If it was missing, she might have a lead on why Mrs. Taylor was killed.

What about Aunt Dottie's copy? My hand shook a little as I reached for the book. I opened it and found the last page of the text.

I almost dropped the book.

Aunt Dottie's copy was one of the rare

ones. There it was, right on the page. *The Clarevoyant's Clew.*

I examined the book. Beautiful condition, I thought. Not exactly pristine, because it had obviously been read a few times. The dust jacket was intact, no tears or chips, and the colors were bright and crisp. My late aunt had loved her books and always took great care of them, even as a child. She had helped instill that love in me.

I had better look after this copy, I realized. There was no way I would ever sell it, and I decided against lending it for the exhibit. I would feel better knowing it was in its place on the shelf upstairs. It would probably be perfectly safe in a locked exhibit case in the library, but I didn't want to take the chance of having it stolen or damaged.

I wondered idly if both Aunt Dottie's copy and Carrie Taylor's had come from a bookstore in Athena. I remembered my aunt telling me about one on the square when she was a child, back in the late thirties. At some point she must have told me the name, but it had gone out of business by the time I came along.

My laptop beeped to let me know I had new e-mail. I set the book gingerly aside and checked the screen. I had a response from Kanesha. Terse, as usual: "Thanks.

We'll check for it."

It was out of my hands now. I knew Mrs. Taylor's house would be subjected to a thorough and painstaking search. If the book was still there, they would find it. The question was, would Kanesha tell me one way or the other? Without my having to annoy her by asking, that is.

If the book was potentially the motive, then who would want it badly enough to kill for it?

My prime suspect was Gordon Betts — a notion based more on my antipathy to the man than on anything concrete. He boasted he had the largest collection in the world of Mrs. Cartwright's books. Did he have a copy of the variant printing of the first book, though?

A whisper of memory teased at me. What was it Mrs. Taylor had said the last time I saw her? Something to do with Gordon Betts.

I thought hard and finally dredged it up. I heard her voice in my head saying, *Gordon may think he has everything, but I know better.*

Could she have been talking about her copy of *Spellwood Mansion*?

No, it couldn't be that, surely, because her possession of it was right there on the

Web for anyone to see. Gordon Betts, obsessive collector that he allegedly was, surely wouldn't overlook a piece of information as significant as that.

No, I decided after further thought. There had to be something else Mrs. Taylor had that he didn't.

If *he* killed her then, he probably did so for a different reason.

Another idea struck me. Unless she had a better copy than he did. I knew serious collectors would *trade up,* as it were, replacing an inferior item in their collection with one that was in better condition in some way. Gordon Betts could have wanted her copy for that reason.

I was tempted to e-mail Kanesha with these speculations, but I came to my senses before I did. I doubted she would thank me for complicating the issue. Better to wait until I knew whether Mrs. Taylor's copy was missing.

A glance at the laptop screen reminded me I hadn't quite finished my e-mail to Bronwyn. I had better get back to work and finish it.

Twenty minutes later I hit Send, then shut down the laptop. In my earlier excitement I hadn't realized that my neck and shoulders ached from hunching over the computer. I rubbed the back of my neck with both hands, and that helped. A hot shower would help even more, but I thought I'd stretch out on the bed for a bit first.

I made myself comfortable and picked up *Spellwood Mansion.* I probably should have put it away without finishing my reread, but I would be careful with it. I needed to get Mylar jacket covers and put them on all the books, I decided. That would protect them much better.

I found my place and began to read.

"Tell me, Mrs. Eden, the source of the danger," Veronica urged once again.

"The story is a long one." Mrs. Eden spoke in a low voice. "I can hardly bear to think of the horrible, vicious man who is at the root of all my troubles. But I must share the details with someone." She paused for a deep, sobbing breath.

Veronica was concerned that Mrs. Eden might lose her fading strength altogether, unless she had some kind of restorative to bolster her strength and her spirits. "Might we ask for some tea? I am quite thirsty myself, and I believe the hot tea would revive us both."

Mrs. Eden nodded gratefully. She pointed with a trembling hand to a bell pull on the wall by the fireplace. "If you will be so kind as to summon Bradberry, he will see that refreshments are brought."

Veronica complied with the request and immediately resumed her place beside her hostess. Moments later the door opened, and the butler entered the room noiselessly.

"What do you require, Madam?" He gazed intently at his employer, and Veronica found his expression slightly menacing.

"Tea, if you please, Bradberry, and a few sandwiches, if Cook will be so kind." Mrs. Eden's voice died away to a mere whisper on the final words.

"Certainly, Madam." Bradberry inclined his head before he turned and glided quietly out of the room.

Mrs. Eden lay back on the chaise, the back of her hand against her forehead and her eyes closed. Veronica hesitated to rouse the invalid, but if she were to help Mrs. Eden, she must hear what her hostess had to say about her danger.

"Mrs. Eden, please, continue your story," Veronica urged in a quiet tone.

The invalid's eyes fluttered open. "Yes, of course, my dear. I was about to name my persecutor." She paused. "He is none other than Langley Braddock."

Veronica gasped. Langley Braddock was a well-known financier and socialite of the highest reputation. He moved in the best circles and called many an important man his friend. Yet Mrs. Eden claimed him as her oppressor. How could this be?

Mrs. Eden nodded weakly. "I see you recognize the name." Her tone was bitter as she continued. "To the rest of the world he is a paragon, a leader of society, but to me he is a heartless, cold tyrant. He is the executor of my late husband's estate, and he has stolen almost everything my husband left me to further his own dark schemes."

Veronica found herself in a quandary. Langley Braddock was an acquaintance of her own guardian and had been entertained by Aunt Araminta on at least three occasions. She recalled him as a distinguished man of somewhat cold and regal bearing. She had not warmed to him herself but knew her guardian admired him. Yet Mrs. Eden claimed him as the source of her danger. Perhaps the woman was deranged after all.

"I see you are doubtful." Mrs. Eden sighed heavily. "That is my great misfortune, because he is such a plausible rogue. I alone know the truth, yet no one will believe me."

Veronica spoke hesitantly. "Have you any proof of his crimes against you?"

Mrs. Eden nodded wearily. "The evidence lies in my late husband's papers, but the villain has them in his own keeping. He has taken great pains to discredit me, and no lawyer will go against him. So you see, my plight is desperate. He means to sell my house and force me into utter penury. I will soon have nothing left."

Veronica held her response, for at that moment Bradberry appeared through the door, pushing a tea tray in front of him. He came to a halt beside Veronica. "Perhaps you will serve, miss, as Madam is not well."

Veronica inclined her head to indicate that she would. "That will be all, thank you," she said firmly.

Bradberry departed, and Veronica poured tea for herself and her hostess. "Here," she said as she handed the cup and saucer to the invalid. "Perhaps this will help restore you somewhat."

Mrs. Eden accepted the tea gratefully and began to sip at it. Veronica took her own cup and began to drink. The tea was strong — stronger, in fact, than she normally liked — but as she was so thirsty, she drank down the first cup and quickly poured herself a second.

There was a plate of sandwiches, and Veronica selected one and placed it on a small dish, which she then proffered to Mrs. Eden. Her hostess waved it limply away. "The tea is enough for now."

Veronica nodded. "Please continue when you feel you can." She picked up the sandwich, but it seemed heavy. Veronica frowned. She felt so sleepy all of a sudden. She was rather tired, she thought. Maybe more tea would revive her.

The cup never reached her mouth, for Veronica could no longer fight off the waves of exhaustion that engulfed her. The plate with its sandwich slipped to the floor as Veronica fell soundly asleep.

Twenty-Two

I smiled as I finished the second chapter. Poor Veronica. I wondered idly how many times during the course of the series she had been drugged or hit on the head. She got tied up a few times, too, as I recalled. Being a feisty girl detective had the occasional drawback.

I turned the page.

From somewhere far distant Veronica heard a gentle voice. It seemed to be calling her name. "Ronnie, oh dear Ronnie, please do wake up. Can you hear me at all?"

Veronica wanted to answer that she could hear, but an overwhelming darkness surrounded her. She tried to open her eyes. The eyelids refused to obey. They felt heavy and lifeless. She struggled, determined to open them, and at last her eyelids moved.

Where was she? Veronica had no idea of her location or what was wrong with her. Why did she feel like every part of her body was too heavy to move?

"I hear y-you," she managed to croak. Her throat was dry, painfully so. "W-w-water, p-please."

A gentle hand slid behind her head and lifted it slightly. Her eyelids closed again, but she felt light pressure against her lips.

"Here's the water, dearest, open your mouth just a little for me."

Veronica knew that voice, knew that it belonged to someone who meant her no harm. But who was this ministering angel?

She managed a few sips of water, and her throat felt better. Next she felt a damp cloth on her forehead, and she welcomed the cooling effect. She began to revive, but with agonizing slowness.

"Where am I?" she whispered. She forced her eyelids open, and in the dim light she began to recognize the familiar outlines of her own room. "I'm home?"

"Yes, dearest, you are," the voice responded tenderly. "You are safe where you belong, with your dear guardian and your devoted friends. It's me, darling, Lucy."

"Lucy?" Veronica felt stronger, knowing that her best chum Lucy was with her.

Perhaps Lucy could explain what had happened to her, why her memory was curiously blank.

After more water and cool compresses, and more of Lucy's devoted attentions, Veronica was able to sit up. Her mind cleared a little of the fog, and she felt a sense of urgency. There was danger somewhere, but where?

And for whom?

My phone rang, and I set the book aside. I suppressed a groan when I saw the number. Kanesha must have done some checking into the e-mail I sent her.

Her first words confirmed it. "Thanks again for the e-mail. At least now I know why that book might be valuable, to somebody anyway."

"You're welcome." I decided to venture a question. "Have you found Mrs. Taylor's copy yet?"

"No, not so far. I don't think it's in the house. They've searched it pretty thoroughly." She paused. "Do you think she might have put it in a safe-deposit box?"

"It's possible," I replied. "But somehow I don't think she would have. Most book collectors in my experience like to have the books easily at hand so they can look at

206

them whenever they want. Remember James Delacorte and his collection? He had books far more valuable than Mrs. Taylor's copy of *Spellwood Mansion,* and his were on display in the house."

Thinking about Mr. Delacorte always saddened me. His untimely end came about in part because of his collection. Had the same thing happened to Mrs. Taylor?

"Yes, I recall." Kanesha's tone was dry. "I'm going to have to check on a safe-deposit box, though. Have to rule that out."

I decided to venture another question, since Kanesha seemed to be in a forthcoming mood — or what passed for one with her. "Do you have any other potential motives?"

"Not yet, but it's early on. We have a lot more fact-gathering to do. Thanks again for that e-mail. If I have any other questions, I'll let you know."

I barely had time to say "Of course" before she ended the call. I'd had no chance to voice my suspicions of Gordon Betts, but perhaps that was just as well. Kanesha's tolerance of my *interference* would extend only so far.

Why had I focused solely on Gordon Betts? That thought struck me suddenly. I couldn't in all fairness concentrate only on him simply because of my antipathy to his combative, self-centered personality. Della Duffy could as easily have been interested in Mrs. Taylor's copy of *Spellwood Mansion*. She hadn't been that much more pleasant, frankly, than Gordon Betts even after I made allowance for her phobia of cats. She and Carrie Taylor obviously knew each other. I ought to find out more about her.

I recalled what Melba told me about the message from Mrs. Taylor. Even though there had apparently been a man at the door when she ended the call to Melba, that didn't mean the man was her final visitor last night. Another person could have come along later, so I couldn't rule out a woman as the killer.

An Internet search might yield information. I wondered, though, how common the name *Della Duffy* might be. I picked up the laptop and typed the name, enclosed in quotation marks, into the search engine.

There were many pages of results. I skimmed the list on the first page, and two of them looked promising. The rest appeared to be obituaries. I checked the links connected to social media, but the pictures didn't match the woman I'd met.

I examined four more pages of links but found only one hit that appeared useful.

The link led me to a mention of Della Duffy on a blog devoted to girls' series fiction. What I read shocked me.

According to the blogger, who evidently went by the bizarre name *ILoveVeronica-Thane,* Della Duffy was involved in an altercation with another collector — unnamed — at a convention devoted to juvenile literature. The blogger gave a brief description of the incident, which took place in the book dealers' room. Duffy and the other collector both allegedly claimed to have spotted a much-desired item on a table and reached for it at the same time. The other collector insisted that he touched it first, but Della Duffy was equally insistent that she did. When the man snatched it up from the table, she pushed him and tried to grab the book away from him. He slipped and fell on his backside. He never let go of the book, however, and purchased it for his collection. Della Duffy protested loudly but to no avail. According to the blogger, sympathies evidently lay with the victor, who was a popular and well-known figure among collectors.

That was definitely interesting, but I wished the blogger hadn't been so coy about the identity of the man Della Duffy attacked. I skimmed through the comments attached to the blog post, but no one named the man, though the discussion was lively. One person claimed to have witnessed a similar incident involving Ms. Duffy at another convention but provided no details. I looked further through the entire blog but could find no other mentions of Della Duffy.

Not much to go on, and not completely reliable since they were really only hearsay, but these incidents left me with the impression that Della Duffy went after what she wanted. She appeared to have a temper, also, and that intrigued me.

If she'd wanted Carrie Taylor's copy of *Spellwood Mansion,* for example, how far would she go to own it?

I hesitated for a moment, but then I decided I ought to share this information with Kanesha. I e-mailed her the link to the blog posting with a note that I had found another item of interest I thought she should consider.

Okay, out of my hands for now.

Beside me, Diesel stirred. One eye opened, then the other. He blinked at me and yawned. He had a good stretch before he sat up. He warbled, hopefully, I thought. He hadn't eaten in a while so he was on the point of utter starvation.

"Okay, boy," I said as I shut down the

laptop and put it aside. "Let's go downstairs, and I'll see if I can find you a morsel or two."

The cat leapt to the floor and disappeared before I could get off the bed. I smiled as I followed Diesel downstairs. I knew he would be waiting in the utility room by his food and water bowls.

After I saw to the needs of my poor starving kitty, I rooted around in the fridge for my own snack. Azalea had baked a ham two days ago, and there was enough left for a sandwich.

Sandwich in one hand and a can of diet cola in the other, I climbed the stairs, intent on further research on the Internet. I might as well see what I could find about my host for the evening, Winston Eagleton. With such a distinctive name to search, I figured I would get far fewer results, and those that I did retrieve would be on target.

I was right. My search on Eagleton yielded only seven pages of hits. There were even images this time, not simply text.

I took a bite of my sandwich and clicked on one of the images, and there was Eagleton, beaming like a cherub into the camera lens. The next image contained a surprise. Eagleton, radiant smile in place, had his arm around none other than Gordon Betts, who looked more than a bit uncomfortable.

The chummy pose appeared staged to me, and I wondered what the occasion for it was. I clicked on the link to visit the page where the image resided, and the resulting explanation gave me another surprise.

According to what I read, Gordon Betts was a major investor in Eagleton's publishing concern.

If that were the case, I wondered why Eagleton appeared so desperate to get his hands on Mrs. Cartwright's unpublished manuscripts. I remembered Eugene Marter's allegations that Eagleton threatened his grandmother over them.

With Betts's alleged millions behind him, surely Eagleton could offer Mrs. Cartwright enough money to clinch the deal.

Unless Eagleton and Betts had fallen out, and Betts had withdrawn his support from the publishing venture.

Interesting fodder for speculation, but could any of it be connected with the murder of Carrie Taylor?

TWENTY-THREE

Stewart was pottering about in the kitchen when I came through on my way to Winston Eagleton's dinner party early that evening. Diesel trailed hopefully in my wake, unaware that he was destined to remain home tonight.

"What ho, Sherlock." Stewart shot me a mischievous grin. "Whither art thou bound? And to what fell purpose?"

"What on earth have you been reading, to spout dialogue like that?" I shook my head in mock sadness. "Such a good mind he had, once upon a time."

Stewart snorted with laughter, and Diesel padded over to him and meowed loudly. Stewart had yet to notice the cat, and Diesel obviously meant to bring this to the man's attention.

"Shakespeare, actually," Stewart said as he rubbed the cat's head. "To be more precise, *Macbeth,* hence the mention of *fell purpose."*

"Why this sudden interest in Shake-speare?" I was curious because Stewart, a chemistry professor at Athena College, tended to read mostly nonfiction, with the occasional lurid thriller or trashy best-seller thrown into the mix.

"Trying to elevate my mind above the mundane table of elements that I spend so much of my life with." Stewart's airy tone didn't fool me. Something — more likely, some*one* — had prompted this interest in the Bard, but I knew Stewart wouldn't tell me who until he was darned good and ready. I didn't think Laura was responsible, despite her avowed devotion to the play-wright. There had to be an attractive man involved somehow.

"Shakespeare is a good elevator for the mind." I did my best to keep a straight face, but when Stewart rolled his eyes at my atro-cious pun, I had to laugh. "Seriously, I hope you're enjoying *Macbeth*. Great play, but my favorite is actually *The Tempest.*"

"Haven't made it to that one yet." Stewart rubbed Diesel's head a few more times before he turned to the sink to wash his hands. "Now where are you going? You never did answer me."

"Sorry." I explained briefly about the dinner party. "Laura said she and Frank would keep Diesel company until I get home. They ought to be here any minute."

"I'm staying in tonight. He can come upstairs and play with Dante." Stewart went to the stove, lifted the lid of a pot, and sniffed appreciatively. "Minestrone. Smells sinfully delicious."

"Sure does," I said as the scent wafted my way. "Where is Dante anyway?" Usually the little poodle bounced around Stewart like a tiny dervish.

Stewart grimaced. "He's having a time-out in his crate for a couple of hours. He was a bad boy earlier today while I was out — he tried to eat one of my expensive Italian loafers."

Diesel started chattering, and Stewart and I exchanged amused glances. I would have sworn the cat was commenting on the poodle's bad behavior, and not politely, either. The chatter stopped, and Diesel looked up at Stewart as if waiting for a reply.

Stewart winked at me. "That's right, honey, you are a sweet, well-behaved kitty, and he's a bad, bad little dog."

The cat blinked, then calmly started washing his left front paw.

Stewart adjusted the heat under the minestrone. "Laura told me about the murder.

That poor woman."

"Did you know her?" I glanced at my watch to check the time. I had a good ten minutes before I had to leave.

"I might know her if I saw her." Stewart grimaced. "That didn't come out right. The name rang a faint bell, but I can't match a face with it, sorry."

"No reason you would know her, I expect."

"Did you really get to meet Electra Barnes Cartwright?" Stewart's eyes gleamed with suppressed excitement, I thought.

"Yes, I did. Don't tell me you're a fan, too." I had no idea he had ever read the Veronica Thane books.

"My mother had a set of the books. She adored Veronica when she was a girl, and she let me read them when I was about ten." Stewart smiled. "I had the biggest crush on Artie. I wanted him to be the hero, not that sappy 'oh I'm so perfectly brave and amazing' Veronica." His voice took on a posh, exaggerated drawl over those last words.

That cracked me up. Veronica had rather outshone Nancy Drew in the perfection stakes. Stewart laughed with me.

"Artie did cut a dashing figure, didn't he? Even though Veronica treated him like a lapdog most of the time."

Stewart nodded. "At least he got the opportunity once a book to show off his brawn. He wasn't all lapdog. Now tell me, what is Mrs. Cartwright like?"

"In surprisingly good shape for a woman who's about to turn a hundred." I shrugged. "She's pleasant, for the most part, but I suspect she's not terribly easy to live with. She and her daughter bicker a lot, but I suppose that's not unusual." I checked my watch. "Time for me to get going. Diesel, you have to stay home tonight. Sorry, boy, but you can't go with me."

The cat stopped cleaning his paw and meowed loudly. He got up, turned around, and sat again with his back to me. Stewart and I grinned. Diesel knew what the words *you can't go with me* meant.

The Farrington House was a five-minute drive from my house. I quickly found a parking space and entered the hotel. A pleasant young woman at the front desk, in response to my inquiry, directed me to Winston Eagleton's suite on the fifth floor. That seemed an odd place for a dinner party. Had I misunderstood Eagleton's invitation?

My host answered my knock on his door right away, almost as if he had been standing right on the other side, waiting.

"Good evening, sir, please do come in." Eagleton gestured grandly with his left arm, and I stepped into the room.

"Thank you." When I moved farther into the main area of the suite, I could see that, as was often the case, I was evidently the first to arrive. I abhorred being late, and had for as long as I could remember. That meant I often arrived early. Even when I tried not to be on time, I seldom managed to be more than a couple minutes late.

"How are you this evening?" I inquired of my host.

"Absolutely tip-top," Eagleton said. "So kind of you to join me for tonight's little soiree." He indicated one of the sofas. "Please, won't you sit down? Can I offer you something to drink? Wine, scotch, a soft drink perhaps?"

"A glass of red wine would be fine." I chose a spot at the end of the sofa next to a small table and made myself comfortable. "I hope I'm not too early."

"Not at all, my dear chap, not at all." Eagleton nodded briskly as he moved to the bar to pour my wine. "Punctuality seems to be a rare trait these days, but it is one I admire tremendously." He brought me the wine, and I took a cautious sip.

I tried not to make a sour face, because

the wine had a sour taste. I forced myself to smile as I swallowed because my host was watching intently for my reaction. "Nice," I said as I put the wineglass down on the end table. I would have to find somewhere to dump the rest of it, because there was no way I was going to drink any more. I thought of Helen Louise and how appalled she would be. She despised bad wines, and this was one of the worst I'd ever had.

"Lovely." Eagleton beamed as he went back to the bar, where he poured himself a tall glass of scotch — with no soda in sight. He downed about half of it in one long gulp, and he beamed even more widely when he came back to stand near the sofa. "There has been a change of plans, I regret to inform you, for this evening's gathering." Eagleton focused his gaze on a point behind me as he continued. "The confounded hotel mislaid my request — so terribly shoddy of them, don't you think? — and informed me at the last minute that they would be unable to accommodate my dinner party. Thus I am unable to offer you and my other guests the repast that I had planned. I do beg your pardon most humbly." He looked down at me again. "But I did manage to find some comestibles that I trust will be suitably tasty and nourishing."

"I'm sure they'll be fine." I offered a polite smile.

"Do help yourself." Eagleton pointed to the dinner table on the other side of the room. "Ah, another guest at the door. Please excuse me." He walked away.

Taking my wine, I got up and moved over to the table to survey the food on offer — the usual chips, dip, and cheese tray one could find at most supermarkets. There were paper plates, napkins, and plastic utensils. Altogether a sad little array of party food.

There was something distinctly odd about this. Donna Evans, the catering manager at the Farrington House, was one of the most organized and detail-oriented people I had ever met. I didn't buy the story that the hotel had "mislaid" Eagleton's request. I was willing to bet the hotel had checked his credit card limit, found that he was maxed out, and turned him down.

Just how desperate for money was he?

Twenty-Four

Even if Winston Eagleton was in dire financial straits, how did that connect him to the murder of Carrie Taylor? Desperation could drive a person to do things he might not otherwise contemplate, but there had to be a link between the need for money and the act of murder.

I realized that it was likely the one had nothing to do with the other in this case. Eagleton's finances could well be a side issue.

Then again, what motivated the killer in this instance?

I mulled it over while I loaded my plate with potato chips, onion dip, a few grapes, and a dozen cubes of cheddar. I turned to see that Della Duffy was the new arrival. When I shifted position, I bumped my wineglass with my elbow. Red wine spilled all over the tablecloth.

At least my clumsiness saved me from

having to dispose of it elsewhere. I set my plate down and grabbed a couple of napkins to sop up as much of the wine as I could. Once I had disposed of them, I took my plate and moved toward Eagleton and Della Duffy. I was embarrassed by my klutziness but I ought to apologize to the man.

My host and Ms. Duffy were engaged in a low-voiced conversation but they broke off when they realized I was approaching them.

"Evening, Ms. Duffy," I said. "Nice to see you again."

Della Duffy, dressed in a low-necked, black linen cocktail dress with flounces around the sleeves and the hem, examined me warily, I thought. "Did you bring that cat with you?"

I didn't care for her tone. Rudeness on her part was bringing out the worst in me. I tried to keep a straight face as I responded. "No, he stayed home. He doesn't like cocktail parties." I stuffed a cube of cheddar in my mouth and chewed to keep from laughing.

Ms. Duffy's eyes narrowed, as she no doubt realized I was poking fun at her. "Nice to see you again, too." The patent insincerity of her tone was payback for my comment.

"Della my dear, may I offer you a drink?"

Eagleton, seemingly oblivious to the tension between his two guests, patted Ms. Duffy's arm. He leaned closer and for a moment appeared to lose his balance before he managed to steady himself. I noticed his tall glass was empty, and I figured I knew why he was oblivious. He was well on the way to getting totally pickled on scotch.

Perhaps I should have stayed home with Diesel. This little shindig had all the makings of a disaster. I munched a few more cubes of cheese.

Della Duffy shook off her host's arm. "Campari and soda, if you have it."

Eagleton stared at her a moment, and I wondered if he was about to fall flat on his face. "What? Confound it, I knew I forgot something. No Campari, my dear. Afraid the catering didn't run to that. How about scotch and soda instead? Plenty of scotch." He smiled.

"Oh, very well." Ms. Duffy sniffed. "I hope it's not that cheap rotgut stuff you served last time."

"I'm sure I don't know what you mean." Eagleton drew himself up, very much on his dignity. "Only buy fine scotch. Connoisseur, you know." He swayed a couple of times.

"Whatever." Ms. Duffy rolled her eyes at me. "I'll get something to nosh on while you fix my drink. Excuse me." She brushed past me, nearly jostling my plate-holding arm. I muttered, "Excuse me," but she didn't slow down on her way to the food.

I followed Eagleton to the bar, concerned that in his current state he might stumble and hurt himself. He made it fine, though, and while he fumbled with the bottle of scotch, I apologized for my mishap with the wine.

He blinked at me. "My dear chap, these things happen. Not to worry, not to worry." He splashed three fingers of scotch in a glass, squirted soda into it, then toddled off to present the drink to Della Duffy.

Could the evening possibly go uphill from here?

When Eagleton went to the door in response to loud knocking and admitted Gordon Betts, I knew uphill was a far distant prospect.

Betts pushed past our host, evidently having spotted the bar. "I need a drink," I heard him mutter as he breezed past me without bothering to acknowledge my presence.

Eagleton remained by the door, his head stuck out into the hallway. I wondered whether he was about to be sick, but then he stepped back and admitted Teresa Farmer. Finally, someone with some couth that I could talk to.

"So lovely to see you, my dear." Eagleton swayed. "Oh, my, the room does appear to be moving rather quickly, doesn't it?" He stumbled past Teresa and plopped down on the sofa. He pulled a handkerchief from his jacket pocket and mopped at his perspiring face. "Rather warm in here, don't you think?"

He must have had another nip or three of the scotch without my noticing, I reckoned. I set my plate on the coffee table as Teresa hurried over to me. "Is he drunk?" she whispered.

I nodded. I stepped closer to our afflicted host. "Mr. Eagleton, could I get you something? Water, perhaps?"

Blearily the man focused on my face. "That would be extraordinarily kind of you, sir."

Marveling at his ability to enunciate clearly while under the influence, I fetched a bottle of water from the bar and brought it back to him. Teresa stood by, watching Eagleton intently for signs of further distress.

I twisted the cap off. "Sip this." I held the water to Eagleton's lips, and his right hand grasped the bottle. He tilted it up and chugged down two-thirds of the contents.

"Thank you." Eagleton grimaced. "I must apologize for my disgraceful behavior. One does tend to fret over these social occasions, and sometimes one forgets to eat before indulging in a wee dram or two of scotch." He started to rise, but I indicated he should remain where he was.

"Let me fix you a plate," I said. "You'll feel better once you've eaten a bit."

"Of course you will." Teresa sat beside Eagleton and patted his arm. "And if there's anything else you need, let us know."

Leaving our host in Teresa's capable hands, I went over to the table. Betts was still at the bar, I noticed, and the scotch bottle appeared empty now. Della Duffy stood at the window, plate in hand, seemingly unaware of the rest of us. She and Betts probably knew each other, given their devotion to their collections, but I guessed they weren't all that chummy. Frankly, it was hard to imagine Betts having friends of any kind — except, perhaps, imaginary ones.

I took a full plate back to Eagleton, and he tucked into the chips and dip with great enthusiasm. How long had it been since the man had eaten? I wondered. I had seen swine at the trough take longer to chew their food.

I motioned for Teresa to join me, and we

ambled over to the bar. I warned her, sotto voce, to avoid the wine at all costs. Betts was rooting around in the cabinets, no doubt in search of more hard booze. Teresa and I grabbed water bottles.

"Gotcha." Betts faced us triumphantly, a bottle of Laphroaig in hand. "I knew he had to have the good stuff hidden somewhere. Never goes anywhere without it." He opened the whiskey, smiling gleefully. "You want some?" he asked after he filled his own glass, sans soda as befit a true connoisseur.

"No, thank you," Teresa and I responded in unison.

"Suit yourselves." Betts shrugged and sipped his whiskey. "What's up with Winnie? He toasted already?"

Teresa frowned. "I think he was suffering from low blood sugar. He simply needed something to eat." Diplomatic of her, I thought approvingly, but sadly, patently false.

Betts snickered. "Yeah, and Nancy Drew was really Frank Hardy in drag. Tell me another one."

I'd bet even his imaginary friends thought he was a jerk.

Teresa and I turned away and walked back over to Eagleton. He had emptied his plate and finished the rest of the water. He smiled and got to his feet. "Thank you both again for your kind ministrations."

"You're most welcome," Teresa said and patted his arm.

We all turned at a loud knocking on the door, and Eagleton started toward it. "Let me," I said and stepped past him. I wasn't sure he was steady enough yet.

Eagleton didn't protest, and I went to admit Marcella Marter and Mrs. Cartwright, swathed once again in black. Marcella pushed in without a word. "Come on, Mother, or you'll never make it in time."

"Marcella, don't be rude." Mrs. Cartwright tried to pull her arm loose but Marcella clung to it.

"Is something wrong?" I asked, careful to move out of the way.

"Mother needs the restroom." Marcella grimaced. "Right away. Where is it?"

I glanced around. This suite appeared identical to others in the hotel I had visited, and I remembered there was a bathroom in the hall between the living room and the bedroom. I pointed. "That way, I believe."

Marcella Marter didn't bother to thank me, though Mrs. Cartwright smiled. Marcella hurried her mother toward the hall.

I shut the door and rejoined Teresa and Eagleton. "Restroom," I responded to their looks of inquiry, and Eagleton actually blushed.

"When, ahem, the esteemed ladies return, we should perhaps propose a toast to the dear departed Carrie Taylor, don't you think? We must acknowledge the lack of her presence tonight, I am sure." Eagleton nodded. "Yes, certainly. I shall prepare myself for the toast, if you will excuse me for a moment."

"Of course." Teresa and I nodded, and Eagleton moved toward the bar.

Teresa whispered, "This is dreadful. I wish now I'd told Mr. Eagleton I was busy tonight."

"Me, too," I said with a quick laugh. "Too late, but it surely has to get better."

"It could hardly be worse." Teresa grimaced.

The room fell silent. Della Duffy remained in position in front of the window. Betts had propped himself against one end of the bar, Laphroaig in hand. Our host retrieved a fresh bottle of water and stood at the other end of the bar.

After what seemed several agonizing minutes — but was probably only five at the most — Marcella and Mrs. Cartwright returned to the living room. Marcella guided her mother to the sofa and sat her down.

"What would you like to drink, Mother?"

"Whiskey, if there is anything decent on offer." Mrs. Cartwright adjusted the scarf at her neck, then her dark glasses. Marcella scowled but headed for the bar.

"Good evening, Mrs. Cartwright, Mrs. Marter." Teresa moved over to the sofa and sat by the author. "How are you tonight?"

"Thirsty." Mrs. Cartwright laughed. "Otherwise, I'm doing just fine, my dear. And you?"

While Teresa and Mrs. Cartwright chatted, I watched Marcella at the bar. She wrested the Laphroaig away from Betts, who offered no resistance. I figured by now he had downed enough of the whiskey to be in a mellower frame of mind.

"Good evening, my dear." Eagleton beamed at Marcella as she found two glasses and poured drinks for herself and her mother. "So pleased that you and your delightful mother could join us this evening. Spending time with you twice in one day is indeed a rare benison."

"Our pleasure." Marcella spritzed the glasses with soda and turned away. I winced at the sight. Though I was not much of a whiskey drinker, I knew better than to insult Laphroaig that way.

Eagleton followed her to greet Mrs. Cartwright. "Dear lady, you are most welcome indeed. I take it as a great honor that you have appeared at this select gathering tonight."

"My pleasure." Mrs. Cartwright smiled briefly before she accepted her whiskey from Marcella.

"Allow me to propose a toast to one who is not with us this evening." Eagleton glanced around. "Della, my dear, do please join us. You, too, Gordon. Gather near."

He waited until Ms. Duffy and Betts drew closer, then raised his glass.

"Would that we could toast dear Carrie Taylor in her living presence, but alas that is not to be. She was a delightful person, a true devotee of our dear Mrs. Cartwright, and a wonderful champion for Veronica Thane in all things."

"What do you mean, 'she *was* a delightful person'?" Marcella appeared confused. "What happened to her?"

Betts giggled. "Somebody murdered her." He downed his drink in one gulp.

Marcella shrieked, dropped her glass, then fainted.

TWENTY-FIVE

Luckily for Marcella, she was standing in front of the sofa when she fainted. She fell backward onto it, about two inches from where her mother sat. The contents of the glass ended up mostly on her, a little on her mother and the sofa. The aroma of the expensive liquor began to pervade the room.

Mrs. Cartwright jerked as her daughter's body landed beside her, but she managed to hang on to her glass of whiskey and soda without sloshing any out. "Oh, goodness, Marcella, whatever is the matter with you?" She glanced around, obviously searching. "Where is my purse? I need my smelling salts."

"Here it is." Teresa grabbed the large bag, almost a briefcase in size, from the floor beside the sofa. She handed it to the author, who quickly rummaged inside and brought out a small bottle. She twisted off the cap, then stuck the salts under her daughter's nose.

Marcella's body flinched as she inhaled. Her eyelids fluttered. After a moment she sat up, shaking her head as if to clear it. "What happened?" she asked in a weak voice. She glanced around, blinking rapidly.

"You fainted." Her mother's tone was crisp. "When you heard the news that Carrie Taylor is dead, you passed right out." Mrs. Cartwright belted back the rest of her whiskey and soda.

"Oh, my." Marcella's right hand went to her cheek. She stared at her mother. "How awful. Who on earth would do such a thing?" She accepted the towel Teresa had fetched and began the attempt to dry herself.

"That's something we'd all like to know." Della Duffy stuffed cheese in her mouth as she stared down at Marcella and Mrs. Cartwright.

Marcella frowned. "You don't think I know anything about it, surely." She dropped the towel on the floor.

"Did I say that?" Della sounded bored. "I was talking to Winnie."

"Dear ladies, I am certain that none of us knows anything about such an unfortunate occurrence." Winston Eagleton cleared his

233

throat as he glared at Della Duffy. "It must have been some local ruffian who did this terrible thing. Why, none of us really knew poor Carrie all that well."

Betts giggled. "Come on, Winnie, you know better than that. I saw you at the con in Boston, cozying up to her, kissing her hand, whispering sweet nothings in her ear. You were sweet on her."

Eagleton's face burned bright red, and for once he appeared to be at a loss for words.

"That's right," Della said. "I saw you, too. Probably trying to get her to invest in your press after Gordon pulled his money out. But I'll bet she didn't fall for it, either."

"Either?" Mrs. Cartwright laughed. "I suppose that means he tried it on you first, eh?"

Della snorted. "He did try it on me, but I ain't buying. Probably tried it on Gordon, too, to get him to reinvest. When it comes to money, dear old Winnie is totally bisexual."

Betts simply giggled again. I think he was too far gone to care what Della Duffy said.

Despite the painful embarrassment I felt at having to witness such a nasty little scene, I took careful note of Della Duffy's indiscreet remarks. I would share the information with Kanesha later, in case it had any bearing on the murder.

Eagleton found his voice. "I am not bi-sexual. The very notion is the height of absurdity." He paused for a steadying breath. "I admit I did pay court to Carrie Taylor. She was a kind, attractive woman of an age suitable to be a companion to a man such as myself." He glared at Della. "I didn't try anything on you. I merely approached you with a business proposition."

Della shrugged. "If you say so." She turned away and wandered over to the food table.

Teresa and I had been standing by, observing the whole distasteful scene. I had no doubt she was every bit as uncomfortable as I was, having to watch such goings-on. I was about to make my excuses and leave, taking Teresa along, but Marcella forestalled me.

She rose from the sofa and extended a hand to her mother. "Come along now, Mother. I want to go home and get out of this dress. It reeks of whiskey."

"Well, if you must." Eagleton's protest sounded pretty weak to me.

"Evidently we must." Mrs. Cartwright let her daughter pull her to a standing position. "Don't forget my bag, Marcella."

"Of course not, Mother." Marcella

grabbed the purse from the sofa and stuck the strap over her arm.

"Let me show you out." Eagleton preceded the women to the door. "Perhaps you will allow me to visit you again tomorrow and continue our discussions from earlier today?"

"I'll call you," Marcella said, her tone not in the least bit friendly. "Do you think you can find your way again?"

"Most assuredly." Eagleton opened the door. "I do hope your agent will be able to join us."

Mrs. Cartwright paused to turn and look back at the man. "If she ever turns up. I'm beginning to think I need to change agents if the girl can't even find my house with clear directions."

Eagleton frowned. "That is most unfortunate. I wonder where she might be."

"She'll show up," Marcella said, clearly impatient. "She's probably at the house with Eugene right now. Come on, Mother, I want to go home. I can't stand being in this smelly dress any longer than I have to."

"Very well, my dear. Good night, everyone." Mrs. Cartwright went along with Marcella, and Eagleton closed the door after them.

Teresa and I approached, ready to say our

own good-byes.

"Might I have a word with you, old chap?" Eagleton smiled at Teresa. "Would you excuse us just a tick, my dear? Shan't be long."

What could he want? I wondered. I was more than ready to get out of this room and on the way home.

"Sure," Teresa said. She moved a few feet away and stared at a picture on the wall.

Eagleton stepped closer to me and spoke in a low tone. "I wondered if you might do me a favor." His eyes flicked away for a moment across the room. I followed his gaze to where Gordon Betts leaned against the bar, his head down on his arms. "Do you think you could possibly see Gordon to his room? I'm afraid I can't manage it myself. Bad back and all that, you know."

I suppressed a sigh of irritation. Why didn't he simply pour water over Betts's head and send him on his way? That's what I was tempted to do. Innate good manners kicked in, unfortunately, and I found myself agreeing to help.

Eagleton beamed with gratitude. "Thanks ever so, old chap. You are truly most kind."

"Think nothing of it." My wry tone seemed to escape him as he bustled away, headed for Della Duffy still grazing at the dinner table. The woman certainly was putting the food away.

Teresa joined me. "Need any assistance? I couldn't help overhearing."

"No, I think I can manage," I said. "Why don't you go on? I'm sure you're as ready to get away from here as I am."

"Definitely." Teresa grinned. "This evening was like something out of a really bad play." She paused. "If you're sure you don't need me?"

"I'm sure. Go on." I patted her arm before she headed quickly for the door and let herself out.

I turned toward the bar and stared at Betts for a moment. He didn't appear to have moved.

I frowned. Was he still breathing? I couldn't detect any signs of life, and suddenly my heart started pounding. Surely he hadn't died? I started toward him.

A loud snore reassured me. When I reached him and put a hand on his shoulder to shake him awake, he stood and blinked at me. Then he frowned. "What happened?"

"You passed out," I told him curtly. "Why don't you let me help you to your room. The party's over."

He shook his head. "Don't need help." He took a couple of steps, almost tripped over his own feet, but managed to steady himself. "Maybe you'd better," he said with a weak grin.

I took hold of his left arm and steadied him. "What room are you in?"

He stared at me. "Room?" He paused. "Oh, right, hotel. Room. Um, seven-oh-three?" He nodded after a moment. "Yeah, seven-oh-three, that's it."

"Do you have the key?"

He thrust his right hand into his pants pocket and pulled out a card. I took it from him.

"Okay, then, let's go." I started leading him to the door. When I paused to open it, I glanced over to Eagleton and Della Duffy, both steadily clearing the table by eating every scrap of food.

I got Betts out the door and down the hall without much trouble. In the elevator I propped him in the corner before I pressed the button for the seventh floor. He had closed his eyes and appeared to fall asleep again. I roused him after the brief ride up two floors and tugged him out and toward room 703. He stumbled alongside me.

I had to lean him against the wall while I inserted the key card in the lock. He managed to lurch in on his own, and I followed him to make sure he didn't fall and bang his head against something, such as the sharp corner of a desk.

His suite was more lavish than Eagleton's, I thought, but I didn't have much time to examine the furnishings. Betts tripped near the sofa and fell headlong onto it. I rushed forward to catch him, but he hit the cushions before I could reach him.

His face, fortunately for him, hit one of the cushions, but his arm flopped over the end table and knocked the lamp to the floor with a muffled thud. The luxurious carpet softened the blow, and the lamp remained intact.

"What was that?" Betts raised his head for a moment, then it dropped back down before I could answer.

I couldn't leave him prone on the sofa. He might suffocate like that. I managed to turn his body so that he was on his back, head on a cushion, and legs stretched out. He started snoring, and I figured the best thing now was to let him sleep it off.

I restored the lamp to the end table and was about to leave when I noticed how cold it was in the room. I had better find a blanket for Betts; otherwise he might take a chill if he didn't wake up soon to find one for himself. I found the bedroom and rummaged in the closet. As I expected, there was a spare blanket on the shelf.

Back in the living room, I unfolded the blanket and covered Betts with it. I turned, ready to go, when I spotted the dining table on the other side of the room.

There were seven or eight stacks of books atop the table, and I simply couldn't resist going over to see what they were. Typical of bibliophiles like me, even though Betts might consider it snooping. He owed me this much, I figured.

The piles consisted of Veronica Thane books, as I'd expected. Beautiful copies, too. Pristine-looking jackets protected by Mylar covers. I bent to read the spines of the first stack.

Several of the titles were in languages other than English. I recognized French and German. Was that one Swedish? I wondered.

I moved on to the next stack, turning it sideways so I could again read the spines. Midway down I spotted a copy of *The Mystery at Spellwood Mansion.*

I walked back over to the sofa, and a quick glance assured me that Betts was still asleep. I went back to the table and carefully pulled the copy of *Spellwood Mansion* from the stack.

My hands trembled slightly as I opened it from the back and found the page where

241

the identifying error would be.

There it was. *Clarevoyant's Clew.* A true, rare first printing of the book.

Was this really his copy? Or was it Carrie Taylor's?

TWENTY-SIX

I examined the book more carefully. There were no labels, no marks of any kind that I found. The book looked like it had seldom been opened, the binding tight, the colors of the jacket fresh and unfaded. A rare copy indeed, to have survived eighty years in this condition.

Nothing to answer my question about its provenance, of course. Betts could have possessed this copy for years. Or he could have stolen it from Carrie Taylor after he killed her.

Then I realized how stupid I had been to pick up the book in the first place. Fingerprints. I had added mine to whatever prints the Mylar cover might hold. I might even have smudged those of another person. Hastily I put the book down on top of the pile from which I had pulled it.

I dreaded the inevitable glare of irritation and disapproval I'd get when I told Kanesha about this. But I had to tell her, in case this copy of the book had anything to do with the murder.

I turned to go, but a question popped into my head. Did Betts have another copy of *The Mystery at Spellwood Mansion*?

Without touching any of the books on the table, I examined the piles, looking for a second copy of the first Veronica Thane book.

I didn't find one. What did that tell me?

I really wasn't certain. Betts had boasted that he had over five hundred Veronica Thane books in various formats, and there couldn't be more than sixty or seventy books on the table. The others were probably somewhere in the suite, but I didn't think it would be a good idea for me to try to find them and go through them all.

I decided I had better get going and not yield to temptation to see what else he had. I glanced at the sleeping man on my way to the door, and he seemed fine.

Before I could open the door, however, I heard a groan emanating from the area of the sofa. I hesitated, but the groaning continued, then intensified. I turned back to see what was wrong. Betts was struggling to get the blanket off and rise from the sofa.

"Going to be sick." He managed to get

the words out before his body convulsed.

I spotted a small, decorative garbage can at the end of sofa and scooped it up. Barely in time, I managed to stick it in front of him, and he vomited into it. He clutched at the can and pulled it to his chest, letting his head hang over it.

He threw up again. I watched, alert for any sign that he was about to drop the can or to collapse. He seemed steady enough. I waited, and though he made a few retching sounds, nothing else issued forth. His grasp on the can loosened, and I took it from him and set it aside, trying not to look at or smell the contents.

Betts stared up at me, bleary-eyed. "Sorry," he mumbled. "Could you get me a wet towel?"

"Sure. Be right back." I hadn't expected to play nursemaid to a drunken man tonight, but I couldn't in all good conscience abandon him at this point, no matter how tempted I was to walk right out.

I found a washcloth, luxuriously thick, in the bathroom and soaked it in cold water. After I'd wrung out most of the water, I carried it back to the ailing Betts.

He mumbled his thanks and wiped his face several times, then folded the cloth and pressed it to his forehead.

Figuring he would be okay on his own now for a few minutes, I took the garbage can, thankfully metal, and carried it into the bathroom. I dumped the contents into the toilet and flushed them, then I stuck the can under the faucet in the bathtub and ran water into it. I sloshed that around a bit, then dumped it again in the toilet.

I did that a couple more times before I was satisfied that the garbage can was as clean as I was going to get it. Back in the living room, I set the can on the floor near Betts, just in case. He raised his head and focused on me as I was about to sit down. "Sorry to trouble you," he said, sounding actually humble, "but would you mind getting me some soda from the bar fridge? And some crackers if you can find some? I think that would help settle my stomach a bit."

"Sure." I found a can of soda along with some peanut butter crackers and brought them back to him. He fumbled with the tab on the aluminum can, so I opened it for him. Then I opened the crackers, too. Once again he thanked me.

He sipped at the cola and ate a couple of crackers, avoiding my gaze for the moment. His color appeared normal again, and his eyes seemed clearer when he did at last look directly at me. He drained the can and set it aside.

"Feeling better?" I asked.

"Much," he said with a faint smile. "Look, I really owe you one for helping me like this. Didn't realize how lit I was getting. I don't often drink like that."

"It can hit you pretty quickly if you're not used to it." I kept my tone mild, though I was pretty irritated with him. Still, I reckoned, he had suffered from his overindulgence, and he was acting much nicer than I had seen him do so far in our brief acquaintance.

"I'm not used to it, despite what you probably think of me." Betts managed a wry grin. "I know I come on way too strong sometimes."

"Yes, you most certainly do." I softened my words with a brief smile.

He leaned back against the sofa and closed his eyes. "I really feel wonky, but the soda and the crackers helped."

"Best thing you can do now is go to bed and sleep." I stood. "Would you like some help? I should probably be going now."

"No, I'll be okay, I think." Betts pushed himself up from the sofa. He didn't wobble on his feet, and I took that as a positive sign. "Thank you again."

"You're welcome," I said. I decided to ask him something before I left, though, and take advantage of his pliant, repentant mood. "Did you get Mrs. Cartwright to sign your books yet?"

Betts shook his head. "No, not yet. I still have to work out the arrangements with her daughter." He paused. "To be honest, the daughter is insisting on one thing that I'm not happy about."

"Really? What is that?"

"She wants me to bring all of the books to their house and leave them there for as long as it takes Mrs. Cartwright to sign them all. I know she's an old lady, but Mrs. Marter said it could take her three or four weeks. I'm not sure I want to leave my books with them that long. They could get damaged, and there wouldn't be much I could do about it."

"That is rather odd," I said, though I could understand that Mrs. Cartwright might not be up to signing several hundred books in a couple of days' time. "But what if that's the only way you can get them all signed?"

Betts shrugged. "I don't have much choice, do I? I gave them the money before Mrs. Marter informed me of that particular condition."

"It sounds like you have a truly impressive collection." I hoped he might volunteer to show me at least part of it.

"Yeah, I do." Betts yawned. "Look, I need to get to bed. You can show yourself out, right?" He glanced pointedly toward the door.

"Sure. I hope you feel better after a good night's sleep." I headed for the door, wondering why he suddenly seemed so ready to get me out of his suite. Was it because he didn't want me to look through his books?

I pondered the question on the drive home. Betts had more facets to his personality than I'd anticipated, given his rude behavior at our first meeting. I had no doubt he could be ruthless when it came to getting what he wanted, but would he go as far as murder?

Diesel greeted me in the kitchen with a chorus of plaintive meows, I supposed to let me know how lonely he had been without me. Naturally I had to take a couple of minutes to reassure him how wonderful he was and that I was abjectly sorry for abandoning him, although I knew Stewart had given him every attention while I was out.

With the cat pacified — for a few minutes, at least — I decided it was my stomach's turn for attention. Winston Eagleton's offerings hadn't lasted long. I made myself a couple of ham sandwiches and sat at the table to eat. Diesel, from his vantage point right beside my chair, took great interest in my food. Before the impersonation of cat-starving-to-death got under way, I offered him several small bites of ham.

After I polished off the sandwiches, I decided I should let Kanesha know about the copy of *Spellwood Mansion* I'd found in Gordon Betts's suite. A brief text message asking her to call me ought to suffice. I didn't feel like getting out the laptop to do e-mail, nor did I want to attempt it via the phone. I hated typing longer messages on those tiny letters. My fingers were big enough to hit two or three at a time.

The house was quiet as Diesel and I climbed the stairs to my bedroom. I wondered idly whether Stewart had allowed Dante out of his crate yet and whether Laura and Frank had ever come to baby-sit Diesel. With Stewart available, they probably decided they weren't needed.

I changed into pajamas, despite the fact that it wasn't quite nine. I felt tired after the events of the evening, but I didn't want to go to sleep just yet in case Kanesha called me back.

Diesel stretched out on his side of the bed

and warbled to let me know he needed more attention. After rubbing his head and along his spine for a bit, I made myself comfortable and picked up *Spellwood Mansion.* I was in the mood to read more Veronica Thane, and it would pass the time while I waited for a response from Kanesha.

Veronica was being ministered to by her best friend Lucy, I recalled, when I last put the book aside. I found my place once again.

"What happened, Lucy?" Veronica reclined against the pillows. "What time is it?"

"It will soon be eleven. You've been asleep all day." Lucy patted Veronica's hand. "We don't really know what happened. When you didn't return home last night, your guardian became worried. She asked Artie and me if we had heard from you, and when we told her we had not, she became even more agitated."

"Dear Aunt Araminta," Veronica murmured. "I regret so deeply that she was worried about me. And dear Artie, too."

Arthur Marsh, known to his intimates as "Artie," was a classmate of Veronica Thane and Lucy Carlton. Tall, handsome, and athletic, he was the son of Mrs. Buff-Orpington's lawyer and chief advisor, Horatio Marsh. He was devoted to Veronica and often escorted her to dances and social affairs. His best friend, Anthony Rutherford, was Lucy Carlton's frequent escort.

"She knew you would not do such a thing on purpose," Lucy assured her. "She suspected that you might be in the midst of another adventure, and she asked Artie if he would search for you."

"I was on my way home from visiting our old chum Mary Ferris in Trentville," Veronica said slowly. "There was a frightful storm."

"Yes, it was certainly fierce," Lucy agreed. "Artie suspected you might have had an accident, driving in such conditions, but he said nothing of that to your guardian."

"Where did Artie find me? And my car? Is my car damaged?" Veronica had great affection for her trusty red roadster, for it had served her well.

"Your car is fine," Lucy assured her with a smile, well aware of Veronica's attachment to the vehicle. "Artie found you, sound asleep in it, just a couple of miles outside of town along the river road. He was unable to rouse you, you were so deeply asleep." Her troubled expression revealed her affectionate concern for her best chum.

"How very strange," Veronica murmured. She did not remember feeling tired driving home from Trentville. But the storm — something about the storm. The memory teased her with its elusiveness. She expressed her frustration to Lucy.

"Dearest, you must not force your poor head to remember. It will all come back to you in time." Lucy again patted Veronica's hand, then offered her more water to drink, which she accepted gratefully. Her throat still felt quite parched.

"What happened after Artie found me in my car?" Veronica asked, still anxious about her roadster.

"He brought you home immediately, of course," Lucy said. "As soon as you were safely in your bed and the doctor called to attend you, he went back with one of his chums to retrieve your roadster. It is in its accustomed place in the garage, never fear."

"Dear Artie," Veronica said, her eyes gleaming with the faint sheen of tears. Really, she did have the most devoted and worthy friends.

"Artie was desperately worried about you," Lucy said. "As indeed we all were, for we could not wake you. Dr. Rhodes tried several remedies, but you remained asleep." She paused, her expression pensive.

"How very peculiar," Veronica said. "In general I do sleep rather soundly, but I am not hard to awaken."

"It was very strange," Lucy agreed. She hesitated before she continued, "Dr. Rhodes concluded that somehow you must have been drugged."

TWENTY-SEVEN

I was about to turn the page to the next chapter — and find out Veronica's reaction to the news that she had been drugged — when my cell phone rang.

To my surprise, the caller wasn't Kanesha Berry. Instead the call was coming from the Farrington House.

The moment I said "Hello," Winston Eagleton launched into speech. He sounded distraught.

"I do beg your pardon for calling you on such a matter, Mr. Harris, particularly after the events of this evening when I am sure you must be rather tired and wanting to rest." He paused for a breath but continued his rapid speech before I could interject a word. "However, I find myself in a most difficult situation, and while one hesitates to presume on the kindness of someone who is nearly a stranger, yet one sometimes has to do these things."

"Do what things?" I felt slightly dazed. I was struggling to hone in on whatever point he was dancing around. His obvious distress apparently only increased his volubility.

"In the situation in which I currently find myself, I desperately need the services of a competent lawyer. I was told by a most reliable source that your son is a lawyer, and while I realize it is the height of presumption on my part, I wondered whether you would ask him to represent me."

"Yes, my son, Sean, is a lawyer, and a very good one," I said. "I am sure he would be happy to help you, but exactly what situation are you in?"

"Oh, dear, I am not explaining things at all well, am I?" Eagleton sighed into the phone. "This is the inevitable result when I am overset by events. The situation is this. The police, in the form of a Kanesha Berry, who I gather is with your sheriff's department, rather than the police department, intends to take me in for questioning. I am hesitant to go with her without the knowledge that I will have adequate legal representation" — and his voice dropped to a whisper — "because one has certainly heard that terrible things can happen to one if one is incarcerated, even briefly."

Good grief, I thought, what on earth had

256

happened now? Was Kanesha going to arrest Eagleton for the murder of Carrie Taylor?

"I will get in touch with my son and have him meet you at the sheriff's office. In the meantime, I know he would caution you not to answer any questions until he has had a chance to talk to you and find out exactly what is going on." I was burning with curiosity to know exactly what was going on myself but I didn't feel like I should ask. Better to talk to Sean and let him sort things out. Kanesha's patience was probably worn out by now. I could imagine the effect that Eagleton would have on her.

"Thank you, Mr. Harris. I shall not forget your kindness in my hour of need, I can assure you. Oh, dear, the policewoman is looking at me rather fiercely now, so I suppose I must end this call and wait for my legal representation to sort this out. But pray do not believe what you will hear, for I am not a thief." The phone clicked in my ear.

Thief? What had Eagleton allegedly stolen? Carrie Taylor's copy of *Spellwood Mansion?* That was the only thing I could come up with that was pertinent to the case.

Diesel nudged my hand, his signal that more attention should be paid, and I rubbed his head with that hand while I speed-dialed Sean with the other.

"Hey, Dad," he said when he answered. "What's up? Everything okay?"

I assured him I was fine before I told him that he had a new client. I explained who Winston Eagleton was and related what I knew of the circumstances — precious little, actually. "It must have something to do with Carrie Taylor's murder, though," I concluded.

"I'll get down there right away," Sean said. "Alex and I were watching a movie, but it can wait. I'll see what I can do for the man."

"Thanks, Son," I said. "I'll just warn you that he tends to use seven words when one will do, particularly when he's excited. So be prepared."

Sean chuckled. "Got you. Talk to you later."

I put the phone down, confident that Sean would advise Eagleton well. If only I could go with Sean, I thought. I burned with curiosity over what happened. Who accused Eagleton of theft? If I knew that, I might have some idea of what it was he was supposed to have stolen.

If he was indeed in financial straits, as I suspected, he might well have stolen a valuable item in hopes of selling or pawning it.

Or maybe he couldn't pay his hotel bill, and the Farrington House management sent for the police.

Would they really do that, though? I wondered.

I was giving myself a headache from the fruitless speculation. I went into the bathroom, found the aspirin in the medicine cabinet, and downed a couple with water.

Too restless to read, I put my book away. Perhaps I should try to relax and get some sleep. I doubted Kanesha would call me tonight when she was busy dealing with Winston Eagleton. Diesel had dozed off again, and I stretched out beside him and switched off the light.

Though my mind buzzed for a while over the happenings of the past couple of days, I eventually relaxed and felt myself slipping into sleep.

When I awoke later, I thought at first morning had come, but the bedside clock informed me it was a few minutes shy of midnight. I turned the light on and sat up. Diesel was gone, and I felt suddenly alert. And hungry.

Time for a midnight snack, I decided. I slipped on my house shoes and headed downstairs in search of nibbles. I could see from the stairs that the light was on in the kitchen, and as I came closer, I heard my children's voices in conversation.

Laura broke off talking when she spotted me. "Hi, Dad. What are you doing up this late?" Diesel lay on the floor beside her chair. He raised his head briefly to acknowledge my presence but didn't vocalize.

Sean turned to greet me. "We didn't wake you up, did we? I didn't think we were that loud."

I laughed. "No, you didn't wake me." I padded over to the fridge. "I guess my stomach did. I feel like a snack. Maybe another ham sandwich."

Sean shook his head at me. "Sorry, Dad, but we polished off the ham about ten minutes ago."

"I think there's still some of the pimento cheese, though," Laura said. She knew how fond I was of it, particularly Azalea's home-made variety.

"That will do." I found the plastic container, retrieved a knife and crackers, and joined my children at the table. Diesel abandoned Laura and came to sit hopefully by my chair. He was destined to be disappointed, though, because cats shouldn't have cheese.

Sean raised his mug. "We made decaf if you want some of that."

"In a minute maybe," I said as I spread pimento cheese on a cracker. "What were you two plotting when I came in?" Diesel batted at my arm with one of his large paws, and I frowned at him and shook my head. He knew what that meant.

Laura grinned. "No plotting, I swear. Sean was telling me about his new client. He sounds like a real trip."

"Were you discussing Eagleton's case with her?" I frowned at Sean.

"Don't worry." Sean gave me one of his surely-you-know-better looks. "I haven't violated the attorney-client privilege."

"He was only telling me about Mr. Eagleton and how eccentric he is." Laura stood and carried her mug to the dishwasher. "Nothing inappropriate."

"Sorry," I said. "Guess I was too hungry to think before I spoke."

Sean grinned. "No offense taken, Dad. I do have Eagleton's permission to talk to you about it, though."

I paused, about to stick another cheese-laden cracker in my mouth. "Really? Why?"

My children exchanged a look, one that I interpreted easily, having seen it countless times, particularly in their teenage years. It meant, *How's Dad going to take this?*

Sean kept a straight face as he answered

me, though I knew it was an effort. "Mr. Eagleton somehow heard about your previous experiences in sleuthing, and he wants you to help me clear his name. He's convinced you're Sherlock Holmes and Hercule Poirot rolled into one." He held up his hands in mock surrender. "And before you say anything, he didn't hear it from me."

"Or me," Laura said with a broad smile. "Especially as I haven't met the man. I'm off to bed, and I'll leave Holmes and Watson to it." She dropped a kiss on my cheek and walked out of the kitchen. Diesel, apparently having decided that no treat was forthcoming, scampered after her.

I finished my cracker before I spoke. "I suppose I shouldn't be surprised. It was bound to happen sooner or later, considering the situations I've been involved with." I grimaced. "I hope no one ever says anything like that in front of Kanesha, or I'm liable to get my head lopped off."

"We certainly wouldn't want that to happen." Sean kept his expression solemn. "At least until you've made out your will."

"Very funny." I got up to fix myself a cup of decaf. "I've already made out my will, and I've left everything to Diesel, just so you know." I smiled sweetly as I sat down again.

Sean rolled his eyes at me. "Back to Mr. Eagleton. He really does want your help. He told me you had already been of considerable assistance to him in a matter of some delicacy."

I knew he was quoting the man. "Yes, I suppose I had been." I told Sean about taking care of a drunken Gordon Betts.

"Too bad you got stuck with that," Sean said. "Now, about my client. He's being held in the county jail."

"On what charge?" I sipped my coffee. "Surely not for murder, or you wouldn't be so casual about this."

"No, not murder. There's no evidence of that." Sean leaned back in his chair and rubbed a hand across his face. Now that I took a good look, I could see how tired he was. "The charge is theft."

When Sean paused and didn't continue right away, I tried to keep my impatience out of my voice. "What on earth did he allegedly steal?"

"Five unpublished manuscripts belonging to Electra Barnes Cartwright."

TWENTY-EIGHT

"The Veronica Thane manuscripts?" I hadn't even considered them. So much had happened since I first heard about them that I had nearly forgotten they existed.

"Yeah, and Eagleton swears he didn't take them." Sean shrugged. "But they were found in his suite at the Farrington House."

I wondered who had found them, but I had another question I wanted answered first. "Who reported them missing?" I decided I'd had enough pimento cheese and got up to put the food away.

"Eugene Marter, the grandson, called the sheriff's department to report the theft."

I had put my odd encounter with Eugene out of my mind, along with the manuscripts. Now, I realized, I needed to tell Sean what Eugene had told me. "I have more questions about the theft, but first there's something you should know." I gave Sean a summary of the meeting when I resumed my seat at the table. My son's eyes narrowed when I related the alleged threat Eagleton had made against Mrs. Cartwright.

"Did you believe Marter?" Sean asked.

"Hard to say. Carrie Taylor told me he was shiftless, couldn't keep a job, but of course I have no idea if that's true." I thought back to the encounter, replayed a bit of it in my head. "He was rather odd. Talked like Hollywood's idea of a Mississippi redneck, when both his mother and his grandmother speak like educated women. He told me he'd had run-ins with the police."

"Maybe not a completely trustworthy character then." Sean looked thoughtful. "I'll have to discuss this with my client. Kanesha didn't mention any threats when she questioned him, so I presume that Marter never talked to anyone else about it."

"Frankly I thought he probably wouldn't," I said. "He didn't seem that eager to have contact with the authorities."

"Other than calling them to report a theft."

"That reminds me of one of the questions I wanted to ask. Who found the manuscripts in Eagleton's suite?"

"Kanesha." Sean leaned back in his chair. "Evidently Marter wouldn't talk to anyone

265

else when he called in to report the theft. He said Eagleton must have taken the manuscripts during a visit to Mrs. Cartwright earlier in the day."

I nodded. I remembered that Eagleton had referred to a visit tonight.

Sean continued, "They weren't able to settle on terms because, according to my client, Mrs. Cartwright and Mrs. Marter were asking for much too large an advance."

Given what I suspected about the man's financial situation, I figured *much too large* might be a relatively modest sum — although they did seem really greedy. I told Sean my suspicions. "You might well be whistling in the wind for your fee if I'm right."

Sean sighed. "My first *pro bono* case then. That's another topic I'll have to discuss with Mr. Eagleton. If he really is desperate for money, that could have spurred him to steal the manuscripts."

"Did Eagleton tell you how much they wanted?"

"Fifteen thousand per manuscript. I don't know enough about publishing to decide whether that's an unrealistic figure or under market value. What do you think?"

I considered it for a moment, but I had to confess to Sean I wasn't sure, either. "The

Veronica Thane books have been out of print for thirty years, and Eagleton has been the only one that I know of to show any interest in reprinting them. I don't know that any big publishing houses would pay that much. I suspect they wouldn't."

"Sounds reasonable to me," Sean said. "I almost forgot. Eagleton mentioned that he expected to be negotiating with Mrs. Cartwright's agent. She was supposed to be there but she never showed up."

"Mrs. Cartwright mentioned that tonight at the hotel." I frowned. "That's really odd. Teresa talked to someone in Ms. Thigpen's office the other day and was informed that she was already en route to Athena. She was flying into Memphis and would pick up a rental car to drive down. I wonder what happened to her."

Sean's expression turned grim. "I don't like the sound of that." He pulled out his cell phone. "Let's call Kanesha and report this. The agent may have gotten lost trying to find the Marters' house or decided to do a little sight-seeing, but if she didn't . . ."

He punched in a number. "Voice mail." He waited a moment, then left the deputy a message with a brief summary of the potential issue.

He set the phone on the table when he'd

finished. "I have to say, Dad, with all that you've told me, I have a feeling there's something hinky going on here. The missing agent could be connected, too. How, I don't know."

"It's all strange." I thought for a moment. "You said earlier that Kanesha found the manuscripts. Did she have a search warrant?"

"She did, but I doubt she would have needed one. Eagleton told me he was convinced the whole thing was a practical joke on Eugene Marter's part. He thought Marter was simply jerking the sheriff's department around and was happy to cooperate."

"But Marter wasn't, as it turned out," I said. "Do you know where exactly Kanesha found the manuscripts?"

"In between Eagleton's mattress and box spring. Not an imaginative hiding place."

I agreed. "What do you think? Did he take them?"

"He's hard to read." Sean gave a short laugh. "He was really wound up. You weren't kidding about the seven words when one would do, except I'd say it was more like seven*teen*. He was highly indignant that such aspersions had been cast upon his character." Sean grimaced. "Now I'm starting to sound like him."

"That last bit did have the ring of a direct quotation." I smiled. "He is loquacious, almost beyond endurance, but is he a thief? And a murderer?"

Sean's eyes narrowed. "You think this is connected to the murder?"

"I don't know." I shrugged. "None of this would have happened if we hadn't decided to do this exhibit and then asked Mrs. Cartwright to appear at the library. Eagleton and the others might never have come to Athena."

"You had no way of knowing a woman would be killed." Sean gazed sternly at me. I knew it bothered him when I went into hair-shirt mode.

"I know, but I can't help a feeling of responsibility." Sean started to speak but I held up a hand. "Let's just leave it at that, okay?"

His expression told me he didn't like it, but he didn't press the point.

"Tell me, did Eagleton venture any theories as to how the manuscripts got in his suite and under his mattress?"

"He kept insisting that Eugene Marter had to be behind it." Sean shook his head. "Though he couldn't explain exactly why Marter would do it. Or when and how Marter got access to his hotel room."

I considered that for a moment. "What if someone is trying to get him out of the way?"

"Out of the way of what?" Sean got up to pour himself more coffee.

"Good question. Perhaps somebody is working for another publisher." I mulled that over for a moment. "No, that seems far-fetched."

"Maybe." Sean sipped his coffee. "It seems even more far-fetched as an attempt to link Eagleton to the murder."

"It doesn't make much sense. Let's look at it from another angle. What if Eagleton really did steal the manuscripts? How could he possibly have hoped to get away with it? If he published them, he'd be putting the evidence right out there."

"He didn't strike me as a stupid man, although he might be desperate for money," Sean said. "He had to know — if he did take them — that he was bound to be found out." He shook his head. "No, it won't wash. Frankly, that's why I'm inclined to believe he didn't steal them. It would be a completely asinine thing to do."

"Could it be what Eagleton claimed then? Eugene Marter playing a practical joke?" I frowned. "But if Marter is truly leery of tangling with the law, he'd know Kanesha would take a dim view of such an idiotic stunt."

"Who else had access to the manuscripts?" Sean asked. He continued before I could respond. "Obviously Mrs. Cartwright and Mrs. Marter did. Anyone else?"

"The agent might have," I said. "She's unaccounted for, but why would a reputable agent do something like that? It doesn't make any sense."

"Unless the person who did it wasn't bright enough to consider all the angles." Sean laughed. "That's why a lot of criminals get caught. They're not all that smart to begin with, and they do dumb things all the time."

"The whole thing looks pretty silly to me."

Sean's cell phone buzzed. He glanced at the screen. "Kanesha. I'll put it on speaker." He punched a button.

Kanesha didn't wait for the customary greeting. "So what's this about a missing agent?"

"My father is with me," Sean said. "I'm going to let him tell you what he knows." He pushed the phone to the middle of the table between us.

I gave the deputy a rundown of the few facts that I knew.

"What is her name again?" Kanesha asked.

"Yancy Thigpen," I said. "She works in New York City."

"My client said he expected Ms. Thigpen to be present at the meeting he had with Mrs. Cartwright and Mrs. Marter earlier today. He was puzzled by her absence, and after talking with my father, I have to agree. It is odd that she wasn't there."

"She might be stuck out on a country road somewhere, lost and out of gas." Kanesha sounded weary. "Cell phone reception isn't always that good in those areas either." She paused. "Or she could be in a hotel room in Memphis. I'll put out the word to be on the lookout for her. I'm sure she'll turn up before long."

"I sincerely hope so." Maybe my imagination was going into overdrive, but I felt uneasy about this situation. I couldn't help thinking there was a sinister aspect to the young woman's nonappearance.

"In the meantime, if you hear anything further, let me know." Kanesha ended the call.

"Nothing more we can do at the moment." Sean yawned and stuck his cell phone in his pocket. "I don't know about you, Dad, but I'm ready for bed. I've got a long day ahead of me tomorrow, thanks to my new client." He pushed back his chair and stood.

"You go on up," I said. "I'm going back to bed as soon as I double-check that the doors are locked."

The back door in the kitchen was secure, as was the front door. I headed down the hall to the back porch door. On impulse I went out on to the porch and looked out at the backyard. The illumination from the streetlights penetrated only dimly here, and clouds obscured the stars. I stood for a few minutes, listening to the quiet of the neighborhood around me.

I sent up a brief but fervent prayer on behalf of Yancy Thigpen, hoping that she would soon be found, safe and unharmed.

My mood somber, I locked the porch door and walked slowly up to my bed.

Twenty-Nine

I had a distinct sense of déjà vu the next morning when the phone rang a few minutes after seven and Kanesha was on the other end.

"Good morning, Deputy. What can I do for you?"

Kanesha sounded tired when she answered. "Sorry to bother you again so early, but I need to talk to you. All right if I drop by?"

"I'm up and dressed, so come on by as soon as you like." I still had a nearly full pot of coffee, too, and I figured she could use some.

"Be there in less than ten." She ended the call.

"We've got company coming." I looked down at Diesel. The cat chirped at me and then went back to washing his left front leg.

I fetched a clean mug from the cabinet for Kanesha and set it by the coffeepot. Before

I could pick up my own cup for a sip, my cell phone interrupted me.

"Good morning, Melba," I said, feeling a bit guilty that I hadn't called her yesterday afternoon to check on her. "How are you doing?"

"As well as could be expected," she said. "Look, is it okay if I come on over? I know you're usually up early, even on a Sunday morning, and I'd like to talk to you about Carrie."

"Sure, you know you're always welcome. But Kanesha called just before you did, and she's on her way here, too."

"That's fine," Melba said. "I need to talk to her anyway. I'll be there in about ten minutes."

"Sounds good." I put my cell phone away. "Diesel, guess who's coming now? Your buddy Melba."

He recognized the name, and he warbled several times. He stopped washing himself and wandered out of the kitchen. He was headed for the front door to wait for Melba, but Kanesha would arrive first.

Hard upon that thought came the sound of the doorbell. I hurried to the front door to admit Kanesha, first telling the cat that this wouldn't be his buddy. Diesel meowed and moved aside.

"Morning," Kanesha said as she stepped inside.

"Come on out to the kitchen. I have fresh coffee waiting."

"Wonderful, thanks."

I could hear the tiredness in only those few words. I wondered if she'd had any chance to rest in the past twenty-four hours. I debated asking her, but she could be so prickly at times. Instead I poured the coffee and handed her the mug. She sank into a chair and rested her elbows on the table while she sipped.

"Rough night?" I asked, figuring that was safe enough as a conversation starter. I took a chair across from her.

"Crazy night," Kanesha muttered. She drew a deep breath and rubbed a hand across her eyes. "Managed about three hours' sleep, I think."

"That's not good," I said. I figured I'd better let her know Melba was on the way, and I broke the news.

"Good." Kanesha downed the rest of her coffee and held out the mug. "Could I have a refill?"

"Of course."

"Thanks," she said. "As tired as I am, caffeine's the only thing keeping me moving and barely upright."

276

I handed her the full mug. Since she appeared to have let her usual defenses down, I decided to probe a little. "Can't you take some time to go home and get a few more hours of sleep? Are things happening that fast that you can't?"

"Not exactly fast," Kanesha said, "just hard-down crazy. But I might as well wait till Ms. Gilley gets here so I don't have to repeat anything." She covered her mouth as she yawned, and I could feel the waves of exhaustion emanating from her.

Less than a minute later the doorbell rang, and I could hear Diesel's happy chirping as I headed for the front door. He knew it would be Melba this time, and he was scratching at the knob when I got there. If he ever figured out how to operate the deadbolt on the front door, we were in trouble. "Let me," I told him.

Melba entered to joyous warbling from the cat, and I moved aside to let the two greet each other. Melba bent so that her face and the cat's were close and rubbed noses with him. She scratched his head and talked to him for a moment before she straightened and looked up at me.

She didn't appear quite as exhausted as Kanesha, but I could tell she hadn't had enough rest. She was impeccably groomed and dressed like she was ready to go to the office, and that was reassuring. That was Melba in control.

"We're in the kitchen." I gave her a brief hug, and she and the cat preceded me.

Melba and Kanesha greeted each other while I poured coffee for the new arrival. Melba took my spot, so I sat at the end of the table between them. Diesel wasn't about to let Melba get more than two inches away from him and crowded against her chair, his head on her thigh.

"Deputy Bates is mighty helpful, I want you to know," Melba said, looking at Kanesha. "I know he must have been worn out, but he never said a word or tried to hurry me up at all."

"He knows his job," Kanesha replied. She glanced at me. "I asked Ms. Gilley to have a look through Mrs. Taylor's house, see if she thought anything was missing. Bates was there to assist."

"And to make sure I didn't take anything myself." Melba smiled. "Far as I could tell, none of Carrie's jewelry or valuables was missing. She didn't believe in having a lot of knickknacks around anyway, and that made things a lot easier. She didn't have much jewelry that was valuable, either, and the two pieces she did have are probably in her safety-deposit box in the bank."

"Then I suppose you can rule out robbery as a motive," I said to Kanesha.

"There was something missing," Melba said before Kanesha could respond to my statement. "I doubt anybody else would consider it valuable, but I know to Carrie it surely was."

Was it one of her books? I wondered.

"What was it then?" Kanesha asked.

"I thought I better have a look through Carrie's files," Melba said. "I wasn't as interested in those kids' books as she was, even though I read some of them when I was a kid myself. But I knew how important all that stuff was to Carrie. Anyway, I had heard her talk often enough about that Mrs. Cartwright. Carrie sure did an awful lot of research on that woman." She paused to sip at her coffee and stare into space for a moment.

Sometimes Melba took a long time to get to the point, and this was obviously going to be one of those times. I was ready to poke her, and I'm sure Kanesha felt as impatient as I did, waiting for Melba to say what she had to say. I suspected she did it on purpose, but she would never admit it.

"Does that mean some of Mrs. Taylor's files are missing?" Kanesha asked, a slight edge to her tone.

Melba nodded. "Yes, ma'am, they sure are. She had just about a whole file drawer on Mrs. Cartwright. I should know, because she showed it to me often enough." There was a catch in her voice, and for a moment I thought she might break down. Funny how those little quirks of a friend's personality could hit you when they were gone, things that annoyed you when they were alive, but now didn't seem all that bad. I knew how Melba probably felt right then.

Kanesha must have sensed it, too, because she didn't press Melba to continue.

After a heavy sigh and another sip of coffee, Melba went on. "When I checked that drawer, it was about one-third empty. There was no sign of that stuff anywhere else in the house, so whoever killed her took it."

THIRTY

"Was there something really valuable in those files?" Kanesha asked.

Melba frowned. "I'm not sure if there was anything worth money. I don't understand all the stuff that goes on with collecting books the way Carrie did. She did tell me a lot of her books were worth a bunch because of their condition. I guess she meant they were in real good shape. She talked about dust jackets sometimes."

I recalled Carrie Taylor's parting words the final time I saw her. She claimed she had items in her collection that Gordon Betts didn't. I wondered now whether she meant documents in her files rather than specific copies of Electra Cartwright's books. Maybe a rare copy of *The Mystery at Spellwood Mansion* didn't enter into the motive for murder at all.

"Do you have any idea what kind of documents Mrs. Taylor had in her files?" Kanesha asked. "Did she ever show you what was in them?"

"She pulled them out a few times and leafed through them with me." Melba shrugged. "Carrie was a dear friend, but I wasn't all that crazy about Mrs. Cartwright and her books the way Carrie was. I would listen to her talk about all that stuff, because sometimes you have to let your friends go on and on about things you're not really interested in, right?"

I nodded. Kanesha remained impassive.

Melba still hadn't answered the critical question. I decided to risk asking it again, hoping that she would finally get to the point.

"What kind of documents did she have in those files?"

Kanesha flashed me a sour look but turned quickly back to stare at Melba.

This time Melba evidently understood the urgency of the question. "She had folders of newspaper clippings, I remember. She showed some of them to me. One that I recollect in particular was when Mrs. Cartwright went to Hollywood. There was talk about making a movie out of her Veronica Thane character, but I don't think anything came of it." Melba paused as if trying to recall more. "Carrie said they ended up

282

making movies of Nancy Drew instead, and so Veronica didn't make it to the big screen. There were articles, though, with photos of Mrs. Cartwright meeting with a producer. I think there was even one with an actress that they were lining up to play the lead."

This was all news to me. I had no idea that Veronica Thane had ever been considered for the movies. I had seen the four movies Bonita Granville made, playing Nancy Drew. While they were entertaining, the Nancy of the films was not *my* Nancy. I wondered what producers would have made of Veronica's character.

"Do you remember who the actress was?" I asked.

Kanesha glared at me, and I realized I could be leading Melba away from the point again.

"It doesn't matter," I said hastily. "I'll look it up later. What else was in the files besides newspaper clippings?"

"Actually the files were mostly newspaper articles with some magazine ones, too," Melba said. "There was a real small file folder with a few letters, and two of them were Carrie's prize possessions."

"Why were they so important?" Kanesha asked when Melba failed to continue.

Melba didn't answer right away. She

283

stared at her mug, but when I offered more coffee, she shook her head. "I'm gathering my thoughts, is all. What I'm going to tell you may sound real pathetic to you, but it's the truth about Carrie and who she was and how she felt." For a moment I thought she was going to cry, but she took a deep breath and looked at each of us in turn.

"Go on, honey," I said softly. "Just tell us."

Melba nodded. "When she was around ten or eleven, Carrie said, all she could think about was Veronica Thane. She started reading those books about then, and she said when she read the first one, it felt like she had found a sister. I know that probably sounds weird, but it was how she felt. See, Carrie was an orphan like Veronica, and I guess she kind of identified with the girl in the books because of that."

Kanesha nodded. "It's understandable."

Looking slightly relieved, Melba continued. "The thing was, Veronica had this rich old lady who took her in, and she had all the nice clothes she could wear, had her own car, and lived in a mansion with servants. Carrie got adopted by a couple who were doing okay when she first went to them, but not long after, her dad went bust somehow, and they were pretty poor. Veronica lived the kind of happy fancy life that

Carrie wanted, and so she latched on to that character and just never outgrew her."

The poignancy of Carrie Taylor's story touched me, and I could tell that it affected Kanesha as well. She presented a hard shell to the world, but I knew there was a compassionate person underneath it. Melba's words affected us both.

Diesel sensed this, too. After sitting contentedly by Melba all this time, he reacted to the emotional temperature change and warbled a few times. Even Kanesha smiled. Melba scratched the cat's head, and after a moment Diesel moved around to me. I had to give him attention and assure him that I was okay. He was still a bit shy of Kanesha, however.

"Carrie loved the books so much," Melba went on, "that she was determined to meet the woman who wrote them. Carrie was adopted when she was about six months old, and she had no idea who her real parents were. If her adopted mama and daddy knew, they never told her, and she was never able to find any records." She paused for a breath. "Carrie said she got it in her head that Mrs. Cartwright was her long-lost mother. She was too young to understand, of course, or even think about the fact that those books were being published twenty years before she was born. You know how kids can be when they want something to be true hard enough, they don't always think logically about it."

What Melba told us made Carrie Taylor's story even more heart-wrenching. I could feel for that little girl who wanted so desperately to know her biological mother and to escape from a life of poverty.

"So Carrie wrote to Mrs. Cartwright." Melba paused. "I think she wrote in care of the publisher maybe. Anyway, she mailed her letter and waited. And waited. And waited. She kept reading the books over and over till they were about to fall apart."

"Did someone give her the books?" I asked. "It doesn't sound like her parents could afford to buy them for her."

"They couldn't," Melba said. "One of the teachers at school felt sorry for her and gave them to her."

"Did she ever get a letter back from Mrs. Cartwright?" Kanesha asked.

"About thirteen months after she mailed her letter." Melba shook her head. "I read it once, the first time Carrie showed it to me, I guess it was. Mrs. Cartwright apologized real nice about answering so long after Carrie wrote to her, but she said that she had moved a couple of times during the year

286

and the post office had trouble keeping up with her and forwarding the mail." She shrugged. "That sounded kind of fake to me, but what do I know? Carrie was so thrilled to get the letter she didn't care. She wrote back to Mrs. Cartwright, and this time got an answer right away. But in that second letter Mrs. Cartwright told her she was going to live overseas and didn't know exactly where she'd be, so she didn't have an address to give Carrie." Melba shrugged again. "That really was a brush-off, I think, but Carrie was only twelve, I guess, and she believed every word of it. She wrote one more letter back to Mrs. Cartwright but it was never answered."

"Was it the letters from Mrs. Cartwright she considered her prize possessions?" Kanesha asked.

Melba nodded. "They were real valuable to her, but do you think they were worth any money? Surely they weren't worth somebody killing her for, were they?"

She was looking at me when she asked the question, and Kanesha also appeared to be waiting for me to answer.

I thought about it for a moment. "Frankly, I can't see that they'd have significant monetary value. Maybe a hundred bucks or so, but unless letters in Mrs. Cartwright's own hand are truly rare, I shouldn't think they'd be worth much. It's not like she was a hugely famous or successful person — although to her fans she was royalty." A thought occurred to me. "Were those letters handwritten?"

"I'm pretty sure they were," Melba said, though she didn't sound completely certain.

"It doesn't sound to me like those letters were valuable enough to kill over." Kanesha rubbed her forehead. "If an item in those files motivated the murder, it surely had to be something else."

But what? I wondered. I couldn't come up with any ideas at the moment.

"Ms. Gilley, would you do me a favor and write down everything you remember about those files? Anything you can recall that you saw or even think you saw?" Kanesha drained the last of her coffee, and I refilled it. She nodded her thanks.

"I can sure do that," Melba said. "If Charlie will find me some paper and a pen, I'll get right on it." She flashed a smile. "That is, if you and Diesel don't mind me hanging around here a little while."

Diesel meowed loudly, and I grinned at Melba. "I think he has spoken for both of us. I'll be back in a minute." I headed for the den at the back of the house and retrieved a notebook and a couple of pens from my desk there. Kanesha and Melba were silent when I returned to the kitchen.

"Before you start making your list," Kanesha said, "can you think of anything else that could be important?"

Melba shook her head. "Not right this minute, but who knows what will come to me when I start writing? Okay with you if I do it here while you and Charlie talk? Or do you want me somewhere else?"

Kanesha eyed me for a moment.

"It's fine with me if she stays here," I said.

Melba flipped open the notebook, uncapped a pen, and started writing.

"Okay, then," Kanesha said. "When you were at the Farrington House last night, did you rifle through anybody's room?"

THIRTY-ONE

I stared back at Kanesha. Was this some kind of joke she was trying to pull?

Melba laughed. "I know Charlie is on the snoopy side, but I'd be surprised if he was going through anybody's room unless he had a powerful good reason."

I started to protest, but I recalled my actions last night in a particular guest's room.

"I did take a look at the books Gordon Betts had out on the table in his suite." I paused because I hated to admit the next bit. "I picked up one of the books and handled it."

"Which one?" Kanesha asked, frowning.

"A copy of *The Mystery at Spellwood Mansion*. Turns out it was one of the rare ones that I told you about." I shrugged. "No way to tell, though, when Betts acquired it. Or how."

Kanesha pulled out her notebook and jotted a few words in it. She glanced back at me. "Anything else?"

"No, that was the only book I touched. I did go in his bathroom, though." I related to them how I had attended to Betts in his drunken state. "I did not, however, go through any of his personal things in the bathroom or the bedroom. I swear to it."

Kanesha nodded. "Were you in any other rooms last night? Besides Mr. Eagleton's and Mr. Betts's?"

"No, I wasn't," I said. "What are you getting at? Has someone actually accused me of breaking into their room and going through their things?"

"Well, I never." Melba was clearly annoyed. "Sounds to me like some jerk is just trying to make trouble for Charlie."

"Not you specifically," Kanesha said, addressing me and appearing to ignore Melba's interjections. "But two of the guests complained to me that their things had been gone through. They were pretty adamant about it, and they both gave me believable explanations of why they were sure it happened."

"Who were they?" I asked. "Like Melba said, it sounds like someone's trying to make trouble for me."

"Not you specifically," Kanesha repeated. "Your name came up as a possibility, and

I'll have to admit I did wonder about it. I know you have a tendency to get pretty involved in these things, and sometimes it's easy to let your curiosity get the better of your judgment."

"I guess I can be a little on the snoopy side, like Melba said." I smiled at my childhood friend. "But I do have my limits. Now, who was claiming their rooms were searched?"

"Gordon Betts and Della Duffy," Kanesha answered. "Frankly, I didn't really think you had done it. I reckoned you might have looked through the books they had lying around in their rooms, but I can't see any harm in that. Or any violation of privacy since they were out for anybody to see. I also didn't think you would have entered their rooms without their knowledge or consent."

"Didn't happen," I said. "I helped Gordon Betts to his room, but I don't even know what room Ms. Duffy is staying in. Or even if she has a room at the Farrington House."

"She does," Kanesha said. "Down the hall from Gordon Betts. Now here's the thing. Whoever got into those rooms knew how to get around those keycard locks they have. Or else a member of the hotel staff helped."

"What if it was a member of the hotel staff looking for something to steal?" Melba frowned. "But you did say nothing was taken, right?"

"Right." Kanesha nodded. "Neither Ms. Duffy nor Mr. Betts had anything stolen. That was what was so odd. What was the snoop looking for?"

I pointed out one obvious flaw I spotted. "First you have to assume that both the complainants were telling the truth about nothing being taken from them. If something linking either of them to the murder of Carrie Taylor got taken, would they admit that to you?"

"I already thought of that." Kanesha sounded testy. "I questioned both of them thoroughly, and my reading is that they were telling the truth. I can't prove it, but that is what my instincts led me to conclude."

I had known Kanesha long enough now to respect her instincts. If neither Gordon Betts nor Della Duffy was lying about an intruder in their rooms, what was the point of the snooping if nothing was taken?

"If you ask me," Melba said, "the whole thing sounds pointless to me."

"Button, button, who's got the button," I said.

Kanesha and Melba stared at me as if I

had lost my wits.

"Nobody said anything about buttons." Melba looked confused. Perhaps she had never heard that phrase before nor recognized the game to which it referred.

I quickly explained. "That came to mind because I had this notion there *was* a point to the search. The intruder was seeking something he knows exists, he simply isn't sure who has it."

"We're back to the beginning then." Kanesha sounded depressed. "What was he looking for? And how is it connected — if it is connected at all — to the murder?"

I had the beginnings of a headache. All this circular speculation was frustrating. Had we accomplished anything? I put the question to Kanesha.

"We know one thing. Files that were important to Mrs. Taylor are missing. There had to be an important item, or several items, the killer wanted. It might be worth money to him, or maybe the value isn't money, but something else entirely." Kanesha paused and thought for a moment. "Actually we knew some of that already. The key thing is, now we know where the valuable item, evidently worth killing for, was located. How are we going to figure out what it was?"

"Research. I'm going to dig into Electra Barnes Cartwright's history as deeply and broadly as I can. Since the contents of those files focused on her and her life and career, then the answer has to be there. If it's on the Internet or in a reference book, then I can find it."

"Because that's what librarians do." Melba grinned at me. She had heard me on this particular soapbox before.

"It would save me time and brainpower I don't have to spare at the moment," Kanesha said. "I can't stay here and watch over your shoulder while you do it, but the minute you find anything significant, call me."

"I will." We had played out this scene between us more than once in the recent past. I was pleased that, though often still wary, she appeared now to trust me to produce results and to share them. To let her take the credit and not to try to put myself in the limelight as the clever amateur who constantly showed up the police. Or in this case, the sheriff's department. I didn't want that kind of notoriety. I was perfectly happy to do my civic duty and give her the credit for the final result.

"Then I believe I'm going to head home and try to catch a couple hours' sleep."

Hands on the table, Kanesha pushed herself upright. She nodded at Melba. "Let me know when you're done with that list."

"I will," Melba said. "You go on and get to bed. You look like you're about to fall over any second now."

I hated to delay Kanesha any further, but a question popped into my head that I had to ask. "Have you had any luck tracing Yancy Thigpen?"

Melba looked confused, but she didn't interrupt to ask who this person was. Kanesha shook her head. "We know she picked up a rental car at the Memphis Airport. After that, nothing. The sheriff's departments between here and Memphis have been alerted to keep a lookout for her and her car. That's about all we can do for now."

"Thanks," I said.

"I'll see myself out." She nodded goodbye and headed for the front door.

Melba waited until Kanesha was out of earshot. "So who is this Yancy Thigpen? What does he have to do with all this?"

"She is Mrs. Cartwright's agent," I explained. "She was supposed to arrive at Mrs. Cartwright's house sometime yesterday for a meeting between her client and Winston Eagleton, a publisher who wants to reprint the Veronica Thane books. According to Mrs. Cartwright and her daughter, Ms. Thigpen never turned up."

"You obviously think there's something sinister about that." Melba frowned. "Sounds that way to me, too, the more I think about it."

"I'm afraid it is connected to Carrie Taylor's murder, and I am praying that Ms. Thigpen is found alive and unharmed."

Diesel as usual picked up on the sudden tension and started meowing for attention. He came to me for reassurance, and I rubbed and scratched his head and back while Melba watched.

"It's amazing to me how he picks up on things." She spoke softly.

"He's very intuitive, that's for sure." I gave my boy an indulgent smile, and he chirped at me. Finally, having had enough attention — for the moment, that is — he wandered toward the utility room. No doubt by now he was starving again.

"Help yourself to more coffee. Of if you'd prefer something cold, there are canned drinks in the fridge. I'm going to get my laptop and sit here with you while I search."

"I'm fine for now." Melba smiled and picked up her pen.

Out of nowhere I suddenly remembered Carrie Taylor's dog. "What did you do with the dog?"

"Zippy, you mean?" Melba laughed. "I thought Thelma, Carrie's neighbor, hated dogs, but now that Carrie's gone, Thelma decided she wants to take him. Says he gets into her yard all the time anyway, so he might as well stay with her because it's familiar. Don't that beat all?"

"As long as she'll provide a good home for him," I said, "it's probably the best thing. Dogs are a lot of responsibility. Cats, too, for that matter."

"I was relieved, actually." Melba waved a hand at me. "Go get your laptop and let me concentrate."

A few minutes later I was seated at the table again, laptop up and running. Diesel had come back and stretched out by Melba's chair. She was engrossed in her task.

As soon as the computer was ready, I opened a browser and prepared to search. I realized I really should think about my strategy rather than start searching with no plan.

What should I search first?

Yancy Thigpen seemed stuck in my head at the moment, so I decided to search her. I might find out something pertinent to her apparent disappearance.

There was actually more than one Yancy

Thigpen out there, I discovered. I honed in on the one I wanted quickly because one of the results included a thumbnail of a young woman. I clicked on that and examined the photo.

I frowned. She looked oddly familiar. I was sure I hadn't met her, but she resembled someone I knew. Who was it?

Suddenly I had it.

Teresa Farmer. She could be Teresa's cousin, if not her sister.

THIRTY-TWO

I stared at the photo of Yancy Thigpen. Did she really look like Teresa Farmer, or was I imagining it? The longer I examined the photo, the less sure I was.

I shifted the laptop on the table so Melba could see.

"Take a gander at this image and tell me what you think. Does this person remind you of anyone?"

Melba glanced at the screen and frowned. "Charlie, you're always thinking somebody strange looks like somebody you know." She leaned forward and peered more closely at the screen. I pushed the laptop a little nearer.

"Well?" I said after a long moment of silence.

Melba shrugged. "I guess she reminds me a little bit of Teresa Farmer from the public library."

"You think in dim light you could mistake

Teresa for this woman?" I recalled the incident when Teresa and I visited Mrs. Cartwright and her daughter and how Marcella Marter reacted so oddly when she opened the door and saw Teresa standing there. I figured she might have mistaken Teresa for Yancy Thigpen.

"I reckon I might," Melba said. She didn't sound convinced. "What does this have to do with anything, though? You think they could be related?"

"I hadn't really thought about that," I said. I told her what happened when we first met Marcella Marter.

"That's weird enough," Melba said. "But does it really mean anything?"

"I don't know," I replied. Melba shrugged and went back to work on her list.

I examined a few more pictures of Yancy Thigpen, and I soon realized that they all had one thing in common. In every single photograph, each apparently taken on different occasions, Ms. Thigpen was wearing a red dress with a scarf. The scarf in each photo was different, but they were all vivid geometric prints. What this had to do with anything, I wasn't sure, but the information could be useful to the authorities looking for her. I fired off a brief e-mail to Kanesha, just in case.

That was enough about Yancy Thigpen for the moment, I decided. I needed to get on to the main subject of my research, Electra Barnes Cartwright. The solution to the murder, the disappearance, the strange theft — she was the common denominator. I was convinced of that.

I typed in her name, hit Enter, and got back over twenty-five thousand results. I knew many of them would be repetitive, but I still had to comb through them to make sure I didn't miss anything significant. As I stared at the screen, I realized I still hadn't formulated a coherent strategy for my research. I needed to have some focus to what I was doing; otherwise I would easily get sidetracked and end up following trails that would yield nothing helpful. That was what made surfing the Internet both frustrating and fun.

"Melba, let me have a couple of pieces of paper. I need to make a few notes."

She glanced up from her work, her expression one of fierce concentration. "What? Oh, okay." She tore several pages out of the notebook and handed them to me.

I found a pen in the jumble drawer and resumed my seat. I stared at the blank page. What should I focus on to start with? Basic biographical information was the logical answer. I made a heading for that on the paper before I turned back to the laptop.

The first result on the screen — after the commercial links to used book sites — led me to a bio of Mrs. Cartwright on a popular Internet encyclopedia. There was only one image attached to the article, a rather grainy photo of her when she was about forty years old. That was during the height of her fame as the creator of Veronica Thane. The first book in the series was published when the author was only twenty-six.

I studied the photograph. Because of the mediocre quality, whether from the original itself or a bad scanning job, I couldn't see the kind of detail I wanted. I could see the resemblance to Marcella Marter and her son, Eugene, however. They both had the same aquiline nose and rather prominent brows, but Mrs. Cartwright's mouth looked smaller and softer. Marcella had rather heavy jowls — from her father's side, I supposed — and Eugene was somewhere in between.

Mrs. Cartwright at the century mark favored the woman of sixty years ago, but of course age exacted a toll on everyone. The younger Electra Cartwright was fleshier, probably plumper in all respects, but I could see the resemblance to the older woman.

I skimmed the basic early biographical details and made a few notes as I went. She was born near Calhoun City, her father a farmer and her mother a schoolteacher. She was an only child who excelled at school — except for mathematics, which she apparently loathed, according to an interview early in her career. There was no money for her to go to college, but apparently she was so eager to get away from small-town life in Mississippi that she struck out for New York when she was barely eighteen. A distant relative offered her a place to live in Connecticut, and off she went. She had performed in plays in high school and was stagestruck, determined to make it on Broadway.

Other than a few bit parts in summer stock and off-Broadway productions, though, Electra Barnes found little success on the stage. She married a young actor named Ellsworth Cartwright when she was twenty, and three years later published her first book, *The Mystery at Spellwood Mansion.* There were few details in the article about her early life as Mrs. Ellsworth Cartwright, other than the fact that her husband was only slightly more successful on the stage than she had been. Mrs. Cartwright quickly became the breadwinner of the family, and Ellsworth faded into the background. The final mention of him in the article was an obituary notice in 1947.

All this was interesting, but I wasn't sure it was helpful. Ellsworth Cartwright certainly could have little to do with the present situation since he'd died more than sixty years ago. I moved on to the section that covered her writing career and the brief flirtation with Hollywood. I didn't find anything particularly exciting or helpful, but the article did name the hopeful starlet who was supposed to portray Veronica Thane in the film.

Her name was Marietta Dubois, and I had never heard of her. Curious, I put her name in the search engine and found a few pages of results. Her career in Hollywood was short-lived, according to one resource. She had minor roles in minor films, and her one chance at a starring role was the proposed Veronica Thane film. Shortly after that fizzled, Marietta married a businessman from her hometown in Iowa and went back there to be a housewife and mother. There were three images of her, and she did fit my mental image of Veronica. Dark hair and eyes, lovely face, enigmatic smile — too bad she hadn't been able to bring Veronica to life.

Funding for the production never materialized, and news of Warner Brothers's plans to bring Nancy Drew to the screen killed the idea completely.

That trail really didn't lead anywhere useful, I realized, but it was interesting. A good example, though, of how easy it was to get distracted and go haring off in one direction when you really needed to be going in another. Back to Electra Barnes Cartwright.

After her disappointment in California, Mrs. Cartwright returned to Connecticut and kept on writing. She gave birth to her only child, Marcella Ann Cartwright, two months after the death of her husband from a heart attack. She never remarried.

In addition to the Veronica Thane books, she wrote thirty-one other titles for children and young adults. Her sales were consistently good, but Veronica was her bestseller. Sales began to drop off in the mid-1960s, and the series ended in 1970 with the thirty-sixth book in the series, *Peril for Veronica Thane*.

Other than information about her books, there was no further mention of details about Mrs. Cartwright's life. She faded into near-obscurity, except among children's mystery series enthusiasts. Even they didn't realize, however, she was still living, much less that she had left Connecticut twenty years ago to share a home with her daughter and grandson.

Now I knew the basic outline of Electra Barnes Cartwright's life. Had I learned anything that shed light on the murder of Carrie Taylor? I couldn't see even a hint of a connection from these basics to the woman who had been killed.

I pondered the next step in my research strategy. Perhaps the best tack for now would be to dig into the history of Carrie Taylor's newsletter. As I recalled, Carrie had never met Mrs. Cartwright face-to-face until this past week, nor had she talked to her directly. She had had contact, however, with Marcella and with the agent, Yancy Thigpen. If issues of the newsletter were available online, scouring through them might yield something useful.

"Melba, I have a question for you."

She looked up from her notes and yawned. "I think I'm pretty much done. I've been racking my poor old brain for every little thing, and I can't think of a blessed thing more." She laid the pen and paper aside. "Whatcha want to know?"

"I'm going to check to see whether Carrie put the issues of her newsletter online. If they are, great, but if they're not, I may need to get hold of paper copies. Did she give you any of them? Or do you think she had spare copies in her files?"

"She gave me a couple now and again." Melba frowned. "I didn't keep them, though, because I couldn't work up much enthusiasm for all that girl detective stuff." She paused. "I know she did keep copies, and of course some of them are probably on her computer. When she started, they were all typed on her electric typewriter. She finally broke down about six years ago and got a computer. I helped her learn to use it."

Her voice choked up on those last two sentences, and I reached over and patted her hand. She sighed deeply. "I still can't believe it. But that's not helping anything right now. I got off the track a little. You wanted to know if there were copies in her files. She had print copies of the ones she did on the typewriter, I believe, but maybe not of the ones she did on the computer. I think any paper ones were part of the files that were taken, though."

While she talked, I did a search on the laptop and pulled up a website for the newsletter. "Thanks, honey. I found her website." I skimmed the page. "Looks like it's basically a one-screen site. There are no links, just information about subscribing, and an e-mail address for inquiries."

That was frustrating. The newsletter might lead me down a completely blind alley, but I had to get a look at the issues. The question was how quickly could I find someone who had copies?

When the answer hit me, I felt like banging my head on the table. I probably had at least several years of them in the house, because I was sure Aunt Dottie would have subscribed.

I hadn't gone through everything in the house after she died, and I definitely would have noticed them. They were probably still here.

Where had she kept them?

Thirty-Three

Again, the answer was obvious after barely a moment's consideration. If Aunt Dottie had copies of the Veronica Thane newsletter, where else would she keep them but in the same room with the books themselves? They were probably in a box in the closet. I couldn't recall ever having gone through that closet, though I'd bet Azalea knew exactly what was in every closet in the house.

Before I dashed up the stairs to check, however, I had a couple more questions for Melba — bits of things that had surfaced from somewhere in the beehive of my brain.

"Got another one for you. Talking about her computer reminded me," I said. "Did they take Carrie's computer from the house?"

"They sure did." Melba nodded three times. "Just like they do on television crime shows. Said they were going to check everything on it."

"I figured they probably would." I hoped they would go through her e-mail in particular. The clue we sought might be lurking in a message. I was happy to leave that particular job to the professionals. In addition to her mail, whoever did the work could go through all the newsletter issues. I would do what I could on my end, especially if Aunt Dottie had copies of the precomputer issues.

"I'm done, Charlie," Melba said as she pushed her chair back and stood. "And I checked the clock. It's almost nine-thirty. I have about enough time to run home and freshen up before church, so I'm going to head out now. Will you see that Kanesha gets my notes?"

"Of course," I said. "You can leave them on the table."

Diesel had evidently been sound asleep, because I hadn't heard a peep from him in quite a while. Melba's stated intention to leave — and the noise of the chair scraping on the linoleum — woke him up. He started muttering and butting his head against her legs, telling her not to go. She laughed and scratched his head and along his spine.

"Sorry, sweet boy, but I need to get to church. I'll see you tomorrow at the office, and I might have a treat for you." Melba smiled down at the cat. He warbled back, sounding slightly happier. The word *treat* always worked. He also knew what *office* meant.

"We'll see you out." Diesel and I accompanied her to the front door, and I gave her a quick hug before she headed down the walk to her car. Diesel meowed after her until I shut the door and he could no longer see her.

I stood there while Diesel ambled back toward the kitchen. I hadn't even thought about church this morning. Nor had I thought much about the fact that it was Sunday. Usually I attended services at the college chapel, and I didn't often miss. Today the fever of the hunt was upon me, and I trusted I might be forgiven nonattendance this once. After all, I told myself semipiously, I was trying to serve the cause of justice.

I wasn't sure Kanesha would see it that way, but she had allowed me to help.

"Come on, Diesel, I'm going up to the third floor." I waited a moment at the foot of the stairs, and he came trotting out of the kitchen toward me. On occasion he ignored such calls and went on with whatever he was doing, but generally he liked to be near me.

On the third floor I opened the door of the room I always thought of as Aunt Dottie's special library. In the dim light through the gauzy curtains, I would have sworn I saw a shape on the bed. When I blinked and looked again, though, the bed was bare. I smiled. If Aunt Dottie lingered anywhere in the house, it would be either in this room or in the kitchen, her two favorite places.

I flipped the light switch and advanced toward the smallish closet. Diesel jumped on the bed, rolled onto his back, and contorted himself into a stretch that made my back hurt just to witness. Chuckling, I opened the door and pulled the string for the closet light. The faint odor of mothballs tickled my nose.

Clothes still hung on the rail, and I recognized a few dresses for Sunday wear that belonged to my aunt. I ran the back of a finger down the sleeve of one for a moment, and the sensation of my skin against the wool triggered memories of Aunt Dottie dressed for church. I could see the enormous handbag she always carried with her. For a long time I suspected her of carrying a book — besides the Bible — with her, but I never caught her reading one in church if

313

she did.

I took a deep breath to bring myself back to the present. Time to focus on the search. I scanned the shelf over the clothes rail. About two feet deep and five feet across, it was jammed with boxes of assorted sizes. I counted seven shoe boxes. I didn't think they were likely repositories for the newsletters. None of the other containers bore a label to give me any hints. I would have to pull out each one and check it.

The first box, heavier than I'd expected, contained five handbags of varying size. I pulled one out and opened it, curious to know whether my aunt had left anything in them. I found four bobby pins, a crumpled tissue, and an ossified stick of gum. I decided I wouldn't look inside any of the others for now. Laura might enjoy looking through them. I never knew what retro item might be fashionable again, but my daughter would. I knew Aunt Dottie would be delighted for Laura to use one. The rest ought to go to charity. I would have to talk to Azalea about clearing this closet and any others with similar contents.

The second container held seven small bags and two large ones. The third box held six more. Quilt squares and fabric swatches filled the next two. Aunt Dottie was an indifferent quilter, but one of my treasured items was a wedding ring quilt she made for Jackie and me when we got married.

Next came a box of yarn and not-quite-finished crochet projects — scarves, one half of a sweater vest, and a blanket that might work for a Chihuahua but not much else. I smiled. Aunt Dottie always preferred reading over handiwork like this, although I knew she sewed competently. Whenever I stayed with her, she repaired rips in my clothes, because I often snagged myself on sharp things. Somehow sharp edges and I seemed to find each other way too easily.

I checked the shelf. Other than the shoe boxes, there were only two cartons left. I selected the larger one and pulled it down. The weight surprised me, and I almost dropped it on my toes. I managed to grab a firmer hold and set it gingerly atop a stack of two of the handbag containers.

The contents, I discovered, consisted of scrapbooks and photo albums. I had thought I knew where all Aunt Dottie's albums were, but I obviously had missed several. I pulled the first one out and began to flip slowly through the pages. The theme of this one was church activities, and I figured I would find nothing relevant to my current search. Particularly since the items appeared to be at least forty years old.

The next album held neatly labeled family photos. I set that one aside for further study. Genealogy was an interest of mine, and I thought it would be fun to go through these pictures with Sean and Laura — provided that I recognized some of the subjects.

By the time I'd finished with the scrapbooks in that box and the remaining one, I was tired and thirsty, not to mention a little sweaty. I was disappointed as well, because I hadn't found a single Veronica Thane newsletter. If they weren't here, where else could they be?

My erstwhile assistant hadn't moved from the bed during my labors. That surprised me because normally Diesel adored boxes — as indeed most cats do — and he couldn't resist snooping in them and trying to get inside.

While I looked at him, though, he began to stir. He yawned and stretched before he rolled over into a sitting position. He stared at me, yawned again, then meowed. He spotted the boxes and immediately leaped off the bed to investigate. I watched, ready to intervene if it looked like he might damage anything, but he seemed content to play with flaps and poke his head inside.

My glance fell on the two boxes of scrap-books.

Scrapbook.

I felt like an idiot. How had I forgotten the one I found a few days ago when I came to pick out books for the exhibit? The one devoted to children's series books and their authors.

"Come on, Diesel, we're going down-stairs."

THIRTY-FOUR

Diesel looked up at me from the box he was investigating and meowed with what sounded like an indignant edge.

"Yes, I know you just started playing with those boxes, but I have something I need to do. You can't stay here by yourself."

He stared at me and meowed again. Then he darted under the bed.

"Diesel, come out from under there. Right now." He was like a contrary child sometimes.

I waited for perhaps thirty seconds before I repeated my command.

Still no results.

Aggravated, I got down on my hands and knees to look under the bed. Luckily for me it was an old-fashioned one, high enough off the floor that I didn't have to lie prone to see exactly where he was.

Against the wall halfway between the legs of the bed, naturally. I wasn't going to crawl under to drag him out, however. I knew a better way to get him to come with me.

I put my left hand on the bed for leverage. I stood, wincing as my knees creaked. As I steadied myself, I glanced across the bed at the wall beyond where an old chifforobe stood.

A six-drawer chifforobe.

Why hadn't I thought about checking there for the newsletters? The antique piece was the only other furniture in the room that could hold them.

I moved around the bed, and momentarily left Diesel to his own devices. I pulled open the door of the wardrobe half, but it was empty except for three hangers on the rail.

The top two drawers held old linens, now yellowed with age. The middle two were empty, but the fifth drawer down held a wooden box of a size appropriate to contain the newsletters. I checked the bottom drawer, and it was empty.

I picked up the box and placed it on the bed. The shallow, grooved lid came off easily, and inside lay a stack of papers — what I had been looking for during the past half hour or more.

I replaced the lid and tucked the box under my arm. I was halfway down the hall, having shut the door behind me before I remembered that Diesel remained under the bed. I smiled. This was what I'd planned to do anyway, because Diesel didn't like being shut in a room by himself.

After standing in place for about two minutes, I moved quietly back to the door. I waited a few moments more, then I heard the cat scratching at the door.

"Come on, then, and I'll give you a treat," I said when I swung it open. "I told you I wanted to go downstairs."

Diesel stared up at me for about three seconds and then shot out into the hall and down the stairs. I knew he would be waiting in the kitchen for the promised treat to materialize.

I stopped by my bedroom to retrieve the scrapbook. When I reached the kitchen, the cat sat near the chair I usually occupied. He warbled, obviously irritated with me for taking so long to fulfill my promise. I set the box and scrapbook on the table and retrieved the treat. I ended up giving him a small handful of the little tidbits, and he scarfed them down in three seconds flat. He stared hopefully at me, but I waved my hands in the air and said, "That's all." He muttered but didn't press me any further. He stretched out on the floor by my chair and started grooming his front paws.

After my labors in the closet, I was thirsty, and before I set to work going through the newsletters and the scrapbook, I washed my hands and drank two glasses of water. Only then did I sit and pull the box toward me. Perhaps three inches deep, the box was filled almost to the brim with paper.

The initial newsletter lay on top. A single sheet, neatly typed and single-spaced, it featured a photocopied image of one of the illustrated plates from *The Mystery at Spellwood Mansion,* but greatly reduced from its original size. I scanned the text quickly. Carrie Taylor described briefly her first acquaintance with the series and went on to discuss her devotion to Veronica Thane and the works of Electra Barnes Cartwright through the years. The verso of the sheet featured a list of the books with their publication dates. The newsletter concluded with Mrs. Taylor's address and phone number. She entreated anyone interested in her subjects to get in touch with her to get on a mailing list for further issues.

I set the sheet aside and picked up the next issue. This one was three sheets of paper, and the heading labeled it as *The Thane Chronicles* and denoted it as volume one, issue one. There was a date and a brief reprise of pertinent information from the initial sheet, followed by the subscription information. There was no mention of a cost for subscribing.

There were three short articles. One was a plot summary of *Spellwood Mansion,* and I skipped that. Next came a brief piece on the setting for the series. Mrs. Taylor speculated that the books were set in the author's native Mississippi, though she admitted there were no direct references to the state, only consistently vague acknowledgments that Veronica and her guardian lived in the American South. The final article discussed the clothing in the series. Laura would find that interesting. I didn't particularly, and I put the pages aside.

The issues grew longer as I moved down through the stack. Aunt Dottie, being the organized person she was, had kept them in chronological order. The publication pattern of the newsletter — as we librarians would call it — was irregular to begin with. There was an eighteen-month gap between the first two issues, and a fifteen-month lapse between number two and number three. After the fifth issue the pattern was more regular with two issues a year, usually spring and fall.

With issue number six, Mrs. Taylor offered content written by other Veronica fans and experts. I didn't recognize any of the names but wondered if eventually I would encounter contributions by Gordon Betts or Della Duffy. I only skimmed most of the content, but one short article I read completely discussed Veronica's injuries through the course of thirty-six adventures. She was knocked out seventeen times, got drugged eight times, was tied up in eleven books, and imprisoned eighteen times — once even in a trunk. The writer observed wryly that Veronica was a neurological marvel because she never suffered any cognitive impairment from all those bangs on the head and the drugging with unknown substances.

After an hour I had examined eleven issues without a hint of a clue — at least one that I recognized — relevant to Carrie Taylor's murder. The newsletters might not end up having anything to do with the solution to the crime, but I felt I had to be thorough and examine every one in the box.

Before I started on the twelfth issue, I needed caffeine to pep up my brain cells. I retrieved a can of diet soda from the fridge and happened to glance at the clock. I felt my stomach rumble as I noted that it was almost eleven thirty. Breakfast seemed a long time ago. I might as well break for lunch.

I stuck my head back in the fridge to investigate the possibilities. I didn't feel like cooking but the prospects for a quick meal seemed scant at best. The ham was gone, and I didn't fancy more pimento cheese, delicious as it was. I could make a salad, but I wanted something more substantial.

"Morning, Dad. Ready for lunch?"

Sean's voice startled me, and I almost banged my head on the fridge door as I turned. He stood grinning a few feet away with a large box emblazoned with the logo of Helen Louise's bakery.

"I sure am." I let the door swing shut. "What do you have there?"

Diesel perked up and warbled. He stood and stretched before he walked around the table to rub against my son's legs.

"Salad and quiche." Sean set the box on the table. "I was at the office this morning, and I decided to stop by the bakery on the way home. Figured you might join me for lunch."

"You're my favorite son." I beamed at him and watched while he retrieved plates and utensils.

"Gee, thanks." Sean laughed as he set the table.

"What would you like to drink?" I opened the fridge again.

"A beer if there's any left." He turned to grab napkins from the drawer.

"You're in luck." I found a bottle, opened it, and set it on the table. We sat and served ourselves. Diesel hovered anxiously by my chair. He was going to be disappointed, though, because the quiche was made with cheese, onions, and ham. A large paw tapped my thigh. I looked down at him. "Sorry, boy, but this isn't Diesel food." He meowed, but I shook my head at him. He stared at me for a moment before he stalked off toward his food bowl in the utility room.

After a couple of bites of salad and a few of the delicious quiche, I said, "You were at the office this morning? You must have left pretty early."

Sean nodded and finished chewing before he answered. "Left about six. I had things to do on this new case, then I swung by the jail to talk to Mr. Eagleton again."

"Any new developments?"

"Something pretty strange." Sean set his fork down. "Evidently a neighbor across the street happened to be looking out a front window and saw a man at Mrs. Taylor's front door about the time she left that phone message for Ms. Gilley."

"That's lucky," I said. "Could he identify the man?"

"He said all he could really see was an outline, and his night vision isn't good. The nearest streetlight is out, and Mrs. Taylor's porch light was pretty dim. He thought the man looked slender."

"Obviously not Winston Eagleton," I said. "No way he could be described as slender."

"No," Sean said with a brief grin. "But here's the weird thing. The witness, Mr. Andrews, looked out again about twenty minutes later — he's not completely sure of the time — and saw someone leaving the house." He paused. "But this time it was a woman."

Thirty-Five

"A woman?" I almost dropped my quiche-laden fork. "So Mrs. Taylor had two visitors that night?"

"Looks like it," Sean said. "And it seems more likely that the woman might have been the killer."

"Could Mr. Andrews describe anything about the woman?"

"Not much," Sean said with a rueful grimace. "The only thing he could say was that she wasn't very tall. Neither was the man, apparently. The significant bit is that she was carrying a big box as she left."

"She was taking away Mrs. Taylor's files. That clinches it." I was excited by the new discovery. Then a question occurred to me. "He was sure the person with the box was a woman? Couldn't it have been the man?"

"He says it wasn't. The head was bigger, like the second person had a lot more hair than the first one."

I mulled that over. "The man might have been Gordon Betts, and I suppose the woman could have been Della Duffy. I think they're about the same height. Well, if Della Duffy was wearing heels, she would be."

"Kanesha said she would question both of them today about their whereabouts that night." Sean sipped at his beer. He gestured with the bottle toward the scrapbook, box, and newsletters on the table. "I presume you're doing research with those."

I explained quickly what they were. "I've been through probably a third of the newsletters, but so far I can't see that I have run across anything pertinent to the murder. They may be one big red herring."

"You might find something significant yet." Sean forked up a bite of quiche.

"Maybe." I felt less sanguine about the prospects, but I knew I had to plow on through the rest of the newsletters as well as the scrapbook.

"I wish I had time to help you," Sean said, "but I need to go back to the office for a couple of hours. Another case I'm working on. There's not much else I can do for Mr. Eagleton right now."

"I appreciate it, but I'll muddle through. Although if Laura or Stewart should happen to wander in, I might co-opt one of them." I grinned.

"You're out of luck," Sean said. "Laura and Frank drove over to Cleveland last night for a visit with his mother. I think Stewart is busy this weekend, too. I doubt you'll see him until this evening."

I had forgotten about Laura's plans with Frank. "So much for that idea. Too bad Diesel can't read," I said.

"I wouldn't be too sure of that," Sean said wryly. "That's one smart cat."

We shared a laugh. Diesel was a bright feline, but there were limits to a cat's abilities, after all.

"Will they release Eagleton once the killer is caught?" I ate more of the delicious quiche. My stomach felt happier, even if my brain didn't. "Unless he was dressed up as a woman, he wasn't the person Mr. Andrews saw leaving with that box."

"That will depend partly on Mrs. Cartwright and her family. If they insist on pressing charges, everything will go forward. Unless, naturally, we can prove that the killer planted the manuscripts in my client's room."

"It will all get worked out. In the meantime I guess I should get back to my research." I got up from the table to put my plate and utensils in the sink. "Thanks again for lunch. My prospects were meager until you showed up."

"My pleasure." Sean popped the last bite of quiche in his mouth. I cleared his place, and he dropped the beer bottle into the recycle bin. "I'm heading back to the office, Dad. Let me know if you find anything to help my client."

"Will do."

Sean waved on his way out of the kitchen.

I thought about stopping him to ask about the status of his engagement but quickly realized he wouldn't welcome my inquiry. He would talk to me about it when he was ready.

I resumed my place at the table and pulled the newsletters toward me. A large paw tapped my thigh. Diesel stared hopefully at me. I had no doubt that, had he been able, he would have pointed to his open mouth to let me know he was all hollow inside. I couldn't help but laugh. I pushed back from the table. "Okay, boy, I'll give you a few treats, but that's it." I had filled his dry food bowl this morning, but by now he had probably cleaned it out. "No more until dinnertime tonight."

My act of mercy accomplished, I went back to work. Over the next hour I made it through another third of the stack. The number of different contributors increased. The content of the articles varied greatly, as did the writing ability of the authors. I winced over a few examples of particularly bad prose. Perhaps Carrie Taylor hadn't felt like she could offend people by tampering with their work, or she might not have been bothered the way I was.

I decided to switch from the newsletters to the scrapbook. I needed a change to refresh my brain, not to mention my eyes. I picked up the scrapbook and opened it to the first page.

Aunt Dottie evidently bought movie magazines during her youth because there were several pages of pictures and articles cut from them that featured Bonita Granville and her role as Nancy Drew. I caught myself reading one of the articles. I didn't have time for that now. *Concentrate on Mrs. Cartwright and Veronica Thane,* I reminded myself.

There were pages of article clippings, most now yellowed with age and stained from glue, that mentioned Nancy Drew or one of the other juvenile detective series. I found a few references to Veronica Thane, but nothing extensive. Toward the middle I noticed a section that focused on Mrs. Cartwright, and I felt a tingle of anticipation. The clue I sought might be under my fingers.

Ten minutes later, having worked my way through the pertinent pages, I was discouraged. I hadn't found anything that seemed relevant. The most interesting item was another photo from a film magazine that featured Marietta Dubois, the actress who was to have portrayed Veronica, and Mrs. Cartwright. Miss Dubois, tall and willowy, smiled — insincerely I thought — down at Mrs. Cartwright, who gazed up at the younger woman with manifest delight. Mrs. Cartwright's head was about level with Miss Dubois's shoulder.

Too bad the movie never came to be, I thought. Veronica might have been even more famous, and it could have boosted the career of Miss Dubois.

I skimmed through the rest of the scrapbook but found nothing else related to either Veronica Thane or Mrs. Cartwright. I set it aside, wondering whether I had missed something.

The remaining newsletters beckoned, but I had little enthusiasm for the task. I decided I needed a complete break from my research. Perhaps if I put it all aside for a couple of hours, I could come back fresher and more alert to potential clues.

"Come on, Diesel." I got up from the

table. "Let's go upstairs for a while. I'm going to read, and you can stretch out on the bed and have a nice long nap. How does that sound?"

Diesel warbled happily and trotted beside me out of the kitchen and up the stairs. I took off my shoes and got comfortable on the bed. My copy of *Spellwood Mansion* lay on the nightstand, and I picked it up. Perhaps Veronica would inspire me. Escape reading might be just the thing to clear my head.

I found my bookmark and began to read. Veronica had just found out she'd been drugged. . . .

THIRTY-SIX

"Drugged?" Veronica gasped. Why would someone drug her? And how? "I'm sure Mrs. Eden wouldn't have done such a thing!"

Lucy stared at her. "Mrs. Eden? Who pray tell is Mrs. Eden?"

Veronica blinked several times, and her right hand convulsively clutched at her throat. "I don't know why I said that." A memory was trying slowly to push itself into the forefront of her mind.

Lucy remained quiet, for Veronica's mental struggle was evident in her expression. She grew considerably alarmed, however, when Veronica suddenly collapsed against the pillows. The huge smile that her friend bestowed upon her quickly reassured her.

"You have remembered something?" Lucy asked, waiting tremulously for the answer.

"Yes, I have," Veronica stated triumphantly. "It has all come back to me now. Mrs. Eden's name was the key to unlocking my memories." Her happiness faded quickly, however, as she wondered what fate had befallen her frightened hostess.

Quickly Veronica related to her dearest friend the details of her harrowing adventure the night before. Lucy appeared suitably awed and frightened in turn over the risks that the intrepid young detective had taken in order to help a terrified stranger.

Veronica threw back the covers and prepared to get out of bed. There wasn't a moment to lose. She must go back to that spooky old mansion and discover the fate of poor Mrs. Eden.

Lucy easily divined Veronica's intention, for she had known the courageous girl long enough to be aware that Veronica relished a challenge. Common sense, however, dictated that she remind her chum of the lateness of the hour. "It is nearly midnight now, my dear, and you cannot rush forth from here at such an hour. You must wait until morning."

"I suppose you are right," Veronica responded reluctantly. "Still, I must get up." She moved away from the bed, and her steps, though tentative at first, rapidly became more assured. She walked around her large, airy bedroom while Lucy watched her anxiously.

"Now that I have my memory back, I feel ever so much better," Veronica declared. "Also hungry. Let's go down to the kitchen and see what Cook might have set aside."

"Now, dearest, you know that Fontaine will scold if you do such a thing," Lucy admonished her friend. "Besides, he instructed me to ring for him should you want anything when you awakened. I shall do that now."

"Oh, very well," Veronica said with an impish smile. "I suppose it wouldn't do to upset Fontaine tonight, for he will be cross with me for days afterward."

Haviland Fontaine, formerly of the British Army, served as Mrs. Buff-Orpington's butler and secretary. Though fond of his mistress's young ward, he often deplored her tendency to find adventures. He was also firmly of the opinion that Miss Veronica should remain above stairs and leave the lower regions to the servants as befit a properly reared young lady.

He appeared quickly in response to Lucy's ringing of the bell in Veronica's room. His stoic countenance revealed little emotion as he beheld his young mistress seemingly recovered from having been drugged and abandoned beside the highway. Lucy told Veronica later that she would have sworn the butler's lips twitched into a brief smile, but Veronica scoffed at the notion.

"You rang, miss?" Fontaine was a man of few words. He did not believe, he had once told Veronica, in wasting time or breath on unnecessary conversation.

"Yes, we did." Veronica nodded at Lucy. "I am frightfully hungry, Fontaine. Perhaps you could find something for us, some victuals that Cook has not yet discarded?"

"Of course, miss." Fontaine coughed discreetly. "I will also inform Madam that you are awake. She has been anxiously awaiting the news."

Fontaine soon returned with a platter of bread, cheese, ham, and various fruits. Veronica greeted the sight with cries of delight and was soon happily sating her hunger. Her guardian joined them as Veronica finished the last of the bread and cheese.

"Darling Veronica, how happy I am to see you looking so well." Araminta Buff-Orpington seated herself on the bed beside her ward and clasped the girl's hand affectionately. She turned to Lucy with a smile. "And dearest Lucy, what a treasured friend you are to nurse our girl so devotedly."

Lucy returned the smile. "I would do anything for Ronnie."

Mrs. Buff-Orpington turned back to Veronica. "Tell me, my dear, how you came to be in such a state."

Veronica related the events of the previous evening, and her guardian appeared suitably concerned, then relieved that the girl had come through such a harrowing adventure in good condition. "I do admire your concern for the welfare of those in need of aid, but I must condemn your tendency to put yourself in harm's way." She patted the girl's hand again. "Whatever would Lucy and I do if something terrible happened to you? You really must be more careful, child."

Veronica squirmed with discomfort. She did not like being the cause of unease on the part of such a loving guardian, but yet she could not curb her appetite for adventure nor her concern for others. "I always try my best to avoid danger."

"I know you do," Mrs. Buff-Orpington said smilingly, "and I won't fuss any more. I am feeling rather tired and will now leave you two to chatter away the night as you like or rest." She kissed each girl on the brow and made her stately way back to her own suite of rooms nearby.

Though Veronica did not feel in the least sleepy, she knew Lucy was tired. Therefore, she did not demur when Lucy changed into her nightdress and crawled into the bed beside her. Veronica switched off the light. They chatted briefly, but soon Lucy was sound asleep.

Veronica lay awake for some time, however, plotting her course. She must go back to that spooky house and investigate further. She could not forget Mrs. Eden's fear or her plea for help. Finally, near dawn, she, too, fell asleep.

I turned the page to the next chapter.

Ten o'clock the next morning saw Veronica, accompanied by Artie Marsh, on her way back to the house she later learned was named Spellwood Mansion. Artie protested, trying to convince the girl that she should not tempt fate by going back. Veronica, however, remained undaunted. She must see that Mrs. Eden was safe.

Veronica found the estate with little trouble, and she drove her roadster into the forecourt and parked before the front door. She gazed at the house for the first time in the light of day. Though it looked less sinister without a storm raging around it, Veronica thought nevertheless there was something forbidding about the mansion. She shivered, and Artie noticed.

"Are you cold?" His words dripped with concern. He feared greatly that Veronica would again be injured. But if he could protect her in any way, he would. With his height and strong build, he felt sure he would prove a capable bodyguard for the young detective.

"No, I'm fine." Veronica smiled at her handsome friend. "Come, let's go knock on the door and see what happens. I have the strangest feeling that more odd and puzzling things will occur."

As he extricated his long legs from the roadster, Artie hoped fervently that Veronica was wrong. Perhaps the inhabitants had fled in the night, and he and Ronnie could head home. Artie did not fear adventure, for he was a courageous young man, yet his concern for Veronica was paramount.

He wielded the knocker vigorously, and he and Veronica waited. Moments later the door swung open, and Veronica glimpsed the creepy butler, Bradberry.

"Good morning, miss," the old man said. "Are you returned to visit the mistress?"

"I am." Veronica boldly stepped past the butler into the entranceway. "My friend Mr. Arthur Marsh is accompanying me today. Please announce us to Mrs. Eden. I trust she is well." Until Veronica spoke to the mistress of the house, she decided she would not tax the servant with the mystery of her drugging and abandonment in her car by the side of the road.

"She is indeed, miss." Bradberry closed the front door behind them. "Please walk this way, and I will announce you." He turned and headed toward the same sitting room in which Veronica had talked with Mrs. Eden the previous day.

Bradberry opened the doors and advanced into the sunlit room. Veronica and Artie, following right behind him, could not at first see their hostess. The butler intoned their names and then stepped aside.

Veronica moved forward. Then her step faltered.

Mrs. Eden arose from her chair and walked toward them, her hands extended, a beaming smile on her face. "My dear, how lovely to see you again. And you have brought a companion. How delightful."

Veronica stared hard at the woman. She

341

looked like the Mrs. Eden she had encountered the day before, but her manner was so completely different that Veronica was stunned by the change.

While Artie accepted the woman's hand and shook it, Veronica continued to scrutinize their hostess. Mrs. Eden's face appeared harder, less fleshy, and more heavily made up than the day before. She also seemed stronger, certainly no longer an invalid.

Veronica relied on her instincts in such situations, and her instincts were telling her that the woman was an impostor. This Mrs. Eden was not the Mrs. Eden she met in this house yesterday.

I chuckled at the melodrama of it. A second Mrs. Eden — as I recalled it, a cousin impersonating the real Mrs. Eden, who was imprisoned somewhere in the house.

Out of nowhere my tired brain connected disparate pieces of information, and I knew who the killer was.

THIRTY-SEVEN

Mrs. Cartwright really *wasn't* Mrs. Cartwright.

My solution to the murder was nuts.

Wasn't it?

If Mrs. Cartwright wasn't Mrs. Cartwright, then who was she?

Eugene Marter. Had to be.

I realized I hadn't seen him and his grandmother in the same place at the same time. Had only seen him once, as a matter of fact.

If Eugene was really impersonating his grandmother, then where was the real woman? Was she even still living?

There was an easy way to check that. The Social Security death index.

I slipped on my shoes and hurried downstairs to where I had left my laptop on the kitchen table. As soon as it was ready, I opened the browser and entered a website address. I knew the fastest way to gain access to the information was via a genealogy service to which I subscribed. I input my search terms, Mrs. Cartwright's name, figuring there couldn't be that many other women with her name in the index.

There was no listing at all for *Electra Barnes Cartwright.* I tried *Electra Cartwright.* No hits. *Electra Barnes* returned several, but I could tell by the dates that none of them was the correct person.

I leaned back in my chair and considered the possibilities.

The fact that I couldn't find her in the death index didn't mean that she was still alive. That thought chilled me. Had they killed her and buried her in the backyard?

Nasty.

Maybe she was alive but mentally incapacitated. No longer able to write or make competent decisions about her books.

That would be tragic, but an alternative preferable to my first thought.

Diesel startled me by meowing loudly beside me. I was so absorbed in my speculations that I had forgotten all about him.

"I'm okay, boy." I rubbed his head. "Thinking hard, that's all. Nothing to worry over."

He warbled a couple of times before he settled down on the floor beside my chair.

How would Kanesha react if I shared this theory with her?

She would demand proof; that's how she would react.

What proof did I have? I had a lot of odd facts that I thought suggestive, but Kanesha needed convincing evidence.

Short of walking up to the fake Mrs. Cartwright and snatching the red wig off her head, what could I do?

I had a sudden vision of grabbing hold of the hair, pulling, and Mrs. Cartwright screaming in protest. I shuddered.

No, I had to be completely sure about my theory before I could test it like that.

What incontestable proof could I muster? Surely there was something.

My gaze fell on the scrapbook. Pictures of Mrs. Cartwright. A vague idea began to form.

Hard on those thoughts came another point. Photographs could be the reason the killer took away Carrie Taylor's files. Why Carrie Taylor had to die. She had the proof right there in her file cabinet.

Surely the killer had to realize, however, there were almost certainly copies of Mrs. Taylor's photos elsewhere. Maybe a photograph wasn't the proof after all.

A memory surfaced. At the meeting with

Mrs. Cartwright and Marcella, Carrie Taylor mentioned a photo of the author in the garden shed where she wrote her books. I didn't recall seeing such a picture in Aunt Dottie's scrapbook.

I went back to my laptop and typed *Electra Cartwright garden shed* in the search engine. The result was a couple of pages of hits. I clicked on the first one, and that led me to an article in a fan publication devoted to children's books — not Carrie Taylor's newsletter.

An examination of the other links revealed nothing useful. I clicked the link for an image search, and the result was a screen full of pictures. Some were of the author as a much younger woman; others were of garden sheds. Not a single one showed Mrs. Cartwright *and* a garden shed.

Back to square one on that idea. I glanced at the scrapbook again. This time I pulled it close and found the section Aunt Dottie devoted to Mrs. Cartwright and Veronica. There were a couple of portrait-type photos from magazines pasted in, but those didn't tell me anything.

I stared at the image of Mrs. Cartwright with Marietta Dubois. Both women wore shoes with low heels, from what I could tell. The actress looked tall next to the writer, but if Miss Dubois had been six feet tall, that would make Mrs. Cartwright about five-eight. How could I find out how tall Marietta Dubois was?

The encyclopedia entry I found earlier didn't have that information. I searched for *Marietta Dubois height* but that didn't get me anywhere, except increasingly frustrated. As a test I entered *Judi Dench height* and retrieved the information right away. Too bad Marietta Dubois hadn't been more famous.

I glanced at the screen again and examined the results of my search on Judi Dench. One link jumped right out at me — an Internet database devoted to movies. Maybe it had what I needed?

I found the entry for Miss Dubois, and there it was. *Height 5' 6"*. I laughed with relief. Whether a court would accept it as evidence was one thing, but it might be enough to convince Kanesha.

At our first meeting I noticed that Mrs. Cartwright — or rather Eugene Marter — was the same height as Teresa Farmer. My friend and colleague was around five foot six as well. There was no way the real Electra Barnes Cartwright had grown a good four inches in the past sixty-odd years.

Now that I had identified the murderer, I

considered how that fact fit into the odd incidents that had occurred, starting with the murder itself.

Kanesha's witness, Mr. Andrews, claimed to have seen a man arrive around the time of Carrie Taylor's phone message to Melba. Carrie Taylor had said something like, "What does he want?" About twenty minutes later Mr. Andrews saw a woman carrying a large box leaving the house.

Two possibilities occurred to me. The first — Carrie Taylor had two guests in close succession. I really didn't think so. The second — Eugene Marter arrived as a man, somehow secreting his wig about his person. After he committed murder, he donned the wig to confuse things. That worked for me. I figured Eugene was doing his best to muddy the waters.

Next odd incident — the alleged theft of the five manuscripts and their discovery under the mattress in Winston Eagleton's suite. When Marcella and Eugene first arrived at Eagleton's party, they went immediately to the bathroom. The bedroom was only a few feet away, and one of them could easily have placed the manuscripts where they would quickly be found after Eugene reported the theft. I recalled the large handbag Eugene carried. He had not carried one in his role as his grandmother before, as far as I could remember.

What about the phone call reporting the theft? Didn't it occur around the time of the party when Eugene would have been at the hotel?

Easily resolved — a cell phone call from the car or even from the lobby of the hotel before Eugene and Marcella came upstairs.

My excitement built as I put the pieces of the crime together.

What about the theft, however? Why had Eugene set it up? Had he seriously thought he could implicate Winston Eagleton in the murder? Or had he simply wanted to make everything more complicated in hopes that the authorities would be too confused to see the truth?

That was the likeliest answer — intentional confusion. It had certainly worked, up to a point. Eugene had even set it up by coming to me with his story of Eagleton's threats against Mrs. Cartwright over the right to publish the manuscripts.

What about Yancy Thigpen? I felt chagrined that I had forgotten about the agent until this moment. Had Eugene killed her because she somehow stumbled into the middle of all this?

I could only hope she was alive and

unharmed, perhaps being hidden as a prisoner of Eugene and Marcella. Like the real Mrs. Cartwright. The Marters had a large house, with more than enough space to lock two women away upstairs and out of sight.

What was at the root of the deception in the first place? That was a significant question, and one I should have considered earlier.

The quick answer to that was money. The Marters were desperate for cash, and thought they could make some quick bucks by hawking the manuscripts and collecting fees from fans like Gordon Betts willing to pay outrageous sums to get a signature. A spurious signature, that is.

I thought about those manuscripts. I would love to get my hands on them. It would be wonderful to see them in print, along with the original Veronica Thane books.

An appalling idea brought me up short, however.

What if they were spurious as well?

THIRTY-EIGHT

I hated the idea that the five manuscripts might be fakes, but there were more important things to consider.

First, though, I had to call Kanesha. I pulled out my cell phone and punched in the number.

After two rings her voice growled in my ear. "This better be good."

"Did I wake you up?" I felt bad about that, considering how tired she had looked this morning. But this couldn't wait.

She ignored my question. "Why did you call?"

"I know who the murderer is." I paused for a reaction. None came right away. I plunged ahead. "Mrs. Cartwright is an impostor. It's her grandson, Eugene, pretending to be her. He killed Carrie Taylor because I'm pretty sure she had evidence in her files that would have exposed him." I paused again.

Kanesha snorted in my ear. "If I didn't know you better by now, I'd swear you were drunk out of your mind to come up with a far-out tale like this."

I decided the wiser course would be not to respond to that sally and wait for her to continue.

"But I do know you better. You wouldn't make such an outrageous claim if you weren't sure you could prove it somehow."

"I believe I can," I said, vastly relieved. "It would be easier to show you, though. I can't really do it over the phone."

"Give me twenty minutes, and I'll be there. That okay?" She sounded more alert, less aggravated.

"That'll be fine." I ended the call and immediately started agitating over the best way to present my evidence. I grabbed the pad of paper I was using earlier to make notes from my research, found a blank page, and started outlining.

Diesel must have sensed my mental turmoil. He sat up and prodded at my leg, then butted it with his head until I noticed him. "Everything is fine, boy." I scratched his head with my left hand while I continued to jot things down with my right. He calmed after a minute or so of attention, and I could concentrate completely on my task at hand.

By the time Kanesha arrived, I felt confident that I had put together a reasoned, coherent case against Eugene Marter. I offered to make coffee, and when she declined, I mentioned other beverages. She shook her head. She wanted to hear what I had to say, obviously. She did take a moment to say hello to Diesel, however, and I appreciated the gesture.

I recounted my fruitless search through the newsletters, but I did suggest that they all needed to be examined carefully in case there was further evidence in them. She leafed through the scrapbook while I talked, and when she found the picture of Marietta Dubois with Mrs. Cartwright, I explained how I'd verified the actress's height.

"That sounds convincing." She nodded at the picture. "Tell me the rest of it."

I took her through each of the strange incidents and offered my explanations for each. She seemed particularly interested in my theory about the planting of the manuscripts in Winston Eagleton's hotel suite.

"I couldn't figure out why he would do something that was so obviously stupid," she said. "But I had to charge him, given the evidence. Eugene Marter has a record — mostly petty crime, but he's a shifty devil. Not as bright as he thinks he is, either."

"I can't say I'm surprised." I recounted the story of my one meeting with him — as his real self, that is. "He did admit to me he'd had trouble with the law in the past."

Kanesha nodded. "For most of his adult life. I felt sorry for his mother when I checked his record. Never did meet the grandmother, though I got the impression it was her money that bailed him out."

"No doubt it was. Tell me, do you think she's still alive?"

"Hard to say. You didn't find her listed in the death index. We'll have to contact Social Security to find out whether they're still sending her checks. That doesn't mean she's living, but it will be another charge against the Marters for fraud."

I hadn't thought of that. "What if she's alive but not in any condition to make decisions for herself?"

"If one of them has the right power of attorney, they're okay." Kanesha examined the scrapbook photo again. "The problem is, I'm not sure I can convince a judge to give me a search warrant. I'd like to go in that house and see just who's there, and in what condition."

"I think Yancy Thigpen is there, too. Alive,

I hope, like Mrs. Cartwright." I shuddered. "If they're not, what will you do?"

Kanesha's answered chilled me further, though it wasn't unexpected. "Start looking for evidence of digging on their property."

"If only there were a way to unmask Eugene in public. That would do it, wouldn't it?"

"It would certainly get the ball rolling," Kanesha said. "But I'm not going to go up to Mrs. Cartwright and accuse her of being Eugene in drag. Too risky."

An idea had occurred to me, but I wasn't sure whether Kanesha would go for it. It was corny and clichéd, but it had worked in the past. "How about this? We get Eugene, as Mrs. Cartwright, to come to the library tomorrow with Marcella. Maybe I can ask Teresa to call them and say that we want to discuss further the idea of paying Mrs. Cartwright to appear at the library. I could ask them questions, see if Eugene squirms, and if all else fails, I could try to get the wig off."

Kanesha almost smiled. "Would you really go through with it?"

I nodded.

"You realize you could be laying yourself open to a lawsuit if by some chance you're wrong. Even if you're right, Eugene might try to sue you or charge you with assault."

"I'm willing to take the chance." My heart thumped harder than usual in my chest, but I would do as I promised.

Kanesha regarded me in silence for a long moment. "Why not? It's unorthodox, but I don't have any better options at the moment. Do you think Teresa Farmer will go along?"

"I'm sure she will. I don't have to tell her everything if you don't want me to, just that we need to get Eugene, or rather Mrs. Cartwright, and Marcella to the library as soon as possible."

"If you can get her to do it without telling her completely why, that would be better. That way she can't give anything away."

Teresa was shrewd and no doubt would realize that I was hatching some kind of plot, but I thought she would trust me enough to go along without asking any inconvenient questions.

"I'll call her right now." I took out my cell phone. She answered almost immediately. After we got the preliminaries out of the way, I said, "I can't tell you why, but I really need to get Mrs. Cartwright and Marcella to the library tomorrow." I explained what I wanted her to do. I could tell by her tone that she was burning with curiosity, but she obviously trusted me enough to agree without pressing me for more information. "Call me back as soon as you've made the arrangements with them."

I ended the call and put the phone on the table. "Now all we have to do is wait. Eugene will bite, I'm sure of it."

THIRTY-NINE

The meeting was set for nine thirty the next morning. After Kanesha left, I kept thinking about my plan, and through the afternoon and the evening, I went over it and over it until my head started pounding.

While I lay in bed, trying to still my brain enough to get to sleep, I realized I had overlooked two of the odd occurrences in this strange affair.

The first was the business with the glaring lights when Teresa and I went to visit Mrs. Cartwright in her home. Now that I knew that Eugene was sitting in for his grandmother, I understood. With all that glare, visitors would have a hard time focusing on details of Mrs. Cartwright's appearance — like an Adam's apple or hands that looked too young for a centenarian. At other meetings Eugene had worn a scarf and gloves.

The second incident was the fainting spell Marcella had at Winston Eagleton's party.

The news of Carrie Taylor's murder caused it, but I wondered whether it was a put-on or whether Marcella really had been shocked by the news. I hoped it was the latter because it would mean that she had no idea her son had committed murder until that very moment.

After an hour of lying in bed wide awake, I decided I might as well finish reading *The Mystery at Spellwood Mansion.* If I focused on that for a while instead of the murder, I might relax enough to go to sleep.

I finished the book in about forty-five minutes, and then I put it aside and turned off the light. The plot of the book gave me an idea for the meeting with Eugene and Marcella, and at last I drifted off. Diesel had gone to sleep right away, stretched out beside me in bed.

The next morning I arrived at the library a few minutes before nine, and Bronwyn let me and Diesel in. After she extended the usual greetings to the cat, I pulled her aside and told her I needed a favor. "I can't explain why I need you to do it, but afterwards I can."

"That's okay, Charlie." Bronwyn smiled. "I can contain my curiosity until you're ready to come clean."

While I headed into Teresa's office, Diesel

followed Bronwyn as she went to unlock the door for the day. I knew he would stay with her, which was just as well.

"Morning, Teresa." I stood in the doorway of the director's office with a nervous smile.

Teresa greeted me, her expression solemn. "This isn't going to be anything dangerous, is it? I know it has something to do with Mrs. Taylor's murder, but I don't want any kind of violence. I almost called you at midnight last night."

"I'm sorry." I sat across from her and put down my briefcase. "I really don't believe there will be any kind of violence. Kanesha and another officer will be here, but I don't expect there will be much of a scene." I doubted that Eugene carried a weapon. Besides he wouldn't be expecting anything but good news about a fee for the library appearance.

Teresa sighed. "I hope you're right, Charlie. I told Marcella Marter exactly what you wanted. She tried to press me for details but I said that I couldn't discuss it any further, that she and her mother really needed to meet with us this morning."

"Thank you. I appreciate your trust, and I promise you this will all be over soon." I couldn't tell her that our plans for the big event would have to be canceled, but she would learn that soon enough. "Once we get in the conference room, I'll take over. You just be on the alert, okay?"

Teresa looked dubious at that bit of instruction. "If you say so." She glanced past me at the doorway.

"Good morning."

I turned to see Kanesha, accompanied by Deputy Bates. "Morning, Officers. Let me show you to the conference room." There was a closet inside the room, where staff kept supplies for meetings, such as bottled water, soft drinks, and so on. It was large enough for two people to wait in comfortably until they were needed — in this case, to make an arrest.

Kanesha and Bates followed me to the room, and I showed them the closet. I explained to Kanesha what I had asked Bronwyn to do, and she nodded. "Good idea. Another deputy will enter the library ten minutes after the Marters arrive. He'll be on hand to assist, and they won't realize he's here."

I felt jittery. "I hate the waiting part. I just want it all to be over."

Bates grinned. "Amateur status." From his tone I could tell he was teasing, but he was right. I wasn't used to this kind of setup, and the professionals were.

I left them in the conference room and went back to Teresa's office. By then it was nearly nine fifteen. I hoped the Marters would be on time. I itched to tell Teresa the truth, but I knew it was probably better not to. I could trust in her courage and good sense to react properly when the time came.

Teresa pretended to work on a document on the computer while I sat across from her and tried to keep calm. The minutes seemed to drag by, but at nine thirty-two Bronwyn brought Mrs. Cartwright and Marcella Marter to Teresa's office.

"Good morning, Ms. Farmer, Mr. Harris. I hear you have some good news for me," Eugene said. As expected, he wore a scarf around his neck and thin gloves on his hands. He carried a cane, but not a handbag. That was good. Marcella fidgeted beside him, darting glances at him. It seemed to me that she was afraid of him.

"Good morning, Mrs. Cartwright." Teresa came from around her desk to shake Eugene's hand. "Mrs. Marter, nice to see you again. I appreciate you coming in on such short notice, but we need to discuss things for your appearance here on Friday afternoon. Let's go to the conference room to talk."

Eugene and his mother followed Teresa,

and I found it interesting that Marcella did not assist her son as she had done in the past. To me that was another indication that I was right. Before, Marcella had always been careful to hover close in case she was needed. This morning she was a step behind Eugene.

When we were all in the room, I maneuvered Eugene to a seat at the end of the table nearest the closet. Best to have him as close as possible to Kanesha and Bates with nothing in the way. Marcella sat to one side, Teresa beside her, while I took a chair immediately to Eugene's left.

Marcella's gaze darted from Eugene to me over and over again. Her uneasiness was beginning to unnerve me slightly. I had better get things going. Eugene looked from Teresa to me expectantly. Without the sunglasses he had worn in the past, I found it easier to see the heavy makeup he wore to feminize his features. He had paid particular attention to his eyes, even adding false lashes and thick, bright eye shadow.

"As Teresa said, we really appreciate your coming out early this morning and on such short notice, but I think you'll be happy with the news I have." I glanced toward the door, and right on cue, Bronwyn stepped in.

"Excuse me," she said. "Mrs. Marter, there's a call for you at the desk. A young lady insists on talking to you."

Marcella stared at Bronwyn. "Wh-who is it?"

Bronwyn shrugged. "I'm sorry, she didn't say. She did say it was urgent, though. If you'll come with me, I'll take you to the phone."

Marcella cast an uncertain glance at her son, and he frowned. I caught the hint of a nod from him, though, and Marcella stood. "Very well," she said. "I'm sure it can't be anything important." She followed Bronwyn out of the room.

I quickly turned to Eugene. "Before I share the good news with you, Mrs. Cartwright, there's something I want to show you." I put my briefcase on the table, opened it, and withdrew Aunt Dottie's scrapbook. "My late aunt was a huge fan of yours — I inherited her wonderful collection of your books, by the way — and while I was looking for things to use for our exhibit, I came across this." I patted the scrapbook.

Eugene eyed it nervously. He licked his lips. "Really, how interesting."

I beamed at him, and Teresa gazed at me blandly, though I knew she was as curious as Eugene to see what I was going to do.

"Yes, it's very interesting. My aunt cut out articles from newspapers and film magazines, lots of pictures, too, and put them in her scrapbook. I just couldn't resist bringing it to show you."

Eugene tittered. "That's all very nice, Mr. Harris, but I don't really need to see all those old things. I lived it all, remember. I'd rather focus on the present."

"Of course you would. But there is one picture I would love for you to sign, if you wouldn't mind." I opened the scrapbook and flipped the pages to the photo of Marietta Dubois and Mrs. Cartwright. "It's such a shame that the movie never got made, I think. Veronica would have been even more famous."

Eugene scowled. "Can we get on with this? I'm not having one of my good days, and I don't have the time or energy to sit around here listening to such foolishness. Tell me about the offer of money."

"I'll get to that. Please, won't you look at this picture?" I shoved the scrapbook in front of him, and he glanced down at it. "That actress surely was tall, wasn't she? You look short standing next to her."

Eugene glared at me, his eyes narrowing. I could feel the fear and anger emanating from him.

"You can find out all kinds of things on the Internet," I continued in a chatty tone. "For example, there's a site you can go to and find out how tall famous people are. Marietta Dubois wasn't all that famous, but I did find out her height." I paused and glanced at Teresa. Her eyes were wide with shock. I reckoned she had figured out where I was headed with this. "Turns out Miss Dubois was only five foot six. Judging by that picture, you must be a good four inches shorter than her."

Two things happened at once. Kanesha and Bates stepped out of the supply closet, and Eugene pushed his chair back so hard it toppled over. He grabbed his cane and headed for the door. Bates surged past Kanesha to grab him, but Teresa was up and out of her chair and stepped in his way. Eugene made it out the door. Kanesha ran past Bates- and Teresa, who disentangled themselves quickly. Bates shot after Kanesha and Eugene, with Teresa and me trotting after them.

Eugene was racing for the door, Bates only inches behind. That was when Diesel darted in front of Eugene. The cane went flying, Diesel got out of the way, and Eugene hit the floor. Hard. Bates fell right on top of him.

FORTY

"Bronwyn had just tossed one of those jingle ball toys, and Diesel darted after it." Helen Louise and I were relaxing on the sofa in her living room with some postprandial brandy on Wednesday evening. Diesel sprawled across our laps. He opened one eye and emitted a lazy chirp. "I've warned her about doing that, but for once I was glad she did."

"Don't you think Bates would have caught him?" Helen Louise grinned. "I've seen the man in shorts and a tank top before, and he's in mighty good shape." She stroked the cat's head. "Not that I want to take any credit away from this clever boy."

I gazed at her in mock indignation. "You're going around ogling buff lawmen behind my back? I am shocked, I tell you, shocked."

Helen Louise laughed. "Darling, if I tried anything with Bates, his boyfriend would scratch my eyes out."

"Boyfriend?" That was news to me. I took a moment to digest this interesting bit of information.

"You mean Stewart hasn't told you?" Helen Louise looked thoughtful. "I guess I shouldn't have said anything. I thought surely you knew."

I laughed. "Stewart has been pretty cagey about it, although I could tell he was involved with someone. He's been happier than I've ever seen him lately. Well, good for them. I hope things work out."

"Me, too," Helen Louise said. "They will have to be discreet, but I'm sure Stewart can be when he needs to."

We sipped at our brandy for a moment. The quiet of Helen Louise's house, the one she and two generations of Bradys before her had grown up in, settled around us.

"I sidetracked you." Helen Louise leaned over the cat in her lap to set her brandy snifter on the coffee table. "Tell me what happened after Bates landed on top of Eugene Marter."

"They both had the breath knocked out of them, but Eugene got the worst of it. Bates fell right on top of him, and he's a big guy. The minute Eugene got his breath back, though, he started cursing. Funny how his voice suddenly dropped about an octave." I recalled that moment at our first meeting when Eugene forgot and let his voice deepen briefly. That was my first clue, though I didn't realize it until later. "The wig came loose in all the hullabaloo, but he didn't realize that. He was still trying to make us believe he was his hundred-year-old grandmother."

"He's not all that bright, is he?" Helen Louise laughed, and I did, too.

"He has a certain kind of low cunning," I said after the merriment subsided. "He just can't seem to think things through clearly and consider the consequences. Otherwise he wouldn't have done some of the lame-brained things he did. Searching Gordon Betts's and Della Duffy's rooms at the hotel was pretty stupid, though of course he tried to lay that off on Eagleton later. I still don't know what he expected to find." I paused as another memory surfaced. "He also tried to con me into thinking he was worried Eagleton's demands would cause his poor granny to have a heart attack and die."

"One mistake after another, like planting those manuscripts in poor Mr. Eagleton's hotel room."

"Exactly. He wanted to confuse things — and he did — but it was a dumb way to do it. It was obvious to Sean and Kanesha that Eagleton wouldn't have done such an asinine thing." I drank the rest of my brandy and put the snifter on the end table beside me. "Eagleton was grateful to Sean for his help, but he hasn't coughed up the fee yet. Sean will probably end up writing it off."

"That's too bad," Helen Louise said. "Speaking of Sean, any movement in the stalemate between him and Q.C.?"

"Not as far as I know." I shook my head. "Sean inherited every ounce of my stubbornness and more besides. They'll work it out eventually."

"I hope so, because he and Alexandra are so good for each other, I think." Helen Louise sighed.

I had to laugh. "Yes, she's as stubborn as he is, and maybe they'll wear each other down a bit and learn how to compromise."

"Back to Eugene," Helen Louise said. "We wandered off track again."

"Kanesha picked up the wig and waved it in front of him, and that shut him up. He was mad, though, and I thought any minute he'd start hopping up and down like a temperamental child."

"Where was his mother during all this?"

"Sitting in a patrol car out in the parking lot. The phone call was a ruse to separate her from Eugene. She walked out to the front desk, where a deputy waited for her. He hustled her out before she could cause a commotion. Apparently the minute he got her in the car, she started crying. She was terrified of Eugene because she never expected him to kill anyone. At least, that's what she told Kanesha later."

"Poor woman. I guess they needed money pretty badly, or surely she wouldn't have gone along with a crackpot scheme like that."

"They had Mrs. Cartwright's social security and some investment income, but Eugene couldn't hold a job, and Marcella couldn't, either. They could get by, but just barely." I explained how the plot of *The Mystery at Spellwood Mansion* mirrored the current situation, including the bogus Mrs. Eden, who turned out to be a penniless, greedy cousin of the real Mrs. Eden. Then I laughed. "Veronica actually snatched the wig off the impostor's head to expose her. I thought about doing that to Eugene, but it wasn't necessary." Helen Louise laughed, too.

Diesel raised his head and yawned. He stretched and turned on his back, exposing his belly. That was a clear signal that Helen Louise and I should rub it. Of course, we